Praise for Rhian Cahill's
Catch 'n' Kiss

"The entire story was perfect, from beginning to end. It was heartwarming with heat inducing sex scenes. [...] I absolutely loved this story and can't wait until the next one in this series comes out."

~ *Night Owl Reviews*

"*Catch 'n' Kiss* is the perfect follow up to *7 Minutes In Heaven* and I can't wait to see what game we get to play next in Rhian Cahill's Are You Game series!"

~ *Guilty Pleasures Book Reviews*

"The plot is well balanced with action, emotion and realism. The characters come alive with the need to be a family and Ms. Cahill does a great job of bringing it all together."

~ *Harlequin Junkie*

"*Catch 'n' Kiss* is a highly readable romance with likable characters and of course not to mention the scorching hot scenes of passion that ups the stakes for this one."

~ *Maldivian Book Reviewer's Realm of Romance*

Look for these titles by
Rhian Cahill

Now Available:

Party Games
Truth or Dare
Spin the Bottle

Are You Game?
7 Minutes in Heaven
Catch 'n' Kiss
Red Light Green Light

Print Anthologies
Party Hard
Party On

Catch 'n' Kiss

Rhian Cahill

Samhain Publishing, Ltd.
11821 Mason Montgomery Road, 4B
Cincinnati, OH 45249
www.samhainpublishing.com

Catch 'n' Kiss
Copyright © 2014 by Rhian Cahill
Print ISBN: 978-1-61922-400-1
Digital ISBN: 978-1-61922-065-2

Editing by Heidi Moore
Cover by Valerie Tibbs

This book is a work of fiction. The names, characters, places, and incidents are products of the writer's imagination or have been used fictitiously and are not to be construed as real. Any resemblance to persons, living or dead, actual events, locale or organizations is entirely coincidental.

All Rights Are Reserved. No part of this book may be used or reproduced in any manner whatsoever without written permission, except in the case of brief quotations embodied in critical articles and reviews.

First Samhain Publishing, Ltd. electronic publication: March 2014
First Samhain Publishing, Ltd. print publication: March 2015

Dedication

For Mr. C. You can *catch 'n' kiss* me whenever you want.

Chapter One

Dan O'Conner reached for the warehouse door only for it to fly open and almost take his hand off. He took a half step back when a curvy behind appeared first through the doorway. Jody. She was bent at the waist, her lust inspiring curves on perfect display as she attempted to drag a huge box outside.

He stepped forward. "Here, let me help you."

"No, thanks. I've got it." She might not have snapped at him as usual, but there was a steel edge to Jody's voice that told him to back off.

"Whoa." Dan raised his hands and stepped out of the way as she cleared the doorway, tugging the box with her. Or trying to at least, but the thing was as wide as the door, and if she wasn't careful it would be wedged good and tight. "I was just offering to help."

Jody turned her head, flicking her blonde ponytail out, and lasered him with stormy-blue eyes. "And *I* said I've got it."

Dan took another step back. He had no clue why this woman didn't like him. It went beyond their initial introduction where he'd been pissed off at his boss, Cassie, for bringing in someone to share his workload. He'd been an arse about it all, and after that first day, Jody had avoided him or cut him off at the knees. The animosity hadn't improved one iota when he'd swallowed his pride and apologised for his behaviour either. For some reason, Jody was still determined to dislike him. Which was a definite shame, because once he'd pulled his head out of his arse he'd realised she was one woman he wouldn't mind getting to know better.

Not that he'd take it beyond friendship even if she did like him. They worked together, and he'd been burned by a workplace relationship before. He wasn't about to tread in that territory again no matter how much his libido stood up and took notice whenever she was near. She wiggled her arse as she attempted to pull the huge box clear of the doorway, and Dan's pants got a little tighter. If she didn't want his help he'd be quite happy to stand here enjoying the view until he could sneak past and go inside.

A car pulled up behind him and Dan turned to see Cassie's boyfriend—and Jody's brother—climb out of the driver's seat. "Hey, Luc."

Luc raised an eyebrow and tipped his chin in Jody's direction. "How's it going?"

"Good. You helping out tonight?" Dan asked.

"Nah, just a quick stop to see Cass before I have to get back to work." Luc stood beside Dan and eyed his sister. "Ah, Jody, do you want—"

"No!" Jody snapped as she yanked hard on the box. It sprang free of the frame and sent her stumbling back a couple of steps.

Dan and Luc both jumped out of the way to avoid a collision. Jeez, she really was in a mood. Good to see it wasn't just him she was lashing out at though. If she was that short with her brother, maybe it was her natural disposition and not anything to do with him. Except she was all smiles and laughs with everyone else at work most days. Stepping around the box, he grabbed the door. Jody huffed out a breath and stared at him. He could see her struggling to hold her tongue, so he smiled and pushed the door wider so it wasn't resting on the box and restricting its movement at all.

She narrowed her eyes and pulled her normally plush lips into a thin, straight line. "Don't you have things to do before we head out to the venue?"

Dan grinned. "Yeah, guess I do. See ya later, Luc." He

wasn't stupid. He knew when he wasn't wanted, and if Jody was going to treat him like crap even the draw of checking out her hot bod couldn't convince him to hang around.

Jody took a deep breath and grabbed the box again. She knew Luc was still standing behind her, could feel his eyes boring holes in the back of her head. She'd been a bitch with a capital B. Damn. What was it about Dan that rubbed her the wrong way? He'd apologised for his initial hostile treatment weeks ago, and yet she couldn't seem to let go of her animosity towards him.

"Wanna talk about it?" Luc asked.

She let go of the box and turned to face him. "Not really."

"Are you pissed off in general or just at Dan?"

"Neither."

Luc's eyebrows hiked up to his hairline.

Jody sighed. "You know he was an arse when I first started working here."

"And?"

She shrugged.

"C'mon, Jody, it isn't like you to be nasty when it's not warranted, and I know Dan apologised for being a prick ages ago."

"I know." She dug her nails into her palms. "He just rubs me the wrong way."

"By offering to help?"

Dammit. Why did Luc always have to be logical? "By breathing," she mumbled.

"What?"

"Nothing." She looked at the ground and tried to clear her thoughts. Something that proved difficult whenever Dan was around. She brought her gaze up to meet Luc's. "I don't want to be a bitch to him, honest, it's just...argh. I don't know why I'm like that with him. It's not like I treat anyone else that way."

Luc shook his head. "You don't even treat Colin that badly, and God knows if anyone deserves to be treated like shit it's your ex."

He had a point. But she'd always kept things civil for the girls' sake. "That's for Leigh and Amy's benefit not his."

"Want to know what I think?"

She laughed. "If I say no, is it going to stop you from sharing?"

"Probably not." He grinned. "I think the animosity between you is hiding some serious sexual sparks."

Jody closed her eyes and drew in a deep breath. God, not only was her brother logical, he was smart. She opened her eyes and her gaze met Luc's knowing one. What could she say? She certainly couldn't argue. Dan did get her sexual juices flowing. Something that hadn't happened in so long she'd begun to think that part of her had died a slow, agonising death along with her marriage.

"Look, I understand if you don't want to acknowledge or do anything about it, but you can't keep acting the way you are. It's not fair to Dan—or you—and you've got Cass worried. She said the two of you had a shouting match yesterday, and while I know you'd never do that at a party, you can see how it might be a concern for her."

"Shit. I thought Dan and I were the only ones here." She squeezed her eyes shut.

"Hey." Luc pulled her into a hug. "It wasn't Cass that heard you. West was here."

"Oh God." Jody buried her face in Luc's chest. "That's even worse."

He laughed.

She pulled back and thumped his arm. "It's not funny."

"Yes, it is." He gripped her forearms and set her away from

him. "You need to sort it out."

"I know. I will."

"All right then. Want some help with that?" Luc pointed to the box.

Jody laughed. "Yeah. Help me get it into my car."

Luc bent his knees, wrapped his arms around the sides and picked it up as if it weighed no more than a box of tissues. She rolled her eyes and led the way to her car. She pressed the button on her alarm and opened the tailgate of her SUV. "Shove it in there."

"What's in here anyway?"

"Decorations for a kid's party next week. I'm going to get the girls to help me put them together on Sunday."

"Isn't there a law against child labour?"

"Probably." She grinned. "But don't tell them."

"My lips are sealed." He mimed zipping his lips.

Tears stung her eyes, and for the life of her she couldn't work out why she was on the verge of crying. As Luc straightened from the back of the car, Jody stepped next to him and threw her arms around his waist. She clung to him and swallowed the emotion clogging her throat.

"Hey, hey. What's wrong?" He held her close and patted her back.

"I just wanted a hug."

Luc squeezed her tighter. "Anytime, you know that."

"Yeah, I know." He'd always been there. For as long as she could remember, her big brother had been watching over her—supporting her. But it was time to stand on her own two feet.

Jody allowed herself a few more seconds of leaning on Luc before she pulled free. He watched her with that all-seeing gaze of his and she fought against the need to wrap herself around him again. It wasn't often that she let her doubts and fears creep in, but since she'd gone back to work fulltime, she'd found her emotions in a complete jumble. She flipped from confidence in her ability to support her and the girls to absolute terror that she'd default the mortgage and not be able to put food on the table. It was irrational and stupid, and she'd had enough of her see-sawing state of mind.

"I'm good." It was a verbal assurance for both of them. Luc would take over if she let him, and that was the last thing she or the girls needed. "I gotta go. We're heading out in an hour."

"I'll walk you in. I want to spend a few minutes with Cass before I have to head back to work," Luc said.

They walked back to the building. "You don't normally work nights."

"I've got a couple of new guys on tonight's detail, so I want to be on hand." Luc held open the warehouse door for her to step through. "Plus, Lachlan is worried about Cameron. This is her first official public appearance since she disappeared from the spotlight years ago."

"Not to mention she's now the future Mrs. McDermott. That's got to garner a boatload of attention." Jody had met Lachlan a few times, and while the dark, brooding man wasn't her type, she could see his appeal and understand why a woman who'd shunned the limelight would step back into it for him. She glanced at Luc. "Are you expecting a late one?"

"I don't think so. As soon as I'm happy with the way my men are working, I'll probably cut out." He stopped at the stairs. "I might even see you later if I get off early enough."

"If not, I'll talk to you next week. We have to sort out Mum's birthday present soon."

"Why don't you just get whatever and bill me," he suggested.

"Ha. You're not getting out of it that easy. Besides, we should decide whether or not to go out for dinner or just have it at my place."

"Why don't you have it at Luc's?" Cassie asked from

halfway up the stairs.

"Hey, gorgeous." Luc spun around and took the stairs two at a time. He wrapped an arm around Cassie's waist and yanked her against his chest. "Ah...just the person I was looking for."

Jody watched as her brother planted a kiss on her boss. It wasn't a quick peck on the lips either. No, this was a carnal assault that made Jody's stomach knot with envy. She turned away.

She didn't begrudge her brother happiness, but she'd been married and had two kids and not once had her husband given her the kind of contentment that glowed on Luc and Cassie's faces. Of course, it had a lot to do with the no-good scumbag she'd married and the huge bubble of denial she'd lived in for years. Well, no more. She might not have someone to share the rest of her life with, but she was determined to find happiness and satisfaction in every other aspect of her life. Starting with her job and the friendships she'd begun to form.

And that included Daniel O'Conner.

Dan stood off to the side and watched Jody shut down the party. He was supposed to be here only as backup, but he'd been helping out all night much to her disgust. She'd finally told him to quit interfering in her event, find a spot and stay in it. And he had to admit, she knew what she was doing. He'd underestimated her abilities and owed her another apology. Of course, he'd wait until after everyone had gone home before he gave it to her.

The host and hostess had disappeared behind their bedroom door hours ago and Jody was currently seeing the last of their guests out the door. Clean up was well underway, and he figured they'd be heading out and locking up within an hour, possibly less. There'd been only one glitch to the evening, and while he'd been prepared to deal with it, Jody had taken the situation—a half-naked partier—out of his hands and dealt with it with speed and efficiency. He really did owe her that apology.

She must have felt his eyes on her, because she turned his way and raised one finely sculptured eyebrow. The question was clear. The answer not so much. He couldn't say why he had the urge to follow her with his gaze. Sure, she was easy on the eyes, more than easy, she was a knockout. Especially when you considered she was the mother of two teenagers. Definitely one for the MILF column. A smile tugged the corner of his mouth and she narrowed her eyes.

He straightened off the wall as she headed his way. Her stride was determined and he noticed her hands were clenched at her sides. This could go either way. She'd either rip him a new one or...actually, he wasn't sure how else it could turn out. Dan waited.

"Is there a problem?" she demanded.

"Nope."

"Then what are you doing?"

"Um, staying out of your way like you asked?" He arched one eyebrow.

"Oh, *now* you back off. Typical." Jody spun on her heel and headed for the kitchen.

"Hey, what the hell does that mean?" he called after her but she ignored him and kept going.

Damn woman. There was no way he was leaving it there. He followed her into the laundry off the kitchen where they'd stored supplies. Dan didn't think about it, he just moved up behind her, grabbed her shoulders and turned her around to face him. Her gasp had warm minty breath fanning over his chin and neck. A shudder rolled down his spine. His fingers flexed and dug into the flesh at the top of her arms as he pulled her closer until her breasts pressed against his chest.

"W-what are you doing?" She tried to push him away but

he held tight.

"Something I should have done weeks ago."

Dan crushed his mouth to hers. He slid his hands over her shoulders and up her neck until he gripped her head. He tilted his head to the left, moved hers to the right and sealed their mouths completely. Her lips parted on a puff of air and he took advantage. Diving deep, he thrust his tongue past her teeth and stroked hers. A hot, wet slide that stole his breath and shot molten blood through his veins. She tasted of peppermint. The Tic Tac's she popped like an addict. Speaking of addicts. He could *so* get addicted to this.

To her.

He pressed closer. Pressed his suddenly rock-hard cock against her soft belly. Her curves cradled him and he lost a little more of his sanity. He'd been in denial. Had ignored the rush of desire that coursed through him whenever she was near. There was no denying it now. With one kiss, he'd smashed every wall blocking the way. He couldn't go back to pretending he didn't want this woman.

She tore her mouth from his. Her breath rasping in and out as she dragged oxygen into her heaving chest. He was pleased to see he wasn't the only one blown away by a simple kiss. Not that what they'd just done was simple. Kissing Jody was the least simple thing he could ever do. His gaze locked on hers and he wanted to yell in triumph when he saw her dazed, lust-filled eyes.

"Jesus." The word whispered over her lips a second before she slipped out her tongue and licked across her red kiss-swollen mouth.

A growl rumbled in his chest and he leaned in to take her mouth again. This time, he took it slower. He still plunged deep, tangled his tongue with hers and explored every dark recess. But he did it with a little finesse, a little less desperation. His chest screamed for air but he wasn't done tasting her. Wasn't done sinking into the most sublime kiss of his life. Easing back,

Dan turned it down a notch until he caught his breath again. He'd planned to dive back in. Planned to submerge himself in the carnal pleasure that was Jody's mouth, but it was the wrong time, wrong place.

"Jody!"

They sprang apart just as one of the servers rounded the corner. Dan sucked in air, his chest lurching with the effort. Jody's eyes widened. He couldn't read the myriad of emotions flashing through her eyes except the last one. That was anger. Her cheeks were a delicate pink, whether from their kiss or her escalating outrage, he wasn't sure, but he could guarantee she'd be lashing out at him in three, two—

She shoved past him, almost knocking him off his feet. "What's up, Kerry?"

Her voice was a little raspy and he took satisfaction in knowing he'd affected her even if it meant she'd avoid him even more now that he'd laid one on her. Dan almost rubbed his hands together. He might not have wanted to tempt fate and pursue her due to their working relationship, but he wasn't an idiot. That kiss did not fall in the bracket of normal by a long shot. If she wanted to bury her head in the sand and run from their explosive chemistry so be it. He'd let her run for now.

He had to think it through anyway. Come up with a plan. Because there was no way he was living his life without a repeat performance. And if he had his way, they wouldn't stop at a kiss. So he'd let her run, but she wouldn't get far. It was a good thing he wasn't afraid of a little chase. In fact, back in school he'd excelled at catch 'n' kiss, and he couldn't wait to start the game.

Chapter Two

Jody splashed cold water on her face and wrists. She couldn't believe Dan had kissed her. Kissed the ever-loving life out of her. Dear God, that had been a toe-curling, panty-melting lip lock of epic proportions, and she wasn't sure she'd ever breathe normally again. The man had serious skills. They'd been seconds away from tearing each other's clothes off. She'd never experienced such mindless lust before. Not even in the heady first days of her relationship with Colin.

She sighed. It couldn't happen again. The last thing she needed was a man complicating her life. Her stomach cramped at the thought of never kissing Dan again. He'd had her on edge for weeks. She'd told herself she was still pissed by his obnoxious behaviour when they were first introduced but she couldn't lie to herself any more. Dan O'Conner made her want things. Sex. God, yes! He made her want sex. Jody couldn't remember the last time she'd even had sex. Five years? Six?

Could it really be that long? The more she mulled it over the more she had the sinking feeling that six years was an understatement. She hung her head and let out a deep sigh. She'd buried her needs along with her marriage. Neither had ever been that satisfying, but at least she'd had them. Sort of. Okay, who was she kidding? Both her marriage and sex life had sucked. And not in a good way. Jody smiled. At least she'd kept her sense of humour. Then again, she'd probably curl up in a little ball crying her eyes out if she hadn't.

She grabbed a towel and used it to pat her face dry before checking herself in the mirror. She needed to get back out there, but she'd needed a few minutes to regain her composure. Never let it be said that Jody Walsh couldn't hold it together no matter what life threw at her. Spine straight, shoulders back, she flung the door open and got on with it. The crew had everything packed up and all that was left was one final walk through. She pulled her phone from her pocket and opened her picture gallery to compare each room to the photos she'd taken before they'd set up for the party. It was cheating, but she had no intention of screwing this job—any job—up.

Each room appeared as it had hours earlier. Looking at the house now, you wouldn't know it had been crowded with people partaking in a risqué adults-only party for the last couple of hours. She glanced at her watch. Three fifteen. It had run longer than expected, but instead of being dead on her feet, she was strangely wired. Her system buzzed, every nerve alive and ready for action. Hopefully, she'd be able to sleep. The girls were due home at seven in the morning and she still had to head to the warehouse and unload the night's equipment.

Rounding the corner, Jody ran into a solid wall of warm muscle. Dan. Why was he still here? "Sorry."

"No worries." He steadied her with his hands on her waist. "All done?"

"Yes. I just need to lock up on the way out."

"Let's go then." He cupped her elbow and steered her to the front door.

"What are you doing?"

"Leaving?"

"So go already." She really didn't want to spend any more time with him tonight.

"I came with you in the van, remember?"

Oh shit. He had. Jody closed her eyes and prayed for strength. They'd spend at least another thirty minutes together. "Right. Sorry." She fished the keys from her pocket and picked up her pace. The faster she got him back to his car, the quicker she could take a breath and clear her head.

"Where's the fire?"

"Huh?" She opened the door and climbed in the driver's side.

"Never mind." Dan buckled his belt and stared straight ahead.

She couldn't be sure, but she thought he was looking at her from the corner of his eye. A shiver skipped down her spine and goose bumps broke out on her skin. Her mind replayed their kiss and she licked her lips as the memory of his taste flooded her senses. No doubt about it, the man was lethal to her equilibrium. She stuck the key in the ignition, turned it and fired up the engine. Hot, stale air blasted through the vents and she quickly wound the window down to let in some of the fresh autumn breeze.

The drive back was quiet. Only the soft sounds of the radio and the early morning filtered through the cabin. She couldn't think of anything to say and had no intention of discussing their encounter, so Jody concentrated on getting them to the warehouse safely. A tall order when her mind wanted to circle back to those few minutes with his mouth on hers.

Jody pulled into the driveway and hit the remote for the loading door. The double-wide metal panel slid up in a smooth, noiseless motion before grinding to a halt. She glanced up as she drove under.

"That reminds me. I need to get the installer back out to check the roller door," Dan said.

"But it's brand new."

"Oh, I don't think it's broken. But the guy did say sometimes they need an adjustment after the first so many uses. Better to be safe than sorry." He opened his door when she brought the van to a stop. "I'll start unloading. You go file the paperwork."

"You're hanging around?" Too late. The door closed behind him before she even got one word out. By the time Jody swung out of her seat, Dan had the cargo doors open and was carrying the first of the equipment boxes to the racks. She might not be rid of him as quickly as she liked, but at least she'd get distance—and possibly some sense—when she went upstairs. Perhaps then she'd manage to catch her breath.

She picked up her backpack and headed to her office. A thrill of delight ran through her. *Her* office. After years of working any part-time job she could get, not only did she have a fulltime job she loved, but she had an office. There was no stopping the grin. Even sharing the workspace with Dan couldn't dampen her excitement. The room appeared a little cramped with two desks, but at least they could share the filing cabinets. In the beginning, she'd worried about the combined work zone, but so far it had worked seamlessly. Not that they'd found themselves in the room at the same time very often since she started working at Are You Game?

Jody thought he'd been avoiding her in the beginning, and with her own turbulent emotions about the man, she hadn't worried about it. But now... Now she figured that her initial assumption the tension between them would cause problems had been correct, and couldn't imagine how they'd work in such close proximity after their latest encounter. Not that the conflict between them had headed in the direction she originally expected it to. She swallowed through a constricted throat when she thought about just how close they'd been a little while ago.

Her body still hummed with arousal. She'd done well to mask her reactions to his kiss up until now, but there was a very real possibility she wouldn't be able to hide them any longer. Definitely time to get out of here. Unzipping her bag, Jody pulled out her clipboard and began flicking through the pages. She grabbed a pen and flopped into her chair. Marking off each task, jotting notes about the evening and signing off on staff timecards took her about fifteen minutes, and it wasn't until Dan cleared his throat that she looked up.

"Done?" he asked as he pushed off the doorjamb.

"Almost. You?"

"Yep." He perched his hip on the corner of her desk and her eyes were drawn to the way his pants pulled tight across his muscular thighs.

Jody coughed and jerked her gaze back to the paperwork in her hand. "I'll see you next week then."

Dan laughed.

"What?" She risked a glance up and regretted it the second his gaze snagged and held hers.

"Trying to get rid of me?" One corner of his mouth tipped up.

"Ah, no, but there's no need for you to hang around waiting for me."

"Good manners dictate that I do." He picked up the picture frame she kept on her desk. The one with her and the girls at SeaWorld last year. "They look just like you."

"Really?" She'd never seen the resemblance, but he wasn't the first to make the observation.

"Yeah. How old are they?"

Crap. She didn't want to have this conversation with him. It brought them closer, this whole sharing of personal lives. But she couldn't ignore him. "Fifteen and thirteen."

"Shit. What were you when you had them? Twelve?"

She smiled. The compliment was nice, but she knew she looked every one of her thirty-four years. "You should know better than to ask a woman how old she is."

"I peg you at thirty." He arched one eyebrow.

"Ah, you sweet talker you."

"Hey, if all it takes is sweet talk I'll lay on the sugar until the cows come home."

She'd have to be stupid to miss the undertone of his remark.

"Seriously, how old are you?"

Jody had the sudden thought that her age would be a good deterrent to his obvious pursuit. "Thirty-five in two months."

"June? What date?"

She nodded. "Fourteenth. Why?"

"Well, how about that. We share a birthday. I'll be twenty-eight. We'll have to celebrate together."

"Ah..." What the hell was she supposed to say to that? "The girls and I usually do something fun—go bowling, see a movie."

"Great. Count me in." Dan leaned over and flicked the pages on her calendar. "Okay, the fourteenth is a Saturday so we can do both. Oh, unless they'll be with their father on the weekend?"

He was fishing for information, and Jody couldn't decide if it was a good or bad thing that he didn't balk at their seven-year-age gap or spending time with her daughters. "No, they're with me most weekends, but the last thing you want to do is hang out with a couple of teenagers on your birthday—"

"Stop." He held up his hand. "Here's the thing, Jody. They're part of you. I want to spend time with you so that means I want to spend time with them."

Her stomach clenched. Their father didn't want to see them half the time, so she couldn't imagine Dan really wanted to spend the day in their company. "Look. I don't know what you're trying to do, but pretending to like my kids won't get you in my bed." Jody's face flushed. Where the hell had that come from? She hadn't even been thinking of sex with him. *Liar.*

Dan laughed. A rich deep rumble that shook his shoulders. He leaned over her desk and got right in her face. "Make no mistake here, Jody. Wanting in your bed has nothing to do with wanting to spend the day with you and your kids. I want both. I'll get both."

Dan watched Jody closely. No doubt about it, he'd put it out there. He hadn't even thought before the words were flying across his tongue. Her assumption about his motives pissed him off. She was the only woman he'd ever met who made him want to shake her and kiss her at the same time. It wasn't the first time she'd questioned his intentions, and he wasn't going to let her get away with it from now on. She'd know where he stood every step of the way.

He wasn't sure when he'd made the decision to pursue her. Probably in that first nano-second his lips had touched hers. Her silent, wide-eyed stare almost made him laugh, but he didn't think she'd find his humour acceptable at the moment. Then again, she hadn't exactly found his statement to her liking either. With a sigh, he pulled out of her personal space and grabbed a pen out of the ceramic mug that reminded him of something he'd made back in high school. One of her daughters must have given it to her.

Marking the fourteenth of June with a big star, he scribbled *birthday celebration with girls and Dan* in red. He underscored the whole thing with two lines. "There. It's on your calendar." Dan pulled his phone from his pocket and he added it to his own planner where he discovered the reminder for dinner with his family. "Oh, and keep the night free too. We'll have dinner as well."

She hadn't said a word, and he glanced at her to check she was still there. Her eyes were comically wide and her mouth hung open, so he reached over and nudged her jaw up.

Jerking back, she pulled away from his touch. "What are you doing?"

He smiled at her. "I think I've made it pretty clear."

"Well, yes, but..."

Finding her inability to voice her thoughts shouldn't be gratifying, but Dan loved that he could knock her off her feet this way. "Here, let's make it simple. I like you. You like me. Uh, uh, don't argue, you can't deny we have chemistry. Not after that kiss." He waited to see if she'd remain quiet and let him finish. "Good. So I like you and you like me."

Her mouth moved, and for a second he thought she'd offer an argument, but in the end she rolled her lips inwards and stayed silent.

"As I was saying, we like each other and I think it's worth seeing where that goes. Actually, I know it's worth it."

"How can you know that after just a kiss?"

"Just a kiss? Jody, that wasn't *just* a kiss. That was a life-altering moment that neither of us saw coming or should walk away from." He had to get her to agree with him. The more he thought about it the more he wanted to know every little thing about her. Wanted to spend hours and hours getting to know her.

"But we work together. When this goes pear-shaped we'll be stuck here, in this tiny room, when we won't want to lay eyes on each other."

Dan could see her point, but he didn't think they'd have that problem. "We'll cross that bridge if we come to it."

"No!" She pushed her chair back and stood. "I won't risk my job. Not for you. Not for anyone."

"It won't come to that."

"You can't guarantee that." She opened the drawer in her desk and pulled out a handbag.

"What? You're running?" He stood up and faced her across her desk.

"No. I'm going home," she said as she slipped the strap of her bag over her shoulder. "I'll finish the paperwork there."

"You are running." He wanted to grab her. Shake her. Stop her.

"There's nothing to run from." Jody rounded the desk and headed for the door. "Lock up on your way out."

She was gone before he could get his legs to move, but once his brain got the signals right, he chased after her. "Jody!"

"No!" She spun around and threw her arm up, palm out, to

stop him. "We're not talking about this anymore. There's nothing to talk about."

"Bullshit!"

Her eyes narrowed. "Bullshit? *Bullshit?* Bullshit is the fact you think you can kiss me and then proceed to tell me what we're going to do about it. We might have chemistry. It might be off the charts, but I'm not a slave to my hormones, and I'm certainly not some meek little woman you can order around to your liking."

With that, she turned and continued down the stairs. Her ponytail swung from side to side and he had the urge to grab it and pull her back. *Fuck.* He was turning into a caveman. He'd never felt this razor-sharp need for a woman. Never wanted on a bone-deep-can't-breathe-without-her level. And why the hell was he suddenly so desperate for her? She was the same woman she'd been this morning. The same snapping didn't-want-to-look-at-him Jody he'd been butting heads with for months. Only she wasn't the same. *He* wasn't the same. Not after that kiss.

"We're not done," he yelled at her retreating back.

"Yes, we are," she screamed back, followed by the slamming of the warehouse's outer door.

"*Fuck.*" He speared his fingers through his hair, dug his nails into his scalp and growled. She'd as good as told him to fuck off. If she'd been anyone else he would have taken her at her word. But he wasn't backing down. Wasn't walking away from something he knew could be special—unique—life altering. "Fuck!"

Dan dropped his chin to his chest and drew in a deep breath. The light scent of vanilla teased his nose. Dammit, he could smell her. He pulled the front of his shirt up and sniffed. It smelled exactly like Jody. Some of her perfume must have rubbed off when they'd been locked together. Like an addict, he sucked in another big breath and let her fill him. His body tightened, his cock going from semi-hard to rock hard in a heartbeat.

It didn't matter what had happened before their kiss or after. He wasn't about to let either of them pass up the possibilities their chemistry offered. Jody might be right. Hormones may be the driving force behind their sparks, but Dan knew lust. He'd spent his whole adult life letting it lead him from one woman to the next, and what he felt when he held Jody—kissed her—was a billion times more potent. She could run as far and fast as her sexy long legs would take her. It wouldn't matter, because he'd catch her in the end. And when he did, he'd kiss her and prove their first lip lock wasn't a fluke.

Chapter Three

Jody jumped as the door of her office burst open.

"Oh, good, you're still here." Cassie marched over to Jody's desk and slapped down a folder. "I need you to handle this for me."

"Sure." She leaned forward to pull the file closer.

"Wait. Before you agree you should know what it entails."

Jody eyed her boss, the woman who'd become her friend, the woman who was dating her brother. And if she was reading the signs correctly, Cassie would eventually be her sister-in-law. "What could possibly stop me from saying yes to a job?"

"It's a full weekend." Cassie chewed her lip. "Away."

"What?" Jody grabbed the folder and flipped it around.

"Not yet." Cassie slammed her palm on the cover. "I wouldn't ask if I wasn't desperate. I know I promised you the weekend off, but I need to replace Jeremy. He just rang and said his mother has been rushed to hospital with a suspected heart attack, and you're the only one without an event this weekend so you can fill the two-day gap. I'd have to cover a shift for anyone else."

"I already said I'd do it." She tugged the file from Cassie's hold and opened it. Air zapped from her lungs and her stomach cramped so tight she swore her belly button hit her backbone.

"What? What's wrong?" Cassie leaned over to see the page Jody was looking at.

"Nothing." *Oh God.* There was no way she could say no now. "Just a cramp from too much lunch." They'd visited a new sushi place down the road together and she'd definitely eaten too much, but that wasn't what had her insides contracting. Jody took a deep breath and smiled up at Cassie. "Leave it with me. Don't worry. I'll get everything sorted out."

"Luc said we can have the girls. He'll watch them while I work Friday night and Saturday afternoon."

"You sure?" Jody's brother had been having the girls more since he'd begun dating Cassie, but having them for the whole weekend might be a stretch, especially when her big brother had always been uncomfortable around their little girly ways. Although now they were both older, he was finding it easier to deal with them.

"Yes. We love having them. Plus, I want to go see that new Pixar movie and it'll look a lot better if I actually take some kids with me." Cassie grinned. "Not to mention we can hit the arcade afterwards."

"Okay, I'll get them to head home after school tomorrow, and Luc can pick them up from there whenever he finishes work." A whole two days without the girls would normally bring a thrill, but not this time. This time she'd be spending those two days with the one person she'd been avoiding like the plague.

"Great. I owe you. I'll let Luc know the plan." Cassie headed out with a wave.

Jody slumped in her chair. It'd been two weeks and six days since the moment. She refused to think of it as a kiss. That just bought back memories and sensations she didn't want to deal with, so it was *the moment*. Either he'd given up, was avoiding her or was biding his time. None of those scenarios made her happy. He'd been so adamant the other night, and then when she'd brushed him off—okay, it had been more than a brush-off—he'd all but disappeared. Well, there'd be no escaping each other this weekend.

Dan was the lead coordinator and she was the assistant. But that wasn't the kicker. No, the huge problem was they were sharing a hotel room. She leaned her head back, closed her eyes and tried to put a lid on the panic bubbling in her chest.

"Sleeping on the job?"

She catapulted forward, her eyes opening wide and her breath rushing from her lungs. "Shit. You scared the crap out of me." Her heart beat against her ribs like a drummer on speed.

It had been like this for days. She'd lived on tenterhooks waiting for the other shoe to drop. Of course, he'd been all smiles and friendly workplace-acceptable talk. All the while, she'd been worrying about touching him—stressing about him touching her. The hairs on her arms and neck stood at attention just being in the same room as Dan. She could only imagine her body's reaction if they actually touched.

"What's got those creases in your forehead?" He sat behind his desk and Jody breathed a sigh of relief. He wasn't coming closer.

"Oh, I was running through my mental to-do list." She held up the folder Cassie had given her. "Lots to get organised before the weekend."

"You agreed to fill in for Jeremy?" He raised his eyebrows.

"Yes." She clamped her mouth shut. As soon as she was alone again, she'd ring the hotel and see about getting another room. She'd pay for it out of her own pocket so Cassie would never find out there'd been a problem.

"It's fully booked." Dan leaned back in his chair and crossed his muscular arms over his chest, the sleeves of his polo shirt stretching tight.

"What is?" She forced her gaze away from his bulging biceps and up to meet his.

"The hotel." A smile curled his mouth. The same mouth that had turned her into a puddle of need two weeks ago.

Oh my God. Was he a mind reader? She wanted to wipe the silly grin off his face.

"But don't worry, the room has two beds. As long as you don't snore, we'll survive."

"Snore? That's all you're worried about?"

"Well, there's also the small issue of me sleeping naked…"

Naked? Heat pooled in her belly, dripped lower and moistened flesh that had been barren only a few weeks ago. With one kiss, he'd brought her body back to life. And now she'd have to share a room with him. A naked him. This couldn't get any worse.

"It's about a three-hour drive from here, so we'll leave at lunch time tomorrow. Make sure we get there with plenty of time to check in and set up for the evening." He scanned a sheet of paper in front of him. "Oh, and don't forget to pack your swimmers. There's a hot tub on our patio."

Jody gulped. Images of a wet, naked Dan flashed through her mind. Her palms grew damp, her skin stretched tight and the crotch of her undies grew wetter by the minute. She had to get out of here. Had to get some fresh air before she did something stupid like throw herself over his desk and beg him to kiss her and take away the ache expanding in her sex. Leaping out of her chair, she all but ran from the room.

Dan watched Jody dash from the room and smiled. She might want to pretend there was nothing between them, but she couldn't hide from her feelings any more than he could. He'd seen the tell-tale reactions her body had presented on more than one occasion over the last few weeks. He wanted to thank his lucky stars that they'd ended up thrown together this weekend, but that seemed horrible when he considered the reason she'd had to come along on this job. Then again, fate was a fickle bitch and he wouldn't look a gift horse in the mouth.

He rolled his chair back and swung his feet up on the desk. He'd wait her out. She had to come back, and he'd been laying low long enough. Time to push her a little. Dan knew he was being arrogant in his approach. Figured she'd call him on it too, but he was enjoying the game. His usual MO when it came to women was simple. Get in, get out. The two long-term relationships—if a few months could be considered long—had been more a convenience than any real need. He wasn't all that sure he liked the man he was.

With Jody, he wanted to savour the chase. His mother had taught him nothing worth having should come easy, and he should always strive to make something better than it was. That probably explained why he'd never stuck when it came to relationships. The women he'd dated *had* come easily, and those that hadn't weren't even a blip on his radar. But this woman. Jody. She was different. Everything about her made him stand up and take notice. From the moment they'd been introduced, he'd felt the buzz.

At first, he'd been so set on disliking her—or the idea of her—that he hadn't registered what was really going on. And if he were honest, he'd admit he'd still been blind right up until the instant he'd laid his lips on hers. He shook his head. Damn, he was an idiot. Blind. Stupid. Ignorant. Each word described him perfectly. Right up until the kiss. In that second, the fog had cleared from his mind and he'd seen with HD-technicolour clarity. Jody Walsh had rocked his world to its foundations. But if he was lucky—and God help him, he wanted to be—she'd help him build them back up again.

Oh, he knew it was too soon to think so seriously, but he'd had days to think about their chemistry, weeks to ponder the absolute rarity of such a connection, and there was no way around it. What he felt for Jody wasn't just simple lust. He knew lust. Christ, he'd spent his whole adult life letting it lead him around by the dick. This was bone deep and raw edged. For the first time in his life, he felt as though he'd be missing out on something amazing if he didn't *get the girl*.

Jody walked back in, her steps faltering when she saw him leaning back in his chair. "Oh, I thought you would be gone."

Hoped more like it. "Nope." He smiled. "Still here."

She headed for her desk. Without looking his way again, she scooped up the file for the weekend job, pulled her bag from a drawer and turned to leave. "Bye."

He could have predicted her snub. She'd made an art of ignoring him for the last three weeks, except he wasn't about to let her get away with it any longer. He pushed out of his chair and met her near the door. "I'm heading out too."

The scowl on her face said it all, and it took considerable effort and a bitten cheek to keep from grinning. Dan let her precede him through the door, let her lead the way downstairs, but once they made it to the bottom of the stairwell, he crowded close behind her. She picked up her pace, and this time there was no stopping the smirk from stretching his lips. When they neared the door, he scooted around her and opened it before she could. He waited for the I'm-capable speech. Women these days couldn't seem to accept a kind gesture no matter how small.

"Thank you," she murmured as she walked past.

His shock was so great it took him a second to follow. He'd expected her to lash out. God knows she never accepted his help when he offered. Suddenly she was thanking him for giving her a hand without asking? Dan wasn't sure what to make of this latest shift in attitude, but he didn't have time to dwell on it. He had something else he wanted to do before they parted ways. Hurrying, he caught her just as she reached her car.

"Hey." As he'd hoped, she spun around, putting her back to her car, and he moved right in.

"Wha—"

Dan lowered his head and slanted his mouth across hers.

Her lips parted as she sucked in a breath—his breath—and he took the opportunity to slide his tongue inside her mouth. The moan that issued from her throat had his blood racing and his balls tightening. Minty fresh, her taste exploded—saturated his mouth with memory and need. He'd wanted this for weeks. Days. Hours.

Forever.

He tangled their tongues and pressed in closer. They touched from chest to thigh, and Dan wanted the barriers between them gone. Wanted to rip the clothes from their bodies and really feel her against him. Except that wasn't going to happen here. There were enough brain cells still functioning for him to know that. Instead, he angled his hips, pushed his leg between hers and rubbed against her pussy. She moaned into his mouth and he increased the pressure. She rocked her hips, the motion growing quicker with each stroke of his tongue—thrust of his leg.

Dan worked his hand from her waist to her breast. He cupped the mound, tested the weight in his palm before pinching the taut nipple between thumb and fingers. Jody murmured, half-demand, half-plea, and the sound egged him on. His cock screamed for action and he twisted a little to the right, pressed his straining length into her hip in an attempt to find the friction he desperately needed. She bucked against him, her spine arching like a bow, and he pulled back, separated their mouths, to see her face.

Her skin was coated in a fine sheen of sweat, her cheeks flushed pink and her pulse hammered at the base of her throat. She was the picture of a woman on the edge, and it blindsided him to think just a kiss and a few well-placed touches could get her there. The swollen flesh of her bottom lip lay wet and inviting, and Dan couldn't resist sliding his tongue over the curved length. He barely registered the traffic metres away, rushing along the road as people made their way home.

He saw the second she realised what they were doing—where they were doing it—and before she could protest, he planted his mouth on hers once more. This time he savoured. Licking and stroking in wet glides that stole his breath and gave him hers. She made that sound again—the one between a demand and a plea, and Dan's good intentions fell at their feet. He squeezed her breast, pressing his thigh into her pussy until she rose to her toes. Off-balance, she leaned in, rocked her hips and ground her sex against him.

Something snapped. In him—in her—he didn't know, but all of a sudden they were moving together in a frenzy of need that left Jody panting in his mouth and Dan clenching every muscle in an effort to hold off the orgasm burning in his balls. She arched, her muscles stretched tight, and her breath stalled. Then it happened. She shattered. The climax tore through her. Her body thrashed between him and her car, and he pulled them away so she didn't hurt herself on the hard metal surface. He held her close, his mouth still devouring hers, soaking in the sounds she made, while she rode out the final waves.

Dan enjoyed the moment. Took it all in and engraved it on his mind, because he knew the second she came down, the moment reality returned, she'd be all over his arse about what he'd done. Sure she'd let him, she'd definitely been willing, but he'd pushed himself on her, taken her by surprise and left her no recourse but to surrender. And surrender she did. Beautifully. Completely. He wanted her to do it again. And again.

Jody dragged air into her straining lungs. Every part of her felt replete—relaxed in a way she hadn't in so long it took her a moment to get her head around what had happened. She'd come all over Dan's leg. Gotten off in the damn parking lot. On his *leg*. She wanted to hate herself for allowing it to go that far, but the pleasure still zipping through her veins, pleasure she hadn't experienced in years, wouldn't let her. He held her close and she buried her face in the curve of his neck to avoid facing him a few minutes more. Not that she could ignore him. Not with the huge erection pressing into her hip.

She couldn't evade the inevitable forever, so she took a deep breath to brace herself. Big mistake. His scent filled her. Soaked into her pores and surrounded her with renewed desire. He smelled like sex. *They* smelled like sex. Her insides quivered. A trembling of nerves and cells brought to life by the man holding her close. She'd never done anything like this before.

Never dreamed she'd climax without stripping naked and spending long minutes building towards an orgasm that often proved elusive.

"You okay?"

The quietly uttered question brought her out of her thoughts. She was more than okay, but she wasn't about to stroke Dan's ego by telling him. Managing a nod, she tried to pull from his grasp.

"No. Not yet." He roamed his hands up and down her back, soothing and arousing, the motion keeping her in place. "There's no one around and nobody can see us from the street."

She sighed. At least Dan was the only witness to her embarrassingly wanton behaviour. As the seconds ticked past, Jody began to realise the full extent of her mistake. She'd been so easy. So ready to ride his leg and take what he offered. Embarrassment didn't begin to cover it.

"Stop beating yourself up," he murmured in her ear, his warm breath flowing over her neck.

She shivered and a groan slipped up her throat. How did he read her so well?

"I know what you're thinking, but don't. Take it for what it is. Mutual pleasure."

Jody laughed. "Not so mutual."

"Oh, you're wrong there." He gripped her arse cheeks and pulled her hard against him. "Feeling you get off is one of the most pleasurable things I've ever experienced."

She highly doubted it. His hard cock still pressed against her. He had to be in some sort of discomfort if not outright pain. "I..." Words failed her.

"Here's what we're going to do. When you're ready, I'm going to let you go and you're going to get in your car and drive home." He gave her arse a gentle squeeze.

"But—"

"Nope. The only butt is the one I've got my hands on. The same one that will be in that driver's seat in a few minutes."

"Dan."

He kissed the top of her head. "'Night, Jody. I'll see you tomorrow morning." With care, he let her go.

No argument came to mind. No words or thoughts or anything that might make this moment easier. Thank you was on the tip of her tongue, but the words seemed out of place and inadequate at best, so she turned around and opened her door. She slid into her seat and felt the stickiness of her come-soaked undies between her legs. Sliding the key into the ignition, she reached for the door only to have Dan close it for her. They stared at each other through the window and she pressed the button to lower it.

"Please, don't say anything." He brushed a finger down her cheek, over the swollen flesh of her lips. "I'll see you tomorrow."

"O-okay."

He grinned and stepped back. "Don't forget to pack your swimsuit."

The reminder of what lay ahead had Jody's insides springing back to life. Thinking about sharing a hot tub with Dan sent a shiver down her spine and a host of sexually charged images through her mind. She needed to leave. Distance would help her think clearly. Turning the key, she started the car then put it in reverse. With one last look at Dan, she lowered the handbrake and reversed out of her spot. It took everything she had not to glance in the rear view mirror to see if he watched as she drove away.

She had no idea what to think or how to feel about the last few minutes in his arms. There was no denying she'd enjoyed herself, the evidence was in her drenched underwear and making the drive home extremely uncomfortable. Stripping out of her clothes and jumping in the shower was the first order of business when she got home. Hopefully, the girls would be busy with homework and she could sneak to her room without having to stop.

Jody flipped the visor down and slid open the mirror. Her face was flushed and her hair was a mess with numerous strands escaping her ponytail and hanging in her face. Any adult would know exactly what she'd been doing, but at fifteen and thirteen, she hoped the girls would be oblivious and assume she'd just had a hectic day at work. A car cut her off and she shook herself free of her thoughts and concentrated on the madness of peak-hour traffic.

It was a bitch. Everyone seemed to be in a big hurry to get where they were going and nobody wanted to let someone else get in front of them. She barely missed being part of a three-car smash, braking hard to miss the vehicle in front and spewing some choice words she'd never utter with her daughters around. Then again, it had been an afternoon of doing things she'd never do with the girls present.

With fingers curled tightly around the steering wheel, Jody negotiated the roads until she hit the quieter suburban streets near her house and she could relax her grip. She lived in an area where the median house price was considered low, but it was a beautiful older area of Sydney that she loved and one that she could afford on her own with two kids to support. As she pulled into her driveway, she wondered what Dan would think of her small fibro house. Would he see the fading, chipped paint? Would he notice the lawn needed mowing and the garden weeding?

Giving herself a mental slap, she switched off the car and got out. It shouldn't matter what he thought. She didn't need his approval of where she lived. Besides, she owned it. Well, she owned three quarters of it, the bank owned the rest. Perhaps the peeling paint and messy yard were the bank's quarter. Jody glanced down the street then back at her house and tried to forget about the man she'd just driven away from. What mattered was what lay before her. Her house and the girls tucked safely inside its walls.

She didn't need a man to give her a home. She'd done that herself without the help of the man she'd married. Nothing Dan offered could compare with what she had. But even as she thought the words, she knew she was a liar. The dampness of her undies and hum of pleasure still vibrating in her blood proved that.

Chapter Four

Dan glanced over at a silent Jody. The woman had barely spoken two words to him all morning at the office, and that was a feat in itself considering they'd had to pack equipment for this weekend's job. They'd loaded the van in silence, climbed in and driven for over an hour and still she'd said nothing. It was starting to get on his nerves, but he didn't know what the right words to disperse the awkward tension humming between them were.

He couldn't tell if she was embarrassed by what had happened yesterday or pissed off at him for taking advantage of her. Again. He'd been angry with himself for ambushing her a second time until he'd accepted the fact that, right or wrong, he'd made a move and he had to live with the fallout. Of course, that was easier said than done, especially when he sat beside a stone-faced Jody. Dan figured he had two choices. Ignore it—which appeared to be how Jody wanted to handle it—or bring it up and discuss it. Right now, neither option appealed.

They had roughly another two hours on the road, so she was effectively a captive audience until they reached the hotel. Once they got to their destination, they'd be caught up in the prep for tonight's welcome dinner, so if he was going to clear the air between them, now would be the perfect time. As much as he didn't want to, Dan couldn't take any more of this strained silence.

"About yesterday—"

"Stop." She turned in her seat to face him. "I don't want to talk about it."

Dan took his eyes off the road for a second to look at her.

"What?"

"I don't mix my personal and professional lives and we're working right now."

Was she for real? "Considering we were on the job both times I've kissed you, I'm not sure your argument holds."

"We weren't yesterday. We'd left for the day."

He could see her squirming in her seat from the corner of his eye.

"Look. Can we just stick with work?"

"Why? So you can continue to ignore the sparks between us?" He couldn't believe Jody thought that was even possible. Any idiot could see there was something going on. The air between them vibrated with the tension.

Dan kept his eyes on the road, but he could see her moving in his peripheral vision so he knew she'd turned away to look out the passenger window. Half of him wanted to leave it alone, not upset her, but the other half wanted to drag it out in the open and deal with it. Hopefully in a positive way—like Jody agreeing they should explore what had them drawing closer together with every breath.

"Jody." He swivelled his gaze from the road to her and back again. "I can't pretend it never happened."

She sighed. "I know. I'm not asking you to forget, exactly. It's just…I can't deal with this right now."

"When then?" He didn't mean to push her, but he couldn't help it.

"Can we just stick to work for now?"

Dan glanced over again to find her still facing the side window. Her shoulders were hunched and she was twisting her fingers together in her lap. As much as he didn't want to drop it, he knew it was pointless to keep pushing. He wouldn't get anywhere at the moment. He let out a breath. "If that's what you want, but the second this job is over we're dealing with us."

"Thank you," she murmured.

Manners had him almost saying you're welcome, but he stopped himself because he didn't want her thanks. Dropping the subject wasn't what he wanted to do, except the only way he'd get his way was to back off and try again later. He leaned forward and hit the switch for the radio. Music filled the cab as they sped down the freeway at a hundred and ten kilometres an hour. Traffic was minimal this time of day so he was able to stick to the speed limit for most of it. If they'd left the office any later, they would have been caught in not only the evening rush home but the weekend travellers as well.

The next two hours were accompanied by the radio, a quiet Jody and Dan's brooding silence, making for a less-than-comfortable trip. By the time he pulled into the driveway of the hotel, he was more than ready to get out of the tomb the van had become. As he hopped out and made his way to the rear of the van, a valet came over. "You'll need a couple of trolleys for what we've got, mate," Dan said.

The valet's eyes bugged out when he peered through the back doors. "Right, two trolleys," he said before scurrying back the way he'd come.

Jody stepped beside him. "I'll check in while you get the equipment unloaded."

"Okay. Make sure you ask for Keith Mooney, he's our hotel contact for the weekend."

"Will do." She turned towards the hotel but glanced over her shoulder before she took a step. "Anything else?"

"No. We just need to get all our gear inside." Jody nodded and Dan watched her walk away. Staring at her, he had to wonder if he'd ever get what he wanted. He always seemed to be staring at her back as she left him in her wake. He'd give anything to be walking beside her. She disappeared into the hotel as the valet came out pulling two trolleys. Dan frowned. It didn't matter what he wanted right now. He had a job to do, and as much as he wanted to blow it off and deal with Jody and the pull between them, he couldn't. Focusing on the van, he began stacking boxes on one trolley while the valet put their bags on the other.

Jody took a deep breath of air-conditioned air and slowed her pace as she walked to the registration desk. Being trapped in the car with Dan for the last three hours had just about broken her. So many times, she'd been a breath away from asking him why he'd kissed her. She wouldn't ask about what had followed, it seemed to be a natural progression whenever their lips met. If they hadn't been interrupted the first time they'd kissed, she had no doubt they would have ended up without clothes and in a similar state of passion as yesterday. Possibly more so. They were combustible.

She couldn't ignore the chemistry any more than she could ignore the man himself when he sat a few feet away. Ten minutes tops. That's all she had before he'd be with her again and all her intelligence went south along with every rational thought. Reaching the counter, she smiled at the woman behind it. "Hi, is Keith Mooney around? I'm Jody Walsh from Are You Game? He's expecting us."

"Oh, yes, he told me to keep my eye out for you. I'll let him know you're here." The woman, Keisha if her nametag was correct, picked up the phone and punched a button. "Mr Mooney, the people from Are You Game? have arrived."

Jody opened her bag and pulled out the credit card Cassie had given her for work use. She also retrieved the run sheet she'd printed off for herself before leaving the office this morning.

"Mr Mooney will be right out. I can check you in while you're waiting."

Jody stopped reading and returned her attention to the young woman. "Great." Rattling metal had her turning to see Dan pushing a trolley laden with their equipment through the front doors, a valet right behind him with their luggage on another. "Could someone take our luggage to our room while we get set up for tonight?"

"Certainly," Keisha said.

"Checked in?" Dan asked as he joined her at the desk.

"Doing that now, and Mr Mooney is on his way."

"Good. I want to take a look at the rooms we'll be utilising before we set anything up."

"Why? I think what you had drawn up was good."

"Yeah, I was lucky the hotel sent me the room sizes and layouts, but I still want to take a look before we unpack."

He had a point. Sometimes something as little as the placement of a power point could throw out an entire layout. "Just let me know what you want me to do and when." As soon as the words left her mouth, Jody realised their unintended double meaning.

Dan grinned and leaned closer, whispering in her ear, "I like the sound of you doing what I want, when I want."

A shiver raced over her skin and her stomach flip-flopped before dropping low and sinking heavy and hot into her pelvis. She took a sharp breath and pulled in his unmistakable scent—a mix of coffee and leather and something uniquely Dan. Without conscious thought, she tipped towards him and would have leaned against him if they hadn't been interrupted.

"Mr. O'Conner. Ms. Walsh. Lovely to have you both with us. I'm Keith Mooney."

A striking blond man in black trousers and light-blue business shirt with the hotel logo on the left breast pocket came towards them. He was almost too good looking, and Jody had to look away or risk getting caught staring at his surprising beauty. She focused on Dan and found herself comparing the two. While Dan wasn't quite as handsome, he wasn't anything to sneeze at either. And while Keith was blindingly attractive, it was Dan who set her pulse racing and her breath hitching.

Dan extended his hand to shake the other man's. "Pleasure

is ours. We're looking forward to working with your employees."

"They're all quite excited about the weekend seminar. I hope the trip up wasn't too long." He turned and offered Jody his hand.

It was the longest drive she'd ever endured, but not in the way Keith implied, so she shook his hand and lied. "It was very pleasant. It's a while since I've driven through this part of the state."

"You're here at a good time too. We haven't hit the freezing temps of winter yet and with the autumn rain all the plants have recovered from the brutal heat of summer." Keith turned to Keisha. "Are they checked in, Keisha?"

"Yes, Mr. Mooney." Keisha placed two key cards on the counter. "Ms. Walsh asked that their luggage be taken to their room while you show them around, so I'll get Dave on that right away."

"Good, good." Keith grabbed both keys and held one out to each of them. "Right, if we're ready, we'll tour the conference rooms. Would either of you like something to eat or drink while we're wandering around?"

"I'm fine, how about you, Jody?" Dan asked as he took his key.

"I'd like a bottle of water if I may." She'd finished the small bottle she'd brought with her over thirty minutes ago, and with her body temperature spiking whenever Dan was around, her mouth had become as dry as the Nullarbor Plains. She took the key from Keith and slid it into the back pocket of her slacks.

"Give me two secs to grab your water and we'll get started." He walked behind the counter and entered a door. Gone less than a minute, he was back with her drink and leading them across the hotel lobby. "This is the original part of the hotel, the section we're about to enter and the one your room is in are the additions. You'll notice the architects and builders did everything they could to marry the old with the new. I think you'll agree they did an excellent job."

Jody cracked the bottle and took a sip while she listened to Keith explain how the hotel had gone from being a small forty-room boutique hotel to a four-hundred room one with conference facilities and five-star-resort amenities. She had to admit it was lovely, in particular the way gardens and seating had been incorporated throughout the public indoor areas to give the place a relaxed atmosphere. She would love to sit in one of the many nooks with a book in her hand. Shame she was here to work really. It would have been lovely to enjoy some down time.

They toured the two rooms set aside for their workshop sessions and neither of them found a problem with the layout and what Dan had drawn up from the specs the hotel had sent him. The larger room they were using for the night events met their demands as well, and with the wall of windows looking out over the gardens that would be lit up after dark, Jody thought it would have a magical feel once the lights were turned down low and the evening's festivities began.

"Jody?"

She spun to face Dan. "Sorry. What?" Looking around, she realised they were alone in the big room. Where had Keith gone? When had he gone?

"Did you hear anything I just said?"

Embarrassed to admit she'd completely zoned out, she tried to bluff her way through. "Sure. Tonight's function is in here."

Dan laughed. "Nice try. But, no. I asked if you wanted to go to the room for anything before we get started with set up."

Her face heated. He'd caught her out. "Um. No, I don't need anything."

"Are you feeling all right?" He stepped closer. "You're looking a little flushed."

She definitely felt warm, but it wasn't illness that made her that way. "It's a little hot in here, that's all. Plus, we've been rushing around for the last few minutes." Okay, so they hadn't been running or even walking fast. As excuses went, it wasn't a very good one.

He stepped closer and pressed the back of his fingers to her cheek. "Are you sure? You feel a little hot to me."

Jody swallowed. It wasn't his words that had her stomach clenching and her blood racing. Dan didn't bother to mask the desire burning in his eyes. His hand might be gentle and innocuous, but those eyes...they were dark with arousal and dangerous to her self-control. She fought the urge to lean into him and instead pulled away. "I'm fine."

Putting some distance between them, she headed towards the door to see if the trolley with their gear had found its way to this area of the hotel. She needed to get busy—distract herself—with work. Not that anything could divert her wayward hormones or her body's reaction to being close to Dan. Jody knew she was in trouble. Pushing him away was becoming more and more difficult, and it was only a matter of time before she succumbed to the volatile chemistry arcing between them.

Dan wiped the sweat from his brow. They'd been working for three hours and the room was finally the way he'd imagined it. He'd wanted the tables set like the house tables in Harry Potter. Each group would have a long table and a house flag, in this case a department logo. Food and beverage, meet and greet and housekeeping. Management would be working alongside their staff—on equal footing—for the duration of the weekend.

Cassie had a marvellous program for her corporate sessions, and this one was tailor-made for the hotel industry. Over the course of two days, the participants would be working together in games designed to teach them problem solving and interacting as a team. He'd run these workshops before so he knew them well, but Jody had had limited exposure to the corporate side of the business. Until now, she'd been dealing with the adult and children's party lines. He wanted her to be comfortable with the seminars she'd be running on her own.

"Okay, we're done." He headed over to where Jody was laying out the house flags on the end of the long tables. "Let's go up to the room and run through the program for each of the sessions you're doing. I want to be sure you're familiar with all aspects of them."

"Oh, I already went over them. I didn't see anything that caused me concern."

"Well, we're done down here anyway. Plus, we have to get ready at some point." Dan placed his hand on her lower back and urged her towards the door. "And I'm feeling a little hungry, so I'm planning to order some room service and sit out on the patio for a few minutes of downtime before the chaos begins."

"I'm not hungry." Was she trying to dodge him? Probably.

"It's been hours since lunch, and it'll be another few before dinner."

"I don't snack between meals," she argued.

"I'll order you a coffee." He wasn't about to let her weasel out of spending some time with him, which is exactly what she was attempting to do.

Dan thought he was home free when they reached the door only to run into Mooney. Who, Dan noticed, couldn't take his eyes off Jody. A growl rumbled in his chest and he had to fake a cough to cover it.

"Hey, you're done." Mooney peered past them into the room. "Good, I thought you might like a guided tour through the gardens." His gaze was focused on Jody once more.

"Actual—"

"That would be lovely." Jody stepped away from Dan's hand and he curled his fingers with the need to grab her shirt and yank her back. "Dan was just heading—"

"I think a walk through the gardens would be great." Dan tried not to grit his teeth. He wasn't about to let this guy sneak off with his woman. *Ah, shit.* She wasn't his. He knew that. But he couldn't let her go off with Mooney on her own. Not when they still hadn't reached an understanding. "Lead the way."

"Oh." The look on Mooney's face almost made Dan laugh. Obviously, the guy had expected only Jody to accept his invitation. Dan smiled and held out his arm to indicate Mooney should lead. "Right. This way then," Mooney mumbled as he turned.

Mooney led them out through a side door and into a lush garden with weaving paths and stone benches for those who wished to sit a while. Dan wasn't into plants or gardening, but he could easily appreciate the beauty of the place. He listened with half an ear to the names Mooney rattled off as they passed each new bed of colour. Jody appeared to be soaking up every word the guy said, and Dan's insides churned. Why couldn't she pay *him* that much attention?

They made their way around the building to the rear where the hillside dropped away to reveal rows and rows of grapes. With the area being one of Australia's premier wine producers, he wasn't surprised to find the fruit vines, but until Mooney explained about the hotel's own line of select wines served only to guests, Dan hadn't realised the place was more than a hotel.

"We'll be offering our wines to a few of Sydney's bigger restaurants in the near future, but until then you're only able to sample them here," Mooney said.

"I'd love to try some. Are you serving them tonight?" Jody asked.

"Yes." Mooney grinned. "Are you a wine connoisseur?"

Jody's laughter echoed around them. "Hardly. I just like the occasional sip."

"That's more than you're allowed." Dan couldn't fight his need to squash Mooney's delight. "We're working."

"Oh, surely you're able to have a glass or two?" Mooney asked.

"Nope. The boss has a very strict rule about drinking on the job." Dan smiled smugly when Mooney frowned.

"Dan's right. Even having a sip could get me fired." Jody gave Dan a narrow-eyed look before turning to aim a smile at Mooney. "Perhaps I'll be lucky enough to try it some other time."

He wasn't overly concerned by Jody's supposed anger at him. She knew as well as he did neither of them would be drinking alcohol this weekend. Although, if she did have a couple of glasses she might soften towards him...

"Oh, look at the time." Mooney held up his arm, displaying his watch in an exaggerated fashion. "I have something I have to do before I finish for the day. I'll see you both tonight."

Before either of them could say a word, the man was striding away and out of sight.

"Ouch!" Dan rubbed his upper arm where Jody had just landed a punch. She was surprisingly strong. "What the hell was that for?" Surely if she was going to hit him it would have been one of the two times he'd planted a kiss on her without permission or warning.

"For being an arse." She turned on her heel and headed in the opposite direction to Mooney.

"When?" Dammit. She was running away from him again. Chasing after Jody was becoming an annoying habit. It didn't stop him from following though.

Chapter Five

Jody slipped into the elevator and pressed the close-door button. Unfortunately, she wasn't quick enough and Dan threw his arm between the doors just before they sealed shut. Of course, that meant the damn things opened again and he stepped right in and kept on coming. The look on his face was a good reason to move back out of his way. When he continued to come at her, she kept reversing until she came up against the rear wall just as the doors closed with a soft thump.

She swallowed over the throbbing lump in her throat. It could only be her heart because the stupid thing was racing so hard there was no way it had remained in her chest. He glared at her with green eyes turbulent with emotion. Anger then arousal flashed before his eyes lowered, his gaze following the sweep of her tongue as she slipped it out to wet dry lips. His pupils dilated and her breath stalled as he bent towards her.

He gave her time. Closed the distance in long, drawn-out seconds that allowed her to escape if she chose to. She knew what was coming. Could read it in his hooded eyes, the angle of his head and the smile kicking up one corner of his mouth. But she didn't pull away. Didn't turn her head. Not at all. Instead, she held her breath, tipped her chin up and waited for him to kiss her.

Their lips touched in a whisper-soft caress that did little to alleviate the need curling low in her belly. Jody couldn't wait for Dan to take them deeper. Rising to her toes, she tilted her face and sealed their mouths fully. He groaned, the sound vibrating across her lips and sending shivers through her jaw. He flicked out his tongue, licked from corner to corner before probing the seam of her lips and seeking entry. Opening for him, she tangled her tongue with his.

Lost in the pleasure of kissing Dan, she moved closer, slid her arms around his neck and tugged him to her, pressed her body along the length of his so every part of her front touched every part of his. It was her turn to groan when he nipped her bottom lip while wrapping his hands around her arse and yanking her sex against his. He was long and thick, rubbing against her intimately as he rocked them together.

Jody moaned and moved even closer. She threaded her fingers through his hair, the soft strands sliding over her skin in a sensual caress as she held him to her. Dan's hands weren't idle either. One still gripped her arse, the other swept over her hip, up her side and between them to cup her breast. He stroked his thumb across her taut nipple and sent a jolt of desire arrowing straight to her core. She couldn't help the whimper of need or the bucking of her hips.

A rush of air blew past and she had a split second to wonder where it came from before she heard a woman gasp. Abruptly brought out of her lust stupor, Jody pulled away from Dan. But he wouldn't let her go. He held her close, cradled her against his chest when he leaned over and hit the button for their floor. Just before the doors slid closed again, she saw the stunned look on the elderly woman's face. Heat filled her face and she buried her stinging cheeks in the curve of Dan's neck.

"Shit. We really have to stop doing this in public places." He smoothed his hands up and down her back in long, sweeping strokes. "One of these days we're going to get carried away and end up getting arrested for indecent exposure."

Jody could hear the humour in his voice, but she didn't smile. She appreciated his attempt to lighten the mood, though she couldn't find the funny side of once again being so caught up in Dan she'd forgotten where she was. The man was lethal to her common sense. He turned up and good judgement went right out the door along with every other reason she needed to ignore the way her body wanted his.

With a sigh, she slipped from his arms and moved to the front of the elevator. She didn't say a word and, thankfully, neither did he. The bell dinged and the car eased to a stop. Breath held, she waited what felt like hours but was probably no more than a second, for the doors to open. Exiting, she scanned the plaque in front of her to determine which direction to go. They were on the executive level of the east wing, and according to Keith, their room would have a view of the valley they'd seen earlier as well as a terrace hot tub.

She turned right and moved down the hall at a clipped pace. Why she thought she could leave Dan behind when they were sharing a room was beyond her and, again, she could only blame the fact he seemed to disconnect her from her brain whenever he was near. She slowed her steps, allowed him to catch up halfway to the room so they could continue the rest of the way side-by-side. He produced his key before she could and slid it into the sensor to deactivate the lock.

The mechanism clicked, the light turned green and he pushed the door open. "After you."

"Thanks." She walked in and was immediately taken by the large window that did indeed give them a view of the valley. But even the spectacular scenery couldn't hide the fact the room was barely big enough for the two double beds. Two beds no more than a foot apart. Beds they'd be sleeping in tonight. Dan slept naked. Naked. *Oh God.* She couldn't do this. Spinning around, she smacked right into Dan's hard chest, jarring her so hard her teeth clacked together.

"Hey." He curled his hands around her shoulders to hold her still. "What's wrong?"

She couldn't tell him, not without appearing as though she were a halfwit. Then again, if the shoe fit... Taking a deep breath, she searched for something believable to say. Spying their bags beside the door, she came up with the perfect out. "Our bags. I was checking to see they'd arrived safely." All right, not so perfect, but it would do if he stopped looking at her like she'd grown a second head or perhaps a third eye.

"They're by the door." He let her go and moved back. "I almost tripped over them when I walked in. Not sure how you missed them."

"Um, well, I..." Why was it she turned into a stammering idiot around him? Oh that's right, her brain disconnected whenever he got within sight.

"Hey, let's see what this hot-tub-terrace thing looks like." Dan walked past her and through a door she hadn't noticed beside the window. He stuck his head back inside. "Wow, you *have* to come see this thing."

With no other option, she followed him outside and found herself in little piece of paradise. Lush green vines covered the side walls designed to give the small space privacy from prying eyes. The tub was positioned against a half wall that allowed for an uninterrupted view of the sweeping hills below. Jody guessed you could fit four people in the hot tub if you squeezed in, but the area was definitely intended for one or two. Dan opened a cupboard that ran along the wall next to the door.

"Hey, there's even a bar fridge out here." He pulled out a Coke. "Want a drink?"

"No. Thanks."

He bent over to replace the drink and Jody couldn't stop her eyes from zeroing in on the way his pants stretched tight across his arse and thighs. Before she could get lost in the whole Dan intoxication again, she turned away and headed back inside. Perhaps a little space was needed, and not the kind found out on the balcony. Space as in miles and miles between them. She'd have to settle for a room and locked door for now. She grabbed her bag and flipped it over before unzipping it. By the time Dan came back in, she had her toiletries and tonight's clothes out.

"I'm going to shower and get ready now." Jody didn't wait for him to comment. She gathered her things and entered the bathroom, making sure to lock the door behind her.

Dan sighed as he flopped back on the bed. She'd run away again. Sure, she'd only gone as far as the bathroom, but a wall and locked door were the equivalent as far as he was concerned. He stared at the ceiling and replayed their kiss in the elevator. He'd never touched a woman who instantly drew need so deep he thought he might drown in it. She wasn't like anyone he'd ever been with in more ways than that though. Jody was mature for a start. As much as it shamed him, he had to admit his usual preference was for women younger than himself. Women less likely to be looking for something more than a few hours of fun.

Call him shallow, God knows his mother had on numerous occasions in the past, and until now it hadn't worried him. Now he wanted to go back and erase history so Jody wouldn't see what kind of man he was. Dan knew he'd never treat Jody in the sometimes callous way he'd treated other women, but she couldn't know that. And if she looked at his behaviour before now, she'd be forced to make the conclusion that he was only after one thing. And he couldn't deny it no matter how much he wanted to.

He dragged his hands through his hair, scraping it away from his face and tugging on the ends until pain lanced his scalp. He'd have to prove to her she was different. Whether she knew about his insensitive—though unintentional—actions before or not, he wanted her to see he could care—*did* care. With every fibre of his being, he wanted to prove he was worthy of her time.

Rolling onto his side, he gazed out the huge picture window at the sun-soaked fields of grapes. The afternoon light left dark shadows and bright spotlights scattered over the vines as the sun slowly slipped beyond the horizon. He wasn't one for appreciating nature, but he had to admit the countryside surrounding the hotel was breathtaking. Almost as much as the woman currently showering a few plasterboards, timber and tiles away.

Just the thought of Jody naked behind that closed door had every muscle in Dan's body stretched tight. The throbbing in his groin hadn't quit since the first time he'd kissed her and had only intensified with each one since. She was like a drug in his system. He'd had a hit and the high had made him crave more. He wanted her worse than he'd wanted his first car. And that had been a six-year yearning that he'd finally managed to quench the day he'd turned seventeen and plunked down the three and half grand he'd scrimped and saved his entire teenage life.

Needing a distraction, he reached over to the bedside table and picked up the room-service menu. Scanning the pages, he didn't see anything that appealed, but then the one thing he did want wasn't on the menu. He'd have to come up with a substitute until he could get his hands on his first craving. Unable to decide, he went with a standard feel-good food. Fries. He snatched up the phone and hit the room-service button. When the woman answered, he ordered two plates of fries and hung up. By the time Jody came out of the bathroom there'd be a snack waiting for her, and hopefully he'd have gotten his libido in check by then too.

Dan sat up and rolled off the bed. He'd unpack while he waited for Jody and food. The hot tub beckoned, but he didn't have time to luxuriate in it like it should be enjoyed. They had a little over two hours before they had to be back downstairs ready to meet this weekend's participants. If he remembered right, they had a four-hour gap between the last session tomorrow and the evening function. He rubbed his hands together. A four-hour window was plenty of time to not only enjoy the tub but to convince Jody to join him.

The door opened behind him and he turned to find Jody wrapped only in a towel. He swallowed. Hard. His throat was dry, his mouth more so, and the erection he'd managed to subdue came roaring back to life. Before he could think, he'd taken a step, causing her to back up. Her reaction was enough to stop him in his tracks.

"I forgot my..." She darted over to where her suitcase lay open on the floor and whipped out a black lace bra.

He groaned and clenched his fists tight enough to cut the circulation to his fingers. His balls retracted into his body as more blood filled his cock. How he stayed in place and didn't rush over and ravish her he couldn't say. All he knew was one wrong move and she'd run farther than the bathroom, and he couldn't live with that. Not when everything he never dreamed he wanted was in front of him all pink and wet from her shower wrapped in a fluffy white towel. If it was the last thing he did, he wouldn't blow it with her.

"I ordered some food." His voice sounded tight, but it was a wonder he could get any words out through his constricted throat.

She paused on her dash back to the bathroom. "Oh."

"Yeah." Dan rubbed his jaw. "Just some fries to see us through until dinner."

"Ah...okay. I won't be much longer." She disappeared behind the door, the soft click of the lock echoing through the room as she shut herself away once more.

He felt like an idiot. He was an idiot. She'd been naked and he'd frozen like a randy teenager getting his first look at a set of boobs. The woman did a number on him, plain and simple. Only nothing he experienced—no emotion, no physical reaction—when he was around Jody was simple. Everything about her—about them—was complicated and confusing and downright scary when he let himself think about what he wanted for longer than a few minutes.

She'd blown into his life and turned it upside down without trying. In fact, she'd tried everything she could to avoid him, but the second they were in close quarters and she quit running, they went up in flames. They just had to find a way for neither of them to get burned. Considering they wanted different things, one of them was at least going to be disappointed. Whether that was him or her remained to be seen, but Dan hadn't given up on something he wanted before now, and he didn't see himself backing away from Jody and all being with her offered.

He'd have to convince her they were a good bet. He knew she was divorced, knew she had two teenage girls, and from what little he'd gleaned from Cassie and Luc, he also knew she hadn't had an easy life up until now. Dan didn't expect things to be smooth sailing between them. He fully expected to fight her every step of the way. She'd already proven her opposition to his intentions. It was a shame her body told a different story whenever he got close. She might have had a chance of keeping him at arm's length if her mouth and body spoke the same language.

Dan would have to make sure her mouth fell in line with her body. And soon. His own body couldn't take much more of this constant state of arousal. Besides, it was getting to be embarrassing walking around with a hard-on all day. He could take matters into his own hands—literally—except he felt no urge to satisfy his needs that way. When he finally found relief it would be with Jody. Inside Jody.

Jody took a deep breath to gather her courage and opened the door. Unlike before, she was dressed. Not that her clothes were a barrier against Dan's probing gaze. Starting at her toes, his gaze slowly slid up her body until those piercing green eyes met hers. He had a way of stripping her bare with just a look—of touching her without laying a hand on her.

A shiver skipped down her spine and goose bumps broke out on her arms and neck. "Bathroom's all yours." She sounded breathless so cleared her throat.

"Excellent. I'll be quick. Keep an ear out for room service."

"Oh, I was going to go down—"

"Plenty of time to be working later. Take a few minutes to relax."

Dan disappeared into the bathroom, leaving her to wonder why she had the urge to run at every turn. She knew their overwhelming attraction played into it, but she'd never shied away from the tough things before. Not like she was doing with Dan. She'd stuck out her shitty marriage in the hope of things improving for more years than were sensible, and while she couldn't compare that with her attraction to Dan, she couldn't help think she'd stayed married because it had been easier than facing the fear of what would happen when she walked. It hadn't even been her decision.

She closed her eyes and pushed the horrible thoughts aside. Colin may have been the one to make the break, but once he had, Jody had moved forward with steely determination to prove to everyone that she and the girls would be fine. And they were. *She* was. Except now she had a thing for a younger man and she didn't have the first clue what to do about it other than run for the hills. If she couldn't do that then she'd ignore it until it went away. Only he wasn't going away. He was getting closer, and with each step he took she wanted to take her own towards him *and* away from him.

Could she be any more screwed up?

A knock on the door made her jump and her eyes popped open. She strode over and squinted through the peep hole to see a uniformed staff member. This would be a good opportunity to observe the food and beverage service. Jody opened the door and held it wide. "Come in."

The young man headed for the small table jammed into the far corner. It shouldn't be there, not when there was so little space in the room that the beds were almost touching. He placed the small tray down and turned with a small folder and pen. "Sign here please."

After a quick check of the bill, Jody signed and handed the

folder back. "Thank you."

"You're welcome. Enjoy." He let himself out with a quiet click of the door.

Grabbing a pen and paper, she made some notes about lack of interaction with guests. While the young man was professionally presentable and polite, he didn't engage in any conversation that wasn't necessary, and she wanted to be sure to bring it up during the sessions tomorrow. She wandered back to the table and lifted the lid on one of the plates. A steaming-hot pile of crispy fries filled the plate. The smell alone had her mouth watering and her tummy rumbling. Maybe she was a little peckish. Lifting the second lid, she saw that Dan had ordered a meal for each of them.

"Hey, no pinching mine. You've got your own."

Spinning around, she found Dan out of the bathroom, towel slung precariously low on his hips, standing not two feet away. He was barely covered. His thighs, thick with muscle and sprinkled with a smattering of dark hair, were on display. Glancing up, she saw his ripped abdomen with a tantalising trail of dark hair running down from his belly button to disappear under the towel. Jody tilted her head to the side in her effort to figure out what was wrong.

Oh my God! It wasn't a bath towel wrapped around his hips. It was a *hand* towel! Good Lord, if he moved too fast the thing would be on the floor in a flash and she'd be getting flashed. Turning back around, Jody stared at the plate of fries and tried to catch her breath. Having a nearly naked Dan in front of her did a number on her libido, but the thought of a completely naked Dan had her pulse racing, her breasts tingling and her sex swelling. She felt his heat behind her and knew he stood close enough to touch. If she turned back around...

He reached around her and grabbed a handful of fries. She heard the crunch as he sank his teeth into them. Heard the moan of delight as he devoured them and reached for more. His arm brushed hers and she could smell the soap on his skin, the damp heat still clinging to him from the shower. Taking a step to the side, she avoided contact and grabbed some much needed breathing room.

"These are great. Aren't you going to eat any?" he asked as he picked up another handful.

"Um, yes, but I want to get a drink first." Scooting past him, being careful not to brush up against him at all, Jody exited the room to the terrace where she got a drink from the mini fridge. She pressed the cool can against her hot cheek.

"Jody, can you grab me one while you're there?" Dan called through the door.

She closed her eyes and breathed deep. As much as she wanted to hide out here, she couldn't. She'd just have to suck it up and deal as Leigh was fond of saying. The thought of her girls made her smile. They were the two most important people in her world and for them she'd make it through this job—the weekend—without doing anything stupid like jumping the man who insisted on tempting her with every breath he took.

Chapter Six

Dan reached over and flicked off the bedside lamp. The red glow of the alarm clock mocked him. One thirty and Jody still hadn't returned to the room. Dinner had been a success and he couldn't fault her in any way when it came to the job. She'd done exactly what she was supposed to. She'd mingled well and spent time getting to know each of the men and women participating in the weekend's workshops with the skill of a seasoned professional. There wasn't a single thing he could be angry about when it came to work.

It was her after-hour's behaviour that had his nerves raw and irritated. She'd been talking with Mooney and two of the other men at the end of the evening. Dan had wanted to interrupt, remind her they had an early start, but playing the demanding boss or worse, a jealous jerk, wasn't something he was comfortable doing. So he'd walked away, leaving her downstairs while he came up to the room. Alone. That had been over an hour ago.

He couldn't help the jealous thoughts rolling around his head. Couldn't stop the images of Jody and Mooney tangled together from flooding his mind and tormenting him. Dan knew his jealousy was unfounded. Other than Mooney's obvious interest in her, Dan had no reason to suspect they were hooking up. And as much as he wanted to, he wouldn't go hunt her down and drag her back to their room. Turning over, he punched his pillow. Again.

Dan took a deep breath and held it before letting it out in a rush. He needed to calm the fuck down or he'd be pinning her against the wall, peppering her with questions of where she'd been the second she set foot in the room. He'd thought sharing a room would be torture, but not this kind. Keeping his hands—and mouth—off her had been his biggest concern. Not once did he think she'd find a way to drive him crazier than worrying about being in close quarters.

A full moon hung low in the sky across the valley. He'd left the curtains open so the room was bathed in a soft glow. He snorted. His brilliant idea of letting in the moonlight to give the room a romantic intimacy had certainly blown up in his face. Hard to get romantic when the object of your desire wasn't even here. Throwing back the covers, Dan jumped out of bed and strode over to stand in front of the window.

The landscape, even in the shadows of night, was breathtaking, but he didn't really see it. He only saw the possibility of Jody being with another man. A man who wasn't him. Why he thought this way when he knew in his gut she wouldn't be with anyone else pissed him off the most when it came to the out of control emotions he experienced when it came to Jody. She'd made it clear she wanted nothing to do with him by avoiding him at every opportunity. Had he listened to her not-so-subtle rebuff? No. He'd taken every chance to get closer to her and he'd continue to do so.

He was a masochist. There was no other explanation for his continued pursuit. Rejected at every turn, he kept coming back for more. He'd never done that before. No meant no, and with the abundance of women available, Dan had always moved on to the next one with ease. Until Jody. She pulled him back, made him more determined to win her over with every rebuff.

Dan ran a hand down his bare chest. True to his word, he was naked. He didn't even own pyjamas, so unless he slept in his underwear and a T-shirt, which he had no intention of doing, she'd just have to put up with the possibility of seeing him naked. The door rattled behind him and he glanced over his shoulder to see Jody, head down and shoes off, sneaking into the room. She didn't look his way, kept her gaze on the floor as she tip-toed across to her bag.

He thought about clearing his throat or moving to get her attention. Instead, he stood perfectly still and watched as she pulled clothes out of her suitcase. She tossed them on the bed behind her. The one he'd crawled out of not ten minutes ago. For someone who'd had a jumble of thoughts in his head, he suddenly found himself with a clean slate. Nothing except the sight of Jody lowering the zipper on her dress filled his mind.

She let the simple sheath slip from her shoulders and drop to the floor, leaving her in only a skimpy pair of bikini pants and bra. Her back was to him and he clenched his hands as the urge to walk over and run his fingers down her spine stole through him. He didn't breathe, didn't make a sound as he watched her turn and scoop up the top she'd thrown on the bed. For a split second, Dan had the glorious view of Jody from the front. One second of sheer bliss before she went perfectly still then screamed loud enough to wake the whole damn hotel.

"Fuck." Dan slammed his palms over his ears and ducked when she threw what was in her hand at him. "It's me. Dan!"

Jody froze on her way to the bedside table and he could only assume she'd planned to toss the lamp at him next. "Dan?"

"Who the fuck else would be in our room?" He bent to pick up the shirt she'd lobed at his head. "Surely you hadn't forgotten I was here?"

"Um, no, but..." She looked at the bed behind her, the one in front of her. "I thought you were asleep."

Thought? More like hoped. "Obviously I'm not."

He stepped up to the bed and dropped the shirt. It was at that moment he remembered how unclothed they both were. Her gaze lowered to his groin and bounced away quickly. Dan thought about covering up but dismissed the idea. He had nothing to hide, whether physically or emotionally, he wanted her to know where he stood. And some parts of him were standing very tall right now. She fidgeted, bare feet shuffling on the carpet, and looked everywhere apart from his direction. Figuring he had nothing to lose, he threw out the question burning in his throat.

"Were you with Mooney all this time?"

Her gaze snapped to his. "What? No."

Everything he was wanted to believe her. "Then where were you?" He had no right to interrogate her, but for the life of him he couldn't stop himself.

She sighed, her shoulders drooping with the release of air. "In the garden."

In the garden? "With who?" he demanded.

"No one." She reached over and grabbed her shirt, quickly tugging it over her head before continuing. "I was hoping to avoid this."

"What?" Him?

"You. Naked."

Ah. He'd always been comfortable without clothes on, so he couldn't understand why others were embarrassed when it was he who was on display, but he accepted most people couldn't handle nudity when they weren't intimately involved. "Does my nakedness offend you? Surely you've seen a naked man before." God, he hoped so. She'd been married for Christ sake.

Jody laughed and headed for the bathroom. "Yes, I've seen a few in my time."

A few? *What the fuck?* The bathroom door banged shut. "Who other than your ex have you seen naked?" he yelled at the closed door.

Jody leaned against the door and took a deep breath. My God, the man was breathtaking. Every sculptured inch of him. She'd seen him earlier with just a towel, but that was nothing compared to the sight of a completely naked Dan. Her mouth watered along with other areas of her anatomy. He hadn't shown one single shred of self-consciousness about his nudity either. If anything, he'd been more commanding—more compelling—than he appeared when clothed. She had to face it. The man did it for her.

Trouble with a capital T. That's where she was. Sighing, she shoved off the door and got ready for bed. She'd left her sleeping shorts in the room but the T-shirt she wore came past her thighs so the essentials were covered. Her bra was digging into her sides and she popped the catch through her shirt then slipped the straps off her shoulders and out through the sleeves in one of those contortionist tricks most women knew. More comfortable, she cleaned her teeth then used the loo before taking a brush to her hair.

Instead of her normal ponytail, she'd worn her hair out, and as usual when she did, it was a tangled mass of knots. She really should think about getting it cut except she liked the ease of long hair. Liked being able to gather it up into a tail out of her way and forget about it. She'd never been the type to bother with fussy hairstyles even in her younger years, and once the girls had arrived she'd barely had time to shower, never mind spend hours blow-drying. Jody yanked the last snag free then gathered it all together and wrapped an elastic band around it.

With nothing else to do, she had no excuse to hideout in the bathroom any longer. Determined to show Dan he didn't get to her even though he did on so many levels she refused to examine them, Jody opened the door and entered the room. The moonlight filtering in lit the area enough for her to see he was lying on the bed closest to the window. He had the sheet drawn up to his waist but the effort was too little too late. She knew what lay beneath the covers and wanted to crawl under there with him. But she wouldn't give in to the urge.

Using the skills she'd learn through years of self-denial, she crawled into the other bed. He didn't say anything and she was grateful. The last thing she wanted to do was rehash the evening. She was dog-tired and just wanted to go to sleep. She'd stupidly stayed away from the room in the hope of finding him asleep when she returned so they wouldn't have to face each other. Fat lot of good that idea had done her. Not only had he been awake, he'd been standing there in all his naked—aroused—mouth-watering glory waiting for her.

"Sorry." Dan's voice broke the quiet.

"For?" Jody didn't think he was apologising for being naked. Or aroused.

"For hounding you about where you've been and with whom." His sigh echoed through the room. "I have no right to question you."

She smiled. She totally understood why he'd asked so she couldn't let him think she'd been offended by his questioning. "It's okay. I should have just come to the room straight away."

"Why didn't you?"

The darkness made it easier to reveal her true feelings and she found herself disclosing more than she should. "I was trying to avoid being alone with you. Especially seeing how I knew you'd be stripping out of your clothes at some point."

"The chance of seeing me naked repulses you that much?" he asked.

Jody laughed. "No. Not repulsed."

"What then?"

"Honestly?"

"Yes." His answer was muffled by the rustling of the bedcovers and she imagined him rolling over. "I wouldn't expect you to be anything but honest with me, Jody."

He sounded closer and she turned her head to find him stretched out on the very edge of his bed closest to her.

"I was more concerned with keeping my distance from you. Naked or otherwise."

"I scare you?"

"No, not exactly." She sighed and returned her gaze to the darkened ceiling. "I can't explain it really, and even if I could I'm not sure you'd understand."

"Tell me about your marriage."

The abrupt change of subject threw her. "My marriage?"

"Yes. How old were you? How'd you meet him? How long were you together? Did you love him?"

"Eighteen. High school. Years past when we should have been and I thought I did. Now I'm not so sure."

"You don't know if you loved him?" Shock laced his words.

Jody turned her head to look at Dan. He lay on his side, elbow bent, head resting on his palm while he watched her. "I loved him with everything I was, but I'm not sure it was ever the kind of love that lasts a lifetime. Or perhaps it was the fact he didn't love me the same way in return."

"You don't think he loved you?"

"I think he did as much as he's capable of." How did she explain her ex without sounding bitter or mean? Because she wasn't either of those. They'd both made mistakes in the relationship and Jody fully owned her side of their failure. "Colin is a very selfish, thoughtless person. I'm not sure he's able to love anyone deeply. He definitely isn't willing to make the effort necessary to sustain a relationship. My error was in thinking I could love enough for both of us."

"He didn't deserve you or the girls."

Dan's quiet words brought the sting of tears. He was right. Colin had never deserved the devotion she'd shown him and he certainly didn't deserve to have two beautiful daughters. Her only consolation was that he didn't really have the girls. They'd never bonded even when she'd been married to their father, and he hadn't made any attempt to maintain the fragile connection they'd had once he'd left. "Thank you."

"I think I should be thanking him."

"Why?" What could Dan possible thank Colin for?

"Because if the guy wasn't such a douche bag, I wouldn't have the opportunity to get to know you. Not the way I want to."

"Oh." Jody didn't know what to say to that. She and Dan had hardly been on good terms after they'd first met and now they seemed to have stepped right past getting to know each other straight into being physically intimate.

"I know what you're thinking." She went to speak but he talked right over her. "You don't want to get to know me. I get that you've erected barriers after your marriage and I accept that getting to know you is going to be an uphill battle, but I think you're worth it. I think what we have between us, and don't deny there's something there, is worth the effort it's going to take for me to climb those barriers."

"Jeez, you don't pull any punches."

"I'm not going to trick you into this, Jody. I'll be honest every step of the way. I'm also going to push you when you won't want me to. But if you really want me to back off. Really want me to leave you alone and only be a workmate, I will."

Stunned speechless, Jody mulled over what Dan had said. On one hand, she wanted him to back off and leave her alone, but on the other, she liked that he was pursuing her. She'd never had that. Never had the rush of excitement that came with a man wanting her above all others.

"Here's what I suggest we do. We take this weekend to think about it. Ask me anything. Tell me anything. I'll do the same, and for just these two days we'll be nothing but honest and open. And when Sunday rolls around, we can decide where we're going from there. How does that sound?"

"Like you're backing off."

"Oh, no, definitely not." He got out of bed and came over to hers. Planting his hands on the pillow either side of her head, he leaned over and put his face right in hers. "I'll be in your face, stealing kisses and touching you every chance I get. I'm planning to stack the deck in my favour and I'll use every trick I have to do it."

She didn't get the opportunity to respond before he followed through on his words. He slanted his mouth over hers, but unlike the hurried, frantic kisses of before, he took his time. He swept his tongue across her lips, probed the seam until she opened and slipped her tongue out to tangle with his. A moan echoed between them and Jody wasn't sure if it was his or hers. The kiss was slow and lush, a gentle exploration of new territory that stole her breath and sped up her heart rate.

Her pulse beat a rapid cadence that reverberated through every nerve—every cell. Just when she thought he'd go deeper, he eased back, took them to soft nips and tender licks until he pulled away completely, leaving her panting for breath and wondering what was wrong. Before she could ask, he placed his lips on her forehead in a quick peck.

"Good night, Jody. Sweet dreams."

And then he was gone. Disappearing into the darkness as the moon slid behind a cloud. The lack of light left her feeling cold and bereft, or was that from the sudden lack of Dan's heat?

Dan lay beneath the covers listening to Jody breathe. She'd fallen asleep not long ago. Before that she'd tossed and turned. He'd been on the verge of going over there and pulling her into his arms when she'd stopped fidgeting and her breathing had evened out as she drifted off. He wished he could find sleep now she'd settled. Unfortunately, his mind wouldn't quit. The discussion about her marriage and ex had been enlightening. She hadn't revealed all that much, but what she had—coupled with what little he'd gleaned from Luc and Cassie—was enough for him to draw some very sad conclusions about her life up until now.

He was relieved to know she had the girls even though they tied her to the man who'd obviously taken her for granted. She'd at least had their unconditional love and affection. There was nothing he could do to improve her past, but he'd do everything in his power to make her future a happy one. If she'd let him.

Turning over, he stared out the window and watched the sky light up as a storm rolled through the valley. The weather matched his mood—dark and brooding—and he couldn't help the gloomy thoughts he had about her ex. Dan hoped Luc had given the man what he deserved at some point, except what he knew of Jody told him his wish had probably gone unfulfilled. She wasn't the type to take revenge or even want it. Her lack of hostility towards the man who hadn't given her any of what she deserved spoke volumes. He figured he'd have to learn to hold his tongue about her ex if he wanted to be a part of her future.

It wouldn't stop him from thinking bad thoughts though. He smiled. He'd definitely make her ex pay in his mind. Over and over again.

Chapter Seven

Jody let out a deep breath as she slipped into her room. Damn, it had been a long, long day. Six hours had seemed like sixty, and she was looking forward to the next four hours off to recharge. This was her first corporate event and she had to admit they were more strenuous than the usual adult's and kid's parties she dealt with. She'd coped with the program fine. There was never a point where she'd thought otherwise. It was being the centre of attention that she found draining. Usually she stayed behind the scenes and let the parties unfold. Today required constant input from her. Not to mention a couple of the men had been a little too friendly and attentive.

She'd soon nipped that in the bud, and Dan's scowl at morning tea had proven a major deterrent that had them backing right off. Unfortunately, she'd still had to deal with Keith Mooney's unrelenting interest. His pursuit had been anything but flattering towards the end, and she'd had to pull him aside and lie about being involved with someone so that he'd leave her alone. The fact he'd immediately jumped to the conclusion that it was Dan she was seeing had her troubled. Jody had no idea what would happen if word got back to Cassie.

She slipped off her shoes and kicked them aside before making her way to the mini-bar and a cold drink. She'd popped the top and had just collapsed into one of the chairs on the terrace when she heard Dan come through the door. Twisting around, she leaned over and peered through the doorway back into the room. He walked towards her, his stride purposeful as he stalked over and yanked her out of her seat. Barely a protest left her throat when his mouth slammed down on hers.

There was nothing gentle in his kiss. He took. Conquered every inch of her mouth without remorse. She couldn't catch her breath. Couldn't think beyond the man holding her so close the name badge on his shirt dug into her chest. Just when she thought she had a handle on it, when she sought to meet his demands, he pulled away. Ripping their mouths apart, he pushed her to arm's length. His chest heaved with each ragged breath and his eyes—greener than she'd ever seen them—studied her with such intensity her heart skipped.

"Do you have any idea how badly I want to smash Mooney's face in?" Dan's words were spoken through clenched teeth and razor sharp.

Jody shook her head. She wasn't following the conversation. Not when her mind was still lost in the darkness of that carnal kiss.

"I saw him put his hands on you and I wanted to break every one of his fingers. Slowly. One. By. One."

She swallowed. The violence vibrating in his words sent a quiver through her belly. She should be appalled by his confession—should be disgusted with the brutality of it. Instead, a thrill of excitement shot straight to her core. She'd never inspired such intense emotions in anyone.

He loosened his grip then slid his hands up and down her arms. "Sorry."

Jody shook her head, confused by his apology. "For what?"

Dan smiled, although it wasn't a happy one, more a twist of his lips. "I was rough with you."

Funny. She hadn't thought so. "Were you? I didn't notice." Jody stepped closer and brushed the backs of her fingers along his jaw. "Want to talk about it?"

"That depends."

"On what?"

"Whether you're into the whole alpha man thing." He let her go and moved away to retrieve a can of drink from the fridge.

"Basically, some guy put his hands on the woman I think of as mine."

She nodded. "I get that."

His gaze met hers. "You get that you're my woman?"

Laughing, she said, "No, I get that you *think* of me as yours."

"Ah, I can think it but it doesn't mean it's true, is that it?" He popped the top on the can and liquid sprayed the front of his shirt as the drink fizzed and bubbled out. "Shit!"

He brought the can to his mouth and sucked the overflowing soda. Her gaze was drawn to the splash of brown covering the front of his white shirt and she immediately thought about the stain that would be impossible to remove if he didn't do something about it now. "You've got it all over your shirt. Take it off and I'll soak it in cold water so the stain doesn't set."

Dan arched one eyebrow. "You're telling me to take my clothes off now?"

She smiled. "Just your shirt, smartarse, and only so you don't ruin it."

Dan hadn't waited for her to finish speaking. He'd put the can down and whipped the shirt over his head before the last word left her mouth. Muscles rippled in his arms and torso, and she ogled his chest with barely concealed desire. The trail of dark hair bisecting his abdomen and disappearing into his pants drew her gaze. Jody swallowed, her throat constricting with the burst of lust zipping through her system. Holding out her hand, she waited for him to pass her his top.

Once he did, she just about ran inside to avoid the temptation of touching his smooth skin. Heading straight to the bathroom, she ignored the man following her and concentrated on taking care of his shirt. She removed his name badge then turned the cold water on in the sink and shoved the stained area beneath the flow. When she was satisfied she'd removed all she could, she stuck the plug in the drain and let the basin fill up until it covered all the material.

"There. We'll leave it 'til later then rinse it again to make sure it's all out."

"You know I could just send it to be laundered by the hotel."

"Nonsense. No point wasting money when I can fix it for you."

She was drying her hands when he moved in behind her and slid his arms around her waist. "You know a guy could get used to being looked after." He nuzzled her nape, his lips warm and soft against her skin.

"D-don't get too used to it." A shiver rippled down her neck. "I'm not your mother."

Dan laughed as he let her go and stepped away. "You most certainly are not. She'd have boxed my ears for spilling the drink and told me to wash my own shirt."

Jody turned to see him reach into the shower recess and flick on the water. "W-what are you doing?"

He glanced over his shoulder. "Jumping in the shower to rinse the sticky Coke off my chest, then I'm going to make use of the hot tub."

Before Jody could blink, he popped the button on his pants and slid the zipper down. She quickly turned away and started out of the room only to catch sight of Dan's naked arse in the mirror as she did. The view stopped her in her tracks. He had the best arse. She'd always been a butt girl. Something about a taut male behind did it for her in a big way, and Dan had a world class rear end.

"Wanna join me?"

Her gaze darted up to meet his in the mirror. "What?" she squeaked. God, she'd actually squeaked.

He grinned at her. "In the hot tub. Although if you want to join me in the shower…"

Before she could be tempted to answer yes to either, she made her escape, closing the door behind her. The timber barrier did nothing to silence Dan's laughter.

Dan sighed as he sank into the warm bubbling water. Jody refused to join him and had found some busy work to do in their room. He wouldn't force her to take a break, but he planned to tempt her until she did. He'd start by letting her know how great it was.

"God. This feels amazing. You really should try this," he called out.

"I didn't bring my swimmers." He turned to find her standing in the doorway, her fingers twisting together in front of her and her teeth biting into her plush bottom lip.

"Well, I'd be more than happy for you to jump in naked, but I doubt you're up for that, so why don't you just wear your undies and bra. They couldn't be any more revealing than a bikini." He slipped lower in the water and leaned his head back on the side of the tub, his eyes closing on a moan. Damn, it really did feel good.

He could hear her moving around but he stayed where he was—head back, eyes closed—as his body relaxed by slow degrees. The day hadn't been particularly taxing. Watching the men fawn all over Jody had though. How he'd managed to get through the last few hours without punching anyone Dan would never know. To her credit, she hadn't encouraged any of them, and the fact she'd lied to Mooney about the extent of their relationship showed him just how much she'd disliked the other man's advances.

Mooney had pulled Dan aside to apologise for poaching on his territory. At first Dan had been confused, clueless as to what the other man was talking about. It didn't take Mooney long to impart the necessary words to enlighten him. Dan wasn't sure what surprised him more—Mooney's apology or Jody's outright lie.

Lost in thought, Dan was surprised when the water surged up over his chin. Opening his eyes, his gaze connected with Jody's. She'd slipped in on the opposite side of the tub. The churning water came all the way to her neck so there was no way to tell if she was in her underwear as he'd suggested or if she'd been brave enough to climb in naked. Either way, his cock stirred at the thought of her lush body all slippery wet and within touching distance.

He smiled. "Feels good, doesn't it?"

She nodded as she watched him warily.

His smile grew. "So are you naked over there?"

Her eyes rounded and her lips parting on a gasp as she dipped lower in the water.

Dan laughed. He loved teasing her. "Don't answer. I might not be able to control myself if you do."

"Are you always so direct?" she asked.

"Yeah, don't see any point playing games—especially when it comes to getting what I want."

"And that's me?"

He stretched his arms out along the edge of the tub. "Yep."

"Why?"

"Why do I want you?" For someone who didn't want to play games, he couldn't seem to come up with a straight answer to that question. He shrugged. "Who knows why we're attracted to each other. All I know is it's there and I plan to act on it. With your consent of course."

"Good to know I have some say in it." Her smile softened the seriousness of her words.

Dan forgot all about keeping his distance—forgot about not crowding her—and reduced the space between them to zero. He put his hands flat on the bench seat beside her thighs and brought his face a breath from hers. "You will always have a say in this." Then he slanted his lips over hers.

He captured her gasp on his tongue as he dove into her mouth. Within a heartbeat, she caught up and tangled her tongue with his. Dan didn't touch her with anything except his mouth, but that didn't deter Jody. Her hands landed on his shoulders, her fingers digging in for a moment before she trailed them down his chest. She dragged her nails over his nipples and the flat discs instantly pebbled rock hard beneath her rough touch.

She splayed her hands and swept them lower. His stomach clenched, every muscle going taut with the anticipation of where she was headed next. He didn't have to wait long to find out. With feather-like caresses, Jody stroked the area between his hips, the stretch of skin where the waistband of his pants would normally be. Yeah, he'd chosen to climb into the tub naked, and right now he was thankful for his penchant for nudity.

She pulled her mouth from his when the back of her hand brushed the head of his cock. "You're not wearing any pants?"

It was a question except they both knew there was no real need to ask or answer. Dan replied by sliding his lips over the soft skin of her cheek up to her ear where he blew a stream of air over the damp shell. She shivered. Then a shudder rolled over her as he latched onto her lobe and sucked it into his mouth. Toying with his teeth, he nipped the delicate flesh before soothing the slight sting with the flat of his tongue.

A moan slipped up her throat, the sexy little sound ramping up his arousal and urging him to take more. An answering groan rolled off his tongue when her hands found his cock, her fingers circling the shaft in a loose grip that made him dizzy with want. God. He wanted to fuck her.

"Jody." Her name was a plea and a demand. He wanted her to grip him harder, to stroke those talented fingers from root to tip and back again. "Please," he breathed in her ear.

"You're so big."

Nothing could have brought him to his knees faster than

those breathless words. Every guy wanted to hear that tone of awe from the woman he planned to bed. He leaned back until their gazes connected. Her hands stayed with him, caressed his straining flesh with a mixture of tentative brushes and firm squeezes.

"If you don't want this to go any further you have to stop." His voice was ragged with need. "Now."

Her eyes studied his. She must have found what she was looking for because she gripped him harder and pulled his cock in several quick strokes. "I don't want to stop."

Dan closed his eyes for a split second before meeting her gaze once more. "Are you sure?" *God, please let her be sure.*

She nodded once then pressed her mouth to his as she continued the incredible hand job designed to drive him mad. Closing his eyes once more, he sank into the kiss and let her take them where she wanted. He wasn't sure how, but he knew Jody needed to lead this first time. If he wanted this to be more than a one-time deal, she had to meet him more than halfway. Had to be the one to take them that next step.

He slid his hands along the seat until they brushed against the outside of her thighs. Letting the water help support his weight, he moved his hands to her hips as he knelt on the bottom of the tub. The thin layer of cloth separating his fingers from her skin had to go. "Undies off," he spoke against her lips.

Their mouths separated, both of them panting for breath as their gazes locked. He thought she might back out. Thought now that he was this close to getting her naked she'd pull back and leave him hanging. But he should have known Jody wouldn't chicken out. With the confidence he'd seen from her at work, she pushed him back and stood. She brought her hand to the front of her bra and flicked the clasp that held the cups together. In an instant, her breasts were free. The lush globes drew his hands and he reached up to cup them—weigh them—while stroking his thumbs over the taut peaks.

"Beautiful."

Her skin flushed a deeper red. "I'm old. They're saggy." She covered his hands with hers as though trying to hide herself from him.

Dan stood, pulling his hands away from her body and capturing her fingers in his before she could conceal those sweet curves from him again. "Don't." He held their arms out so he had an unobstructed view. "The only thing I see is a gorgeous woman who sets my blood on fire."

Leaning forward, Dan buried his face in Jody's cleavage. He groaned at the silky feel of her skin against his face. Moaned when he slid his tongue over one curving slope until he reached a puckered nipple and sucked it into his mouth. With a shake of her hands, she broke his hold and tangled her fingers in his hair and tugged him closer—holding him to her. Dan growled and drew harder on her rigid flesh. The tight bud fit between his tongue and palate as though it were made specifically for that spot.

Jody moaned and arched her back, pressing her breast deeper into his mouth. Her grip on his hair tightened—pulled—and sent a sharp sting across his scalp, drawing a rumbling groan from deep in his chest. Dan increased the suction on her nipple then scraped his teeth over the ribbed tip. She jerked, her body jack-knifing in his arms and popping the tasty nub free of his lips.

He nuzzled her silky skin as he made his way up her chest. Her pulse fluttered beneath his tongue when he licked her neck. The sexy little noises she made drove him mad and he had to taste them. Nibbling his way to her mouth, he sampled every inch of her delicate throat before finding her lips and joining their mouths in a breath-stealing kiss that threatened to turn his bones to liquid and shatter his control.

Dan slid his hands down her ribs to her waist then over her hips where he hooked his fingers in the sides of her undies as he continued to feed on her mouth. Her hands joined his and together they pushed her underwear off. He let go of her mouth and lowered his gaze, but he couldn't see beyond her hipbones where the bubbling water swirled between them. Stepping back, he bent forward and shoved her pants to her knees. His mouth was inches from her waist and he couldn't resist leaning in and placing a trail of tiny kisses from her belly button to her hip.

Her stomach trembled beneath his lips and he took great pleasure in making her shudder further. Memorising the more sensitive areas for later use, he continued his journey south. But when his chin dipped into the water he straightened, put his hands on her waist and urged her to sit on the side of the hot tub. Jody kicked her undies free under the water before sitting up on the edge. Pressing his hands on the inside of her thighs, he nudged them apart so he could step between them. He didn't look down. If he did, he'd never be able to resist sampling her sweet pussy, and he wanted—needed—to slow things down, to savour every second of this moment with her.

He moved closer until his cock fit snug against her sex. The heat of her surrounding him drove him a little further into the fierce need and want being with her delivered. Dan shuddered when she dragged her fingers through his hair and tugged his mouth to hers. They slid into the kiss as though they'd done it a million times. Each stroke of tongue, brush of lips, nip of teeth was a perfect caress in a sensual slide deeper. In seconds, they went from lazy to frenzied. Neither of them satisfied with a leisurely ride any longer.

Jody skimmed her hands over his shoulders and down his back, making his groin throb with want. Dan gripped her arse and yanked her closer as a bolt of lust speared him. He tore his mouth from hers and nibbled his way along her jaw. She arched her neck, offering him free rein, and he took all she gave. Her breath panted in his ear, the sexy sounds floating on those small puffs of air firing his blood and filling his cock with white-hot need until he couldn't wait to have her.

Pulling back, he cradled her face in his hands and waited for her gaze to meet his. "I want you."

"Yes."

"Now."

She moaned. The cry cut short when he sealed his mouth to hers once more. The kiss was quick, barely long enough for their lips to touch, before he pulled away. Dan flexed his hips, rubbing his length on the slick folds of her pussy, drawing a whimper from her, a groan from him. Wet heat coated his shaft and he couldn't wait another second to sink his cock inside her. He rocked against her, sliding his engorged flesh through the welcoming clasp of hers, coating them both in her creamy essence.

"Please," Jody pleaded.

Protection. He needed to suit-up.

He froze. He didn't have any condoms. He'd never expected to get here with her so soon. Stupidity on his part, because whenever they touched it was like match to flint. Instant flame.

Dan laid his forehead on hers. "I don't have any protection. I didn't expect..."

"What?" Jody murmured, her breathing laboured.

Dan pulled back to meet her desire-filled gaze. "Condoms. I don't have any."

"Oh." She chewed the corner of her lip. "I-I'm on the pill. And I'm clean. I haven't—"

"Me too. Clean that is. I've never had sex without a condom."

Jody stared at him and he realised she was waiting for him to say more.

"We don't have to." He made the offer but prayed she wouldn't take him up on it.

"You want to stop?"

"Hell no, but I'm not expecting you to take me at my word on something like this."

"I trust you. I wouldn't be here—naked—if I didn't."

What was she saying? Did she mean they could continue? That they could have sex without a condom? "Are you saying we don't need a condom to have sex?"

She nodded.

"You're sure?" Dan sucked in a breath and held it.

Chapter Eight

Jody couldn't think—didn't want to think—if she did she'd put a stop to this madness. Instead, she agreed to have sex with Dan. Without a condom. They might have only known each other a few months, but those months were sufficient time for her to know she could trust him with her safety. And she did. Her marriage had taught her all about mistrust, and Dan didn't evoke any of those all too familiar suspicions.

"Jody, are you sure?" His gaze searched hers "I don't want to do anything you're not comfortable with."

Even now Dan was showing her she could trust him. He'd never force her, and he hadn't been the one to suggest continuing regardless of their lack of protection. She'd told him she was on the pill, safe from disease and willing to have sex without a condom. She refused to second guess herself now.

"Yes. I'm sure."

"Not here." He placed his hand on the edge of the tub and vaulted over the side onto the terrace. "C'mon. I want you on a bed."

Before she could think about moving, he slid his hands under her arms and lifted her out of the tub. Her toes barely touched the floor when he spun her around and picked her up, holding her against his chest. With quick, long strides, he walked them into the room.

"I can walk." Her protest was weak. She was enjoying this macho side of him far too much.

"Yep."

He didn't put her down. He just continued until he reached the closest bed and fell forward, turning at the last second so his back hit the mattress and she came down on top of him. Her legs bracketed his, her sex lined up with his erection, and she couldn't help the little roll of her hips that dragged her clit across his length. She moaned as sensation shot through her core. Bracing her knees on the bed, Jody rocked against him in a slow rhythm. Each pass sent heat and moisture flooding her pussy.

Dan tangled his fingers in her hair, holding her still so he could devour her mouth. With each rock of her hips, he thrust his tongue between her lips. The duel assault drove her higher, pushed her closer to that jagged edge she craved like air. She'd been there before. He'd shown her how good he could make it, and Jody wanted to experience it again with blinding intensity. Breaking free of his kiss, she pushed herself up to her knees and hovered her sex above his.

"Now." She panted. "I want you in me now."

She reached between them and grabbed his cock. Dan gasped and shuddered beneath her. Lowering an inch, Jody lined his body up with hers and slowly began to sink down. The bulbous head breached her opening, stretching her drenched hole with a delicious combination of pleasure and pain. It had been far too long. Her muscles fought against the invasion and she bit her lip, concentrated on relaxing her pelvis until she'd taken more of him.

"Fuck. You're so tight." Dan bared his teeth. "Don't want to hurt you."

"You're not." She took a little more of him. "Just need a second."

Jody took a deep breath and willed her body to accept his. She'd never dealt with this level of discomfort. Not even when she'd lost her virginity had it been this difficult to take a man inside her.

"You're not ready." He gripped her waist and raised her up.

"No." Her hands surround his. "I just need a second. I'm

more ready than I've ever been, but it's been so long." Jody couldn't believe they were discussing this.

"I'm not going to hurt you."

Before she could argue, Dan lifted her off him completely and reversed their positions. From one breath to the next, she went from being upright to flat on her back with Dan looming over her.

"We'll do this my way."

"But—"

His mouth came down on hers. He stroked his tongue across her lips, pressed between them and swept inside. She moaned into his mouth when he slipped his hand over her hip and along her thigh. Shifting to the side, he dragged that questing hand towards her centre. Her breath stalled, her muscles tensing as she waited for the moment he'd touch her.

He didn't disappoint. With skill, he played her. Slid his fingers along her slit, back and forth, never venturing between her folds to where she wanted him most. She rocked her hips, tried to force his fingers deeper only to have him pull away from her completely. His mouth. His hand. He took them both away and she cried out in protest.

"Easy." He chuckled against her neck. "I'm not going far. Just moving down here."

Jody whimpered when he moved his mouth over her collarbone. He licked across her breast until he reached her nipple and sucked it between his lips. Using his teeth to hold the bud still, he lashed it with his tongue, making it pucker tighter. The other breast didn't go unattended. With finger and thumb, Dan pinched her other nipple while increasing the suction on the one in his mouth. Streamers of sensation unfurled, rolling out into her abdomen to tickle her core. Her pussy clenched. Her walls weeping with want.

Letting go of her breasts, he wiggled lower on the bed. He slipped his legs between hers and moved lower still. His intent was clear. She held her breath and looked down her body to watch him settle his face over her sex.

"Damn, I can't wait to taste you." He ran his fingers through the short hair covering her mound. "I can smell you."

To Jody's embarrassment, Dan bent forward and took a deep breath. Her face heated and her thighs tensed against his shoulders as she tried to close her legs.

"Oh, yeah," he breathed against her wet centre.

There was no more time for discomfort. Not when he was swiping his tongue through her folds and sending her to the moon. He lapped at her. Licked up one side and down the other. And when he latched onto her clit, sucked it between his lips and flicked it with his tongue, her world splintered into millions of tiny sparkles. But he wasn't finished. As she came down off that surprising peak, he drove two fingers into her pussy and pressed the flat of his tongue against the now super-sensitive bundle of nerves.

"Oh, God." The whimper whispered over her lips as he found a tender spot deep inside her core.

He worked his fingers in time with his tongue until she was panting for breath and begging for him to stop. To never stop. None of the words leaving her throat made sense. Nothing but the devastating pleasure rocketing through her registered in her overwhelmed mind. And then he did it again. Took her up and over and into that burst of blind relief that left her spent with satisfaction so great Jody doubted she'd ever move again.

Dan crawled up her body, dropping kisses every few inches until he reached her mouth and nibbled on her bottom lip. He licked the slight sting before joining their lips in a scorching kiss. Her mind still reeling, Jody barely managed to keep up. Her body still tingled, her limbs like lead weights that her muscles refused to move. Her chest rose and fell in rapid succession as her lungs worked overtime to keep up with her galloping heartbeat. She opened her eyes to find Dan staring at her, a silly, smug grin on his face.

"Do you have any idea how gorgeous you look all flushed with release?" he asked.

She shook her head, words still beyond her.

"Gorgeous and hot, and I'm so close to losing my load that if I don't get inside you in the next few seconds you'll be wearing it all over your leg." He thrust his cock against her thigh to prove his point.

Jody found the strength to move and spread her legs until he slipped between them, her hips cradling his. "We can't let that happen." She arched her back, angled her hips so his crown nudged at her opening.

"No, we can't." He drove forward, his cock sliding in with little resistance as he sank his entire length into her. "Fuck, that feels amazing."

She had to agree. She'd never felt so full and yet so empty. The two opposing emotions warred inside her and drove her to move. Wrapping her legs around his thighs, Jody used him to propel herself back and forth. Her movements were limited but she managed to slide up and down his shaft a few inches with each squeeze of her legs. It wasn't enough.

"Move." When he didn't respond, she dug her fingers into his arse. "Move, dammit."

"This is going to be over way too quick," he growled in her ear just before he exploded into action.

Jody cried out as he withdrew and slammed back in repeatedly. Over and over, he impaled her on his length. Her back bowed, her feet dropping to the bed, her hips rising to meet his thrusts. He was breathing hard, panting in her ear as he pushed himself deeper and deeper. His pace increased, his cock tunnelling in and out in a pounding beat that left her breathless.

"Are you close?"

The question startled her.

"I can't hold off any longer."

She didn't want him to wait for her, didn't think she'd be able to come again anyway, so she rolled her hips, clenched her vaginal muscles and sent him soaring.

Dan came with a roar. Blood rushed in his ears and pounded in his groin. Fire shot up his spine and out his dick as Jody's pussy milked him of every last drop of come. She did something with her muscles. Something that felt as though she was squeezing him in a rolling touch from root to tip. And the heat. Jesus, he'd never experienced anything like it. Her body surrounded him in a blistering grip he'd give anything to feel over and over again. His arms shook—hell, his whole body shook—his muscles on the verge of giving out as the last of his seed spilled inside her.

With a groan, he fell forward. Half on, half off, he braced his arms and tried to keep from crushing her. His cock remained hard and buried deep in her rippling pussy, totally oblivious to the fact he'd just come hard enough to lose brain cells. He wasn't sure if he could find the words to express how he felt right now. Or if he had the wherewithal to get his vocal cords to form them. She squirmed beneath him and he forced himself to pull free of her body—the action drew a shudder and a groan from each of them. Dan rolled to the side and took her with him, not willing to let her go just yet.

"That was..."

"Uh-huh." He couldn't manage more than a murmured sound.

Jody sighed, the puff of air rushing over his neck and shoulder where her face was tucked against him, and goose bumps rose in a shivery wave down his back. He couldn't recall his body ever being so sensitive. Then again, he couldn't remember the last time he'd held a woman in his arms after sex either. His usual mad dash out the door held no appeal. Not this time. For once, he wanted to hold his bed partner close, and it wasn't with the hope of a second round. Although he wouldn't knock that back.

For now, all he wanted was to lie here and cuddle Jody—feel her softness pressed against him. She satisfied him on so many levels, and yet he couldn't seem to get enough of her. Wanted so much more from her—with her.

"What are you thinking?"

Her question surprised him, though it shouldn't have. As much as she'd avoided him she'd never held back. Her genuine honesty appealed more than he cared to acknowledge. *She* appealed. The thought of possibly screwing this thing with her up terrified him.

She poked him in the ribs. "Did you do the typical guy thing and go to sleep on me?"

Dan laughed. "No."

"Good, because my arm has gone to sleep." She wiggled the arm pinned beneath him.

"Shit. Sorry." He rose up so she could slip her arm free. "You should have said something."

"I just did."

"I meant before it went to sleep." Dan cuddled her close once more.

"Well, I didn't know it wasn't fine until it went numb."

"Oh, right." He scooted over, rolling to his back and pulling her with him. She laid her head on his shoulder, her body plastered to his side. "Better?"

"Mmm."

Dan held her close, his mind replaying everything that had happened from the minute he entered the room. He wasn't sure at what point she'd changed her mind about them or even if she had. It was quite possible she'd back away after today. Dan was prepared for her to do that. He just had to have a plan to keep her from running too far. If he could work out what had convinced her to let him closer, he'd be able to use the same tactic in the future.

Jody moved her leg over his and the residual heat in her pussy pressed against his outer thigh. His cock stirred, pulsing as his body responded to her nearness—to the memory of the pleasure he'd found between her legs. He'd roll over and pin her beneath him if he had the strength, but he still couldn't get his muscles to work properly.

She rocked her hips, that hot centre rubbing on his leg and driving his arousal higher. He groaned when she pushed herself up. Thinking she was going to pull away, he was surprised when she crawled over the top of him and stretched her body out along his. From breast to ankles, skin touched skin, and she wiggled her sex on his as she settled herself against him. Her mouth was an inch from his and he wrapped his hand around the back of her neck and tugged her down until he could fit her mouth to his.

He took his time. Explored every inch of her mouth while he used his hands to map her curves. She wasn't skinny like the fashion mags dictated women should be. Her body was rounded like a woman should be, and he took great pleasure in running his hands all over her. But his arms could only reach so far and he wanted to touch all of her. Trail his fingers across each valley, every slope, and follow with his lips.

Pulling back, he separated their mouths and searched out her gaze. Her eyes were hooded, her lashes shielding her expression, but there was no missing her flushed cheeks or her shallow pants for breath. She was climbing towards that peak again, and this time he wanted them to go over together. He gripped her hips and urged her up. "I want to be inside you again."

Her eyelids fluttered, her searing blue gaze meeting his. She didn't speak. She didn't have to when she sat up, rose to her knees and reached between them to grab his cock and hold it still while she lined up their bodies and slowly sank back down. The moan that left her lips matched the one caught in his throat. Heat surrounded him, engulfed him as Jody took him all the way to the root in one long slide of carnal delight.

They held perfectly still when her pelvis sat snug against his. One heartbeat. Two. Neither of them breathed. Moved. Then Dan's fingers tightened. Dug into the flesh of her arse where he held her. That was all it took to bring them out of the daze their physical contact put them in. She rolled her hips, rocked back and forth, making his cock slide in and out in minuscule increments. His gut clenched, his thigh muscles tightening as pleasure seared him.

"Faster. Deeper," he growled as he used his hands to guide her. But she wouldn't be led. Instead, she kept her slow, shallow pace and just about drove him out of his mind. "Fuck!"

Left with either the option of letting her have control or flipping them over, he took a breath, ready to move when she kicked things up a notch. Using her legs, she rose and fell at an ever-increasing speed and distance until she was riding him like a cowgirl rides a bucking bull. Root to glans, Jody slid up and down in a mind-blowing rhythm. He gripped her hips, holding on for all he was worth as she drove them both towards that ultimate prize.

Dan bucked his hips, thrusting up on each of her downstrokes. She braced her hands on his chest, digging her nails in to his flesh as she upped the tempo once more. Her breathing came in ragged bursts, her breasts bouncing in an erotic tease that keep his gaze firmly trained on her jiggling tits. He wanted to wrap his tongue around her nipples, except he wasn't ready to give up the view of Jody riding him as though her life depended on it.

He stayed with her, arching up as she plunged down, slamming their bodies together time after time until he had to grit his teeth to stop from coming apart to soon. Letting go of one hip, he trailed his fingers over her skin towards her pussy. Her folds were slick, the wet heat coating his fingertips and making the slide across her flesh slippery smooth. Dan searched out the knot of nerves guaranteed to have her joining him on the edge.

Jody jerked, her rhythm stuttering as he circled her clit. Stroked. Pressed. Pinched. Then he did it again. And again. And watched while she ground against him and finally let go. Her pussy squeezed him in a breath-stealing vice that pulled his release from him in a bone-jarring punch to his groin. Fire lanced his cock as spurt after spurt erupted from his balls.

His body throbbed. His ears rang. And his chest ached as his lungs struggled to function. Jody collapsed forward, draping her body over him in a damp blanket of satisfaction. Dan's eyes had shut at some point, and when he opened them he was seeing double. Lowering his lids, he sucked in a deep breath and wrapped his arms around the woman sprawled on top of him.

Her breathing came in jagged puffs and her body vibrated against his as the last of her orgasm ebbed away. He could feel the final ripples of her release along his softening length. His body seemed to have been satisfied this time. Stroking his hands up and down her back, he held her for as long as she'd let him. Dan figured they'd both sated the hunger between them for now and wouldn't be at all shocked if Jody retreated. What they'd shared—twice—wasn't just sex, and he had no doubt she wasn't ready to accept anything more.

With a sigh, he pushed the troubled thoughts from his head. He turned to the side and glanced at the clock. They had two hours before they had to be anywhere, so he closed his eyes and savoured holding Jody in his arms. He'd give anything to make this a regular occurrence, but with the way they'd come together he didn't see that happening any time soon. Dan just hoped having sex hadn't taken them back a step.

He wanted to move their relationship forward, and he didn't think Jody would see sex as a step in that direction. If anything, she'd see it as a reason to avoid him. There was no way he'd stand for that. Not now that he'd had her beneath him—above him. Around him. He'd need to make a connection outside of the bedroom, and the only way to do that would be to insinuate himself into her life.

Dan smiled. He'd make it his mission to woo her. To slowly seduce her into not just letting him between her legs. Because even though he wanted to be there, he knew it wasn't all he was after. He could only hope he had the skills and patience required to win her over. Now that he'd been inside her, there was no chance he'd settle for anything less than possessing all of her. Body, heart and soul.

Chapter Nine

Jody woke wrapped around a warm body. Startled, she jerked back and came face-to-face with Dan. "Oh."

"Hey." He smiled, but the corners of his mouth wobbled and the uncertainty in his eyes troubled her.

"I fell asleep." Stupid conversation considering they'd just had sex. Twice.

"Yeah." He reached up and brushed the hair off her face with his fingertips. "You weren't out long. Ten minutes tops."

"Oh." She glanced away, his penetrating gaze made her nervous.

The phone on the bedside table rang, making her jump. Who would be calling their room? She scrambled over Dan, snatched up the receiver and brought it to her ear. "Hello?"

"Mum?"

Jody bolted upright and dove off the bed. "Leigh? What's wrong? Where's Uncle Luc?"

"Nothing. He's here. Can I go to the movies with some friends tonight? Uncle Luc and Cassie said it was okay if you said yes. They'll be at the same cinema with Amy so I'll be safe."

The movies? With friends? "Why—?"

"I know it's last minute, but we only just organised it and I really, really want to go. Everyone will be there. Please."

"Leigh, put Uncle Luc on for me." If Jody didn't get her brother on the phone Leigh would launch into another stream of babble in order to get a yes. It wasn't the first time her daughter had used the ploy.

"Hey, Jody, how goes it?" Luc's deep voice rumbled across

the line.

Jody glanced at Dan. How did she answer that question? "Um, good. Listen. Leigh can go, but make sure you see her with the group before you leave her. I'm going to ask her who's going when you put her back on but I'm pretty sure it'll be the usual crowd."

"No worries. We'll be there. Cassie and Amy are going to watch some cartoon flick that neither Leigh nor I are interested in, so if I don't find something else to see I'll be hanging out in the coffee shop."

"Okay. Let me know what I owe you. I didn't give either of them any money before I left." She wanted to slap herself in the forehead. She'd left her kids with her brother and not only hadn't she given either of the girls cash, she'd neglected to give any to Luc or Cassie for anything the girls might want.

Luc laughed. "I think I can manage to shout a movie or two. But you know popcorn doesn't come cheap..."

Jody smiled as she knew he'd have expected her to. "Fine. I get the hint."

"Good. Now I'll put Leigh back on so you can grill her. Text me if you find out anything I should know. Catch ya tomorrow night."

Leigh squealed in her ear. "I can go? Oh my God. You're the best mum ever!"

She pulled the phone from her ear and waited for Leigh's enthusiasm to calm down.

"Thank you, thank you, thank you." Leigh finally ran out of steam.

Jody brought the phone back to her head with a smile. "Not so fast. Who's going exactly?"

"Oh, Jenny, Michelle, Monica, Erika, Drew, Claudia and Jason. Oh, and Monica's mum is taking her little brother and sister to the same movie Cassie is taking Amy to so there's plenty of adults going to be there."

Jody loved that her daughter still felt comfortable with parental concern and supervision. She knew there'd be a day when Leigh wouldn't want her to know what she was up to, but until then Jody would make the most of their open, close relationship to build a level of trust between them. "Say hi to Monica's mum for me and make sure you mind your Uncle Luc and Cassie."

"I will. Hey, Amy wants to say hi."

She could hear the phone being passed to an excited Amy and wondered if she should pull the phone away so her other daughter didn't burst her eardrum.

"Hi, Mum. You should see what I helped Cassie make." Amy may have been animated, but unlike her sister, she didn't do it at an ear-splitting decibel.

"What did you make?" Jody lowered herself to the bed behind her.

"These really cool paper-flower bouquets. They're for some party next weekend."

Jody knew the event Amy was talking about. It was a last-minute baby shower booking. "I can't wait to see them."

"Cassie said I could make an extra one for my room so you can see it." Jody could hear the grin in Amy's voice.

"That was nice of Cassie. Make sure you say thank you." Jody jumped when Dan draped the blanket around her shoulders. Glancing over to the side, she saw he sat behind her listening to her conversation. Seeing him reminded her of what she'd done—what they'd done—and she couldn't stop the ripple of fear that flowed through her. Amy's voice jarred her out of her thoughts and a slam of guilt hit her. She should be paying attention to her child, not the naked man next to her. "Sorry, Amy, what was that, the phone cut out a bit." It was a lie and Jody hated telling it.

"I was trying to describe my bouquet, but you can just see it tomorrow when you pick us up from Uncle Luc's house."

Dan's hand landed on her shoulder and she shook it off and stood, putting some distance between them so she could keep her head in gear. "Okay, I'll see you tomorrow, baby girl. Love you. Hug your sister for me."

"Bye, Mum." Amy hung up before Jody could reply.

Jody replaced the receiver and wondered why they'd phoned the hotel and not her mobile. Gathering the edges of the blanket, she wrapped it more tightly around her and headed for her handbag. Rummaging inside, she found the reason her child had found it necessary to ring the hotel to track her down. Her battery was dead. She'd meant to plug it in when she got to the room, but Dan had distracted her. Boy howdy, hadn't he. She looked at the clock and almost choked on her own tongue. They'd been in the room for over two hours and she hadn't thought about anything except Dan and sex.

"I don't think I like that look." Dan moved beside her. Naked.

"Huh?" Jody tried to follow the conversation except her mind couldn't focus on anything other than the very attractive male body in front of her. Her breasts grew heavy and her sex tingled and clenched in remembered sensation.

"You're feeling guilty about something to do with your daughters."

"How do you know that?" Was her face that revealing?

"I've seen the look before. My mother wore it a lot the year my sister slipped on the wet kitchen floor and broke her back." He frowned, sadness pulling at the corners of his eyes.

"Oh my God, is she all right now?"

"Yeah, both of them are. Mum got over her guilt of being the one to drench the floor and Reagan's back healed without major damage. She never played sport again, but her bones healed and she leads a normal life."

Jody couldn't imagine what it must have been like for Dan's mother to go through something like that. Or his sister. "I don't know what to say. My forgetting to charge my phone or leave the girls with money seems like petty issues now."

"Oh, don't go feeling guilty about doing what comes natural to a mother. That wasn't my aim. All I wanted to do was explain why I knew what you were feeling and maybe make you feel a little less that way. Obviously I screwed that up." He shrugged and headed for the bathroom.

Jody wasn't sure what to do or say and found herself following him. "About earlier—"

He spun around, arm up, palm out. "Stop. Before you say anything you don't mean or I don't like."

"Ah..."

"Let's just get ready for tonight and not overanalyse the situation."

"We can't pretend it never happened," she argued.

Dan stepped forward until he was right in front of her, his chest brushing against her hands where she held the blanket bunched in her fists between her breasts.

"I have no intention of forgetting—pretend or otherwise—what happened in this room this afternoon. But I'm not about to let you make me regret what we did, and I'll be fucked if I let you either."

Jody gasped. The firmness of his words, the confidence that radiated off him had her taking a mental step back. "I—"

He placed two fingers over her lips. "No. Don't say anything." Bending forward, Dan replaced his fingers with his mouth. The kiss was quick. Hard. And then he was turning away, leaving her floundering in confusion.

She didn't know which she felt more. Guilt, shame or embarrassment. Or satisfaction. There was no ignoring the hum of contentment infusing every part of her with a lightness she hadn't experienced in years.

For a long twenty-four hours, Dan had tried his hardest not to pressure Jody. The weekend hadn't gone anything like he'd expected. There had been some good and bad, and as he loaded the last of their boxes into the van, he wasn't sure if he dreaded the trip home or not. She'd barely spoken to him since their strained conversation the day before. They'd remained civil and pleasant in public and private, but the intimacy he thought they'd developed in those few stolen hours had proved as elusive as fog.

"We're all checked out and I grabbed us each a bottle of water for the trip home." Jody stepped up beside him and held out a plastic bottle.

He looked at the drink then back at Jody. Her eyes were a little wild—fearful—and he hated that it was him who'd put that anxiety there. "Thanks."

"You're welcome." She turned on her heel and headed for the passenger side.

Scrubbing a hand down his face, Dan wondered if he shouldn't try to smooth things over. The problem was, he didn't have a clue how to do that. He'd fucked up with that whole let's-not-over-analyse-it speech. He'd known it the minute the words left his mouth, but he hadn't backed down. Instead, he'd gotten in her face and spoken without thinking first. It was even worse that his words were said in anger. She'd pissed him off when she'd assumed he wanted to pretend they hadn't shared such an intimate moment.

She could hide or run for as long as she liked, but there was no way she could take back those hours of openness she'd shared with him. She'd let him in. Further than any man in a very long time, and if it was the last thing he did, he'd make sure she knew what that meant to him.

Fishing the keys out of his pocket as he made his way to the driver's door, he decided to ignore the tension between them and carry on as though they hadn't had a few heated words. Climbing in, he said, "What time do you have to pick up the girls, or is Luc dropping them off?"

"Oh, I'm picking them up."

"Well, we better get on the road so you're not too late. They've got school tomorrow, right?" Dan slid the key into the ignition and started the engine.

"Yes."

He glanced at the dashboard clock. "It'll take us three hours to get back to the warehouse, so you should be on your way to Luc's by six." Checking his mirrors, Dan pulled out of the parking spot.

"Six? We'll have barely gotten back then, and we have to unpack."

"I can do that. You need to get home to the girls. Spend some time with them seeing how you've been away all weekend." He wanted her to know he understood and respected her role as a mother.

"I can't let you do that."

"Don't be silly. It'll only take me a few minutes to unload the equipment and then I'll be heading home. We can both do the paperwork tomorrow in the office." Dan wanted to give her space, not too much, but enough to forget the tension of the last two days and perhaps let the good bits float to the top of her memory.

"Are you sure?"

He smiled. The tone of her voice told him she wanted to accept his offer. "Yep. Besides, it'll probably take me less time to unpack on my own than with you."

She sputtered until he turned his grin on her. "Jeez. You had me going for a second there." Her laughter filled the cabin and Dan breathed a sigh of relief.

Reaching over he turned the radio on. "Mind if I play a little music?"

"No, go ahead. I think I'll text Luc and let him know what

time to expect me."

"Do you mind sending Cassie a text with the info about the date Mooney wants us to come back and do the second batch of staff?" he asked as he turned onto the expressway.

"Sure. Might be best if I just ring."

"Probably." Dan leaned over and flicked the volume on the radio down while Jody made the call.

She ended up on the phone for twenty minutes. Both girls wanted to talk to her after she'd spoken to Luc and Cassie, and from what he heard of Jody's side of the conversation, her eldest wanted to have a sleepover next weekend. Jody had said no because she had to work Saturday afternoon. Dan could hear the yelling all the way across the cab. He glanced over to see Jody's cheeks were bright red and figured she was embarrassed about her daughter's outburst. With the skill only a mother had, she ended the call and the conversation.

"Teenagers. There's no reasoning with them." He tried to infuse his words with humour but he didn't think he pulled it off.

"Mmm. Normally Leigh is the more reasonable of the two."

"She's the older one, right?"

"Yeah, fifteen. Amy's two years younger."

"I remember Reagan at fifteen. She was a hellion. I think my mother went gray overnight when my sister hit puberty." Dan overtook a slow moving truck.

"We hit that a few years ago. I'm not sure what prompted that shouting match. I just hope she isn't horrible to Luc or Cassie because I've gone from being the best mother in the world to the worst in the space of twenty-four hours."

"If you go by that standard you'll be the best again by tomorrow."

Jody laughed. "Thanks. I needed that levity. You're right, come tomorrow she'll have forgotten all about it and moved on to the next thing she wants me to say yes to."

"You're doing a great job, you know." He bounced his gaze from the road to her and back again. "From what you've said and what I've gleaned from Luc, their father isn't involved in their raising."

She sucked in a breath. "No, he's not."

"That must be hard. Having to do it on your own now."

Her laughter sounded hollow. "Yeah, because I had so much help before."

Dan would have to be stupid to miss the sarcasm in her words. "Sorry, didn't mean to bring up a sore point."

Jody sighed. "You didn't. I'm not bitter or angry, just sad really. The girls don't deserve to be an afterthought, and with their father that's all they'll ever be."

"At the risk of repeating myself...he didn't—doesn't—deserve you or the girls."

"Thank you. I know that in my head, but sometimes it's nice to hear someone else say it."

They were quiet then. Only the sound of the tires rolling over the road and the whoosh of the air-conditioner pumping the cab with cool air to fill the silence.

Jody pulled up in front of Luc's house and took a deep breath as she switched off the engine. She wasn't sure how she felt about Dan sending her home as soon as they got back. The gesture was nice, and she appreciated it, but she couldn't shake the feeling he was being overly nice because of what had happened yesterday. They should clear the air. Needed to clear it. If they didn't, working together and moving past the shift in their relationship, would be impossible.

She didn't want to give him the wrong impression. There was no room in her life for a man, she didn't need the added complication another person would bring. She'd finally gotten to a point where she was happy with her life—content. Okay, if she were honest, she'd admit the sex had been amazing. Better than amazing. And she'd certainly been shown what she was missing, but she wasn't the type to have a no-strings affair, and she didn't have it in her to attempt another serious relationship, not now, possibly not ever.

A tap on the window made her jump, and she looked over to see Luc standing on the curb watching her. Pulling the keys from the ignition, she steeled herself to face her brother and hoped to hell he wouldn't be able to tell she'd had sex with Dan. She'd barely opened the door when he started talking.

"Cassie has the girls distracted."

"Okay." Jody had no idea where he was going with this.

"I thought you might need a moment to talk before you turned back into super mum."

She smiled. His uncanny ability to judge her moods had always bewildered her. "Talk about what?"

Luc shrugged. "Anything you don't want to say in front of the girls."

"Thanks, but I think I'm good."

"Are you sure?" He studied her for a moment. "I can take Cassie's place and send her out here."

Jody loved her brother, but there was no way she'd discuss her sex life or her confused emotions about Dan with him or her boss. She patted Luc's arm. "I'm fine. Let's go in and I'll get those girls out of your hair so you and Cassie can have some peace and quiet."

"Actually, it hasn't been that noisy. I think Cassie makes more noise than the girls put together." He slung his arm around her shoulders and led her along the path. "We've had a great weekend and I'm beginning to see how much I missed when they were little. Why didn't you make me see more of them?"

Jody couldn't help but laugh. "Lucas Wilhelm, you were terrified of them. Neither of them could move without you freaking out."

He had the grace to colour up. "Well, they were tiny. Hell, compared to me they still are."

"Here's the thing." They stopped on the front step. "When they were little they didn't need more of your attention than you gave, but now that they're older and their father really isn't around, I'd like you to have a bigger role in their lives. They have Dad, but they need a good male influence as well as a grandfather, and I'd like that to be you."

"You know I'd do anything for you and those two."

She smiled and stood on tip-toes to kiss his cheek. "I know, and I thank you for always having my back."

"Anything for you, Budgie." He grinned as he used the nickname he'd given her as a child because he said she chirped like a bird.

Jody slapped his arm. "C'mon, let's go inside." She followed him in, but she couldn't help wishing he wasn't the only good male role model in the girls' lives, which totally went against her earlier thought of not needing a man in her life. No doubt about it, Dan had her brain going haywire. And if she didn't sort out her emotions soon she'd be in all kinds of trouble.

Chapter Ten

Dan stretched out on his couch, phone in hand. Undecided about calling her, he'd hovered his thumb over Jody's number for the last hour. He wanted to check she'd picked up the girls and returned home safe. Which he really had no right to wonder. Only he did worry and he knew he'd give in to the urge to ring her eventually. Checking the time, he figured if he didn't do it soon he'd wake her up.

Giving in to temptation, he pressed the call button and brought the phone to his ear. It rang four times before she answered.

"Hello?" She sounded out of breath.

"Did I catch you at a bad time?"

"Dan?"

"Yeah." What other guy did she expect to call her? "I wanted to make sure you got home safe."

"Oh, well, we did."

"Good. I'm glad."

Silence filled the line.

"Right, well, I bet you have things to do..." He shouldn't have rung her.

"Actually, you caught me just getting ready for bed."

X-rated images filled his head. He'd seen her in her pyjamas. He'd seen her out of them too. His throat and mouth suddenly dry, he swallowed. "Oh, um, I should let you go then."

"No, it's okay." Did she answer a little too quickly? A little breathlessly?

"I don't want to keep you up."

"You're not. I was going to read for a while."

"Anything interesting?" Dan wanted to know what type of book held Jody's attention.

"Not to you I wouldn't think." Her words held a smile.

"How do you know that? We might have the same taste in reading material." He hoped they did. It would give them something in common as well as something to talk about.

"It's a romance novel."

"Is it one of those that are all the fad at the moment?" The genre escaped him, but he knew the books were full of sex. His sister read them. "You know, the ones with explicit sex in them."

"Um..."

He could almost hear her blushing. "It *is*."

"Ah, maybe."

"Read a racy bit to me."

"W-what?"

"Read me something hot."

"No."

"Aw, c'mon, just a paragraph," he coaxed.

"I can't."

"Why not?"

"Because."

"Because why?"

"Jeez, now you sound like the girls when I can't think of a reasonable explanation when I say no to something." She laughed, the sound echoing down the line and tightening Dan's groin.

"C'mon. Just one little bit. Pretty please." He put as much pouty whine into his voice as he could, hoping to convince her to read him something.

"Fine. Give me a second to find a good spot."

He could hear her moving around and imagined she was crawling into bed. The idea alone had his pulse racing and his cock growing thicker. She was silent for so long he began to wonder if she'd changed her mind and was waiting for him to hang up. "Found a good bit yet?"

She cleared her throat. "Yeah."

"Hang on. Let me get comfy." Dan popped the button and lowered the zipper on his jeans. "Okay. Go."

"'Harley leaned back on the bed and spread her legs. The view her position gave Todd had his eyes widening and his pants bulging. She knew what he'd see. She'd made sure there was no hair to hide her cunt.'"

"Fuck. Say that again." Dan shoved his hand in his pants and pulled out his throbbing cock.

"S-say what again?"

"Cunt." He squeezed his eyes shut as he stroked his hard-on. "That sounded so fucking hot coming out of your mouth."

"I'd prefer to just keep reading."

"Does it get hotter?" Dan slowly dragged his hand up and down his length.

"I-I think so."

Jody sounded a little breathless and he closed his eyes and pictured her in the position she'd described. He almost swallowed his tongue when he thought about her pussy stripped of hair. "Keep going," he urged.

"'Todd came towards her, stripping his shirt over his head as he did. The muscles in his chest rippled and her cunt wept with joy. If his chest looked that good she couldn't wait to see his cock. "Lose the pants," she demanded. He stopped beside the bed and did as she asked. He'd gone commando and his magnificent rod sprang free and slapped against his washboard abs. She licked her lips. She'd taste him first, then when he'd blown his load down her throat she'd make him eat her out until she screamed his name, yanked on his hair and came all over his face.'"

Dan groaned. His balls tucked up into his body and pre-come oozed from the slit in his cock. "Stop. Shit. Jody." He wasn't sure what he was trying to say.

"W-what?" She was breathless and he could only imagine how wet she was from reading that passage.

"Hearing you read that is so fucking hot. I'm close to blowing my load, only there isn't anyone to share it with."

"Oh..." Her breathy little sigh sent a shiver over his skin.

"Talk to me."

"You mean read more?"

"No. Tell me what you want me to do to you. Tell me what you'd make me do if that was you and me in that scene."

She was quiet so long Dan didn't think she was going to grant his request. And when she did finally speak, he had to strain to hear the words at first.

"I'd want to lick you while you licked me."

"Man, I'd love to do that. Sixty-nine is my favourite number."

"I've never done that before." Her words whispered through his ear.

"Never?" What the hell was wrong with the guy she'd married? "Next time I get you in a bed we're doing that first."

"Oh. That won't—"

"I'll lie on my back with you on all fours facing the other direction and I'll lick you from front to back and front again. Over and over until your pretty pussy is dripping all over my face. Put your hand on your pussy, Jody. Are you wet for me right now?" Dan tightened his grip but slowed his strokes so he didn't come before he could convince this amazingly innocent woman to indulge in a little phone sex with him.

"Um..."

"Are you wet?"

"Yes," she hissed, and he visualised her fingers sliding through her slick folds.

Fuck. "Play with you clit, Jody, pretend it's my tongue circling and flicking and driving you crazy with lust." Dan's breathing grew jagged when she panted in his ear. "Are you playing with your cunt, Jody?" He used the word from her book, prayed it would make her hotter, because this whole thing had him so close to coming his eyes were about to cross.

"Y-yes."

He heard the hitch in her breath, heard the little whimpers he remembered from Saturday and knew she was close. "Use your other hand and slide two fingers inside that clasping cunt for me. I'm not there to do it so I need you to do it for me."

She moaned and gasped, and Dan closed his eyes and stroked his cock harder. Faster. They were nearly there. Just a little more and she'd go over and then he'd follow.

"Do it harder. Faster. Fuck that wet cunt with my fingers, Jody."

A muffled cry tore through the phone line and he could picture her biting her lip to keep the sob of pleasure from breaking free.

"Oh, God." Her voice shook and he could hear her thrashing about. It was all he needed to go over.

With a growl, he came. Hot spurts of come coated his hand as he milked his cock with a punishing grip. When the last pulse left him, he sagged into the leather cushions and listened to Jody's breath settle back into a normal rhythm. Neither of them spoke. It wasn't necessary when they could hear the other breathing. How long they lay there, he couldn't say. It could have been seconds, minutes or hours. Time didn't matter when they'd connected in such an intimate way. And no matter what she said or did, Dan knew she trusted him.

To do what they just had, to be open enough to have phone

sex with him, showed him more than anything else that she was letting him in. He still had a long way to go, but he was making progress and that was all he cared about. As long as they kept moving forward they could go as slow as a snail and he'd be happy, because they'd be doing it together.

Jody figured she'd lost her mind. Why else would she have had phone sex with Dan? *Phone sex.* She'd never done anything so bold. Hours later, her body still hummed with the release she'd given herself but couldn't take all the credit for. Reading the scene from the book had her so wound up it hadn't taken much to push her over. And when he'd started to describe what they'd do together, how he'd lick her, well, even if he hadn't suggested she touch herself she would have.

She glanced at the clock and groaned. Four in the morning and she'd barely slept. Disturbingly dirty dreams of her and Dan doing every single one of her secret fantasies kept waking her up in a frenzied state that had her breath harsh and her body aching. Tomorrow was going to be bad if she couldn't manage a few more hours sleep. As it was, the alarm went off at six so she could shower and get ready for work before she dragged the girls out of bed and got them moving.

With a sigh, she threw her arm over her face. Hours ago, on the long drive home, she'd decided the thing with Dan couldn't go anywhere. She had her girls, a job she loved and family and friends who filled her life with as much happiness as she needed. And then Dan had rocked her world—again—with a single phone call. The man was lethal to her sanity. Every time he was around or she thought about him she did something out of character—like having an orgasm in a parking lot for God's sake.

Moaning, Jody rolled over and stared at the wall. The picture that hung there should remind her of all the reasons she should keep her distance. It was one of her favourite pictures of her and the girls. They were all laughing and happy, and it wasn't until now that she could see the sadness of the image. Colin hadn't been able to make the family-portrait sitting. Even back then, barely five years into their marriage, she should have walked away. Instead, she'd stuck it out for another five.

Hindsight was all good and well, but it didn't change the fact that she'd wasted most of her adult life on a man who'd never loved her or the girls. Her biggest shame was she'd picked a man who couldn't—or wouldn't—connect emotionally to be the father of her children. She'd overcompensated for Colin's lack of involvement over the years and she honestly thought she had a stronger bond with her girls because of that. Still, she wished they had an interested dad in their lives.

After another ten minutes of lying in the dark wide awake, Jody gave up on sleep and figured she'd catch up on things around the house that had gone undone over the weekend. She started with her bathroom and moved on to the girls' one in no time. Heading for the kitchen next, she wiped down cupboard doors and counters, finishing with the stove. Opening the fridge, she decided to put a slow cooker on for dinner and quickly found some carrots and sweet potato to toss in with the steak she pulled out of the freezer.

While the steak defrosted in the microwave she chopped the veggies along with a couple of onions and threw them into the crockpot. She pulled the meat out before it was fully thawed and cut it into cubes. A litre of stock and a few herbs and spices and she turned on the power and switched the machine to low. By the time the girls got home from school it would be ready. She'd leave a note to ask them to turn it off and some money so they could walk down to the local bakery and get a crusty loaf of bread to go with it.

Satisfied she'd been productive instead of lying in bed mentally flipping through her messed-up life she smiled. Next she'd tackle the washing. It didn't take her long to realise the washer was broken. Again. Last time it had been a coin caught in a hose. The machine wasn't even a year old. She'd have to ring the repairman first thing tomorrow—no, today—and beg Luc to use his if she couldn't get hers looked at before Wednesday.

Heading back to her room to get her phone, Jody wondered what else she could do to occupy her until it was time to get the girls up. She grabbed her phone and went back to the kitchen where she opened her bag and pulled out the paperwork from the weekend and spread it out on the breakfast counter. Putting a memo in her calendar to ring the repairman, she quickly got to work finalising the weekend's papers.

It took longer than expected because her mind kept wandering off on a Dan tangent every few minutes. The man had definitely taken over her thoughts in recent weeks. Ever since he'd laid that first kiss on her, she'd been helpless to stop her memory and imagination from bombarding her with real and dreamed-up pleasure to be found with him. He was trouble whether she gave in to him or fought against him.

Disgusted with herself for losing track of what she was meant to be doing yet again, she tossed down her pen and pushed her stool back with a screech. She'd grab a shower now. With any luck, the hot water would wash away all thoughts of a certain man and everything he made her feel.

The day had been tense. Dan hadn't brought up last night's phone call and neither had Jody. But for all the personal apprehension and strain between them, they'd worked together seamlessly and finalised the weekend's job and locked the second date on the calendar. Dan had spoken to Mooney and emailed the questionnaire Cassie wanted the first group of employees to fill out. Those would be returned by the end of the week so now he could put the file away and call it a day.

Jody was on the phone and as he didn't want to leave

without talking to her and possibly heading out together, he waited. He couldn't help overhearing her conversation and it didn't take him long to work out her washing machine was broken and the repairman couldn't fit her in until next week. When she hung up the phone with a sigh, he ventured over to her desk and rested his hip on the edge.

"I could take a look at that washer for you."

She glanced up. "What?"

"Your washer. I worked for my dad all through my teens and he ran a repair business, so I'm pretty handy when it comes to fixing anything mechanical." Dan smiled. He tried not to let his need to spend more time with her leak into his voice.

Jody's forehead crinkled, her eyebrows rising almost to her hair line. "Really?"

Her scepticism didn't sit well with him. "Yep, and because you're obviously convinced I can't fix it, I'll add an incentive to take me up on my offer. I'll buy dinner for you and the girls, and if I don't have the machine working by the time you finish eating, I'll buy you a new one."

She rolled her eyes. "Jeez, what is it with men and proving they can fix things?"

"What do you mean?" Had someone else offered to repair her broken washer?

"You and Luc. He's already tried to convince me to let him look at it."

"Does he know anything about the mechanics of a washing machine?"

"Probably not, but that wouldn't stop him from pulling it apart if I said yes. But never mind that, the damn thing is less than a year old, so it's covered under warranty. I'm pretty sure I'd void that by letting you look at it."

"Probably, but what if it's something simple that me fixing wouldn't void the warranty, and you wouldn't have the expense of calling out the service company." Dan was reaching. Unless she'd forgotten to plug the machine in and switch it on, she'd still have to call the repairman or risk voiding the warranty even if he could fix the problem.

"Thanks, but no." Jody bent over and retrieved her handbag. "Now if I don't head home and get organised I won't get to Luc's before midnight, and if I don't have a washer for the rest of the week I need to wash tonight."

"Isn't Luc a thirty-minute drive from where you are?"

"Yes, why?"

"Well, my place is only about ten and my washer works. Drier too." Dan held his breath.

"You're offering to let me use your machines? What's the catch?" She eyed him sceptically.

"No catch. Well, other than you actually have to spend time with me outside of work." He grinned.

"Why?"

"Why not?" He wasn't sure why Jody needed a reason, but he'd give her one. "It's just one friend loaning their washer to another. No strings."

"In my experience there's always a string or two."

Dan held up his hands. "Nope, no strings." He grabbed a pen and her sticky note pad, and scribbled down his address. "Here. If you want to take me up on my offer I'll be home all night. If not, no worries."

Jody eyed the note then met his gaze again. "You really do only live ten minutes from me."

"Yeah, a lot closer than your brother's place." Dan pushed to his feet. "Anyway, come or don't, doesn't matter to me, but with the girls having to get up for school tomorrow, I would think cutting some time off your evening might guarantee them getting into bed at a reasonable hour."

Dan got all the way to the door before she stopped him.

"Wait." She hustled to catch up with him. "If you're serious

I'd love to use your washer, but there's one condition."

He didn't think it was the kind of condition his body craved. "Shoot."

"I'll bring dinner."

"I don't—"

She grabbed his arm. "Please. It's already made anyway. I put a hotpot together before I left for work this morning. I'll just bring it with me. Oh, and the girls. I don't like leaving them home alone at night." She smiled.

"What time should I expect you?" Dan wasn't about to argue. If she felt comfortable enough to introduce him to her kids he wasn't about to say anything to make her change her mind.

"Seven? That gives me time to get home, gather the dirty washing, dinner and the girls."

"Great. See you then."

Chapter Eleven

Jody wasn't sure what Leigh's latest outburst was about. She'd been hostile from the moment Jody had gotten home. Amy on the other hand was being the perfect child. She wouldn't have worried if they weren't currently pulling up to Dan's house. There was nothing worse than a child misbehaving in front of others, and Jody turned in her seat to look at both girls.

"Please be on your best behaviour. Dan has been kind enough to let us use his washer and drier, so I don't want to thank him by bringing a couple of naughty kids into his house."

"Then why'd you bring us?" Leigh sat in the front seat, arms crossed and a frown on her face.

"Why wouldn't I bring you?" Jody asked.

"Because we might cramp your style."

"What? Why would you say something like that, Leigh?" Jody was flabbergasted. Who was this child and where had her pleasant daughter gone? One weekend away for work and she'd turned into a monster.

"Never mind. You don't get it." Leigh grabbed the door handle and yanked it open.

Before Jody could reply, Leigh slammed her way out of the car and stomped towards Dan's front door. What the hell was going on?

Amy sighed dramatically from the backseat. "Sometimes she's so selfish."

Jody turned to look at her youngest daughter. "Why do you say that?"

"Because Leigh wants to be home so that *Benji* can ring her."

"Benji?"

"He's some stupid boy at school that's going to ask her out or something." Amy's cheeks flushed with colour. "I overheard her talking to Monica on the way home."

Ah, so Leigh had finally discovered boys. Jody took a deep breath and let it out slowly. She'd been dreading the whole boys talk and she had hoped for another year of ignoring that particular subject, but obviously she couldn't put it off any longer. The girls both knew the basics, they'd had those talks often enough. But Jody had avoided talking about dating, what was okay, what wasn't, and what to expect from any boy interested in them.

Jody found it mildly amusing that both she and Leigh were dealing with interest from the opposite sex. Then again, she hoped Leigh wasn't dealing with the same level of interest. She didn't want to even think about the possibility of her daughter having sex yet. Christ, she was only fifteen. Except she'd heard kids were becoming sexually active a lot younger now days, and the thought of her child being one of them terrified her.

"Mum, are we going to sit here all night?" Amy asked.

"Oh, no." Jody pulled the keys from the ignition and put them in her pocket as she climbed out of the car. By the time she'd opened the tailgate on her SUV, Dan was beside her.

"Here, let me carry that for you." He reached in and picked up the basket of dirty clothes. "Is that dinner I smell?"

"Yes. It's just a basic beef stew." Jody didn't want him to think she'd gone to any trouble on his account.

"Nothing basic about that smell. My taste buds are already watering with anticipation." He grinned at her then walked towards the house. "C'mon, I'm starving."

Jody followed Dan into a nicely decorated house. Most of what she saw had a woman's touch and it suddenly struck her that he might have a woman in his life. Her gaze darted over to him to find he was watching her carefully.

"Do you like it?" He indicated the living room with the lift of his chin. "My mum and sister helped me decorate when I first bought the place."

Relief swamped her. She wasn't sure what surprised her more. The fact she'd never thought to ask if he was involved or the spike of jealousy that had stabbed her in the belly when she thought of him with someone else. "It's great. Very homey."

"That was what my mum said they were going for. C'mon, let's get a load in the washer and then we can have some of that yummy smelling food." He turned and headed down a ceramic-tiled hallway. "Girls, there's a Play Station and computer down this way in the family room," he called over his shoulder.

"Oh, no. I didn't even introduce you to the girls. Dan, this is Amy and Leigh." Jody felt her cheeks heat with embarrassment as she pointed to each of her daughters in turn.

Dan paused and spun around to face them. "It's nice to finally meet you both. I've heard so much about you from your mum, Luc and Cassie that it feels like we've already met." He smiled. "C'mon, I'm sure I've got a game or two you'll like."

Jody had to prompt both girls to say hi before they followed Dan deeper into the house.

Amy walked ahead of her, bouncing along right behind Dan and asking a million questions while Leigh dragged her feet about ten paces behind Jody. The two couldn't be more polar-opposite in mood if they tried. Resigned to spending the evening with grumpy and happy, she hoped Dan didn't mind sharing his time on the teenage emotional roller coaster with her.

"Wow. Leigh, you have to come see this." Amy disappeared into a room at the end of the hall.

"Jeez, could she be any more juvenile?" Leigh muttered as she brushed past Jody and followed her sister through the doorway.

Jody raised one eyebrow at Dan. "What?"

His smile seemed shy and totally un-Dan like. "She's found my electronic game collection."

"Game collection?"

"Yeah, I have every one ever produced." He shrugged. "I've been collecting them for years."

She popped her head in the door to see the girls both had devices in their hands. "Hey, don't touch—"

"No. It's okay. They all work and they're supposed to be played with," Dan said.

"But what if they break them?"

He laughed. "If they've survived this long, I'm sure they'll come out unscathed today. And if not I'll just fix them."

"You can do that?"

"Yep, washers aren't the only thing I know how to repair." Dan turned and walked into the kitchen. "The laundry is this way."

Jody followed him through a gorgeous kitchen. Stainless-steel appliances, gloss-white cupboards and black-marble countertops made the space a cook's dream. She'd love to have a kitchen like this, but on her budget that wasn't going to happen anytime soon. "This is amazing. You must cook up a storm in here."

"Ah, yeah, no. I'm not much of a cook. My mum uses it when I host the family dinners though," he called out from the room on the far side.

She joined him in an area far too fancy for a laundry. "My God, even the dirty clothes get a great room to hang out in."

Dan looked around them then shrugged. "The people who remodelled the kitchen did the laundry and bathrooms as well. I got a cheaper deal getting them all done together."

"Well, if these two rooms are anything to go by the bathrooms must be gorgeous."

"Let's get a load on and I'll take you on a tour."

Jody looked for somewhere to put the crock-pot in her arms.

"Here, I'll take that into the kitchen while you sort your wash. Do I need to plug it in?" He took the heavy pot from her.

"No. It was just easier to grab the whole thing than pull out the inner pot and worry about burning something on it."

"Okay, I'll set the table while you get a load on."

She watched him walk away and wondered what the hell she was doing in his house. She'd managed to sabotage her decision to keep her distance at every turn. Rolling her eyes at herself, she crouched down and began sorting the washing into lights and darks. By the time she'd thrown the lights in the machine, Dan was back, leaning against the doorjamb. His close scrutiny made her nervous, but that was nothing compared to the look in his eyes. They smouldered, the desire he felt for her going unchecked as he watched her.

"Um, I'm not sure how this works..."

Dan pushed off the wall and stalked towards her. Her pulse spiked and her breathing turned choppy—jagged. "Here, let me show you." He crowded in close and leaned over her to press the buttons on the control panel. His breath fanned out over her neck, sending a shiver down her spine and goose bumps racing to catch up.

"Mum! Leigh won't let me play with the Game Boy!" Amy yelled from out in the kitchen.

Jody jumped and Dan immediately moved away. When Amy came charging into the room they were no longer in a compromising position, and Jody turned her attention to her daughter.

"Please don't yell, Amy."

"But Leigh's hogging the Game Boy and I want a turn."

"You can have a turn when she dies or whatever it is that happens when a game is over."

Dan laughed. "You obviously aren't a game fan."

"Well, no, not really." Jody smoothed a hand over Amy's hair. "We'll be eating in a moment, so go tell you sister to put the game away and wash her hands."

"There's a bathroom across the hall from the games room, Amy," Dan added.

"Sorry about that. They've been at each other's throats since I walked in the door this afternoon." She headed in the direction of the kitchen. "I better make sure there's no blood spilled in your bathroom."

Walking quickly, Jody made her way to find the girls and make sure they weren't embarrassing her further by fighting over the soap.

Dan sat on his sofa in a death match with Amy. Leigh was sulking on the other side of the room with the Game Boy she hadn't let out of her hands since she'd arrived. Momentarily distracted by the brooding teenager, the younger one took him out.

"Yes!" Amy pumped her fist in the air. "Die, sucker, die."

"Language!" Jody called from the kitchen where she'd insisted on cleaning up after dinner.

"Fun police strikes again," Leigh murmured.

Dan arched an eyebrow and looked at Amy who shrugged and said, "She's pissed at Mum for making us come here tonight. Some guy from school was supposed to call and ask her out, but she's not home to answer."

"Amy! Shut up!" Leigh looked ready to launch across the room and strangle her sister.

"You two aren't fighting again are you?" Jody asked from the doorway.

He glanced over and saw the frown on Jody's face, the concern in her eyes, and tried to pacify her a little. "Amy beat me again. She's a tough one."

Jody smiled. "She always thrashes me at Wii bowling."

Ah, so they did have a game console at home. "I didn't know you played. I can hook up the Wii and challenge you to a game if you want."

"No, it's okay. I'm going to fold that first load of washing while the other takes its turn in the drier."

When Jody left the room, he glanced back at Leigh who was still shooting daggers at Amy. "You think this guy won't call back if you're not there to pick up?"

She shrugged. "I don't know. I'm not even sure he'll call. He told his best friend who told my best friend, so it might not even be true."

Dan could tell she wanted it to be, and while he wasn't sure where Jody stood on the whole dating thing, he felt he should at least try to make Leigh feel better. "You know, if he likes you, really likes you, he'll keep trying until he talks to you."

Her face brightened. "You think so?"

"Definitely. But if he doesn't, he's not the guy for you."

"Why not?" She'd gone on the defensive again, her brow wrinkling up in the same way Jody's did when she was about to go to battle over something.

"Because if he's not prepared to put in some effort to be with you, then he doesn't deserve to spend time with you."

"Oh, so I should play hard to get? That's what Monica's older sister said."

"No, I just mean if he gives up after ringing you once then he obviously wasn't that interested. But I'm betting he either talks to you at school tomorrow or rings tomorrow night." He'd probably stepped over the line by giving Jody's daughter dating advice. He'd have to tell her what they'd talked about before Leigh or Amy mentioned it to their mother. "Who wants some ice cream?"

"Me. Me. Me," Amy chanted.

"Chocolate or vanilla?"

"Both." She grinned at him and he couldn't resist tweaking her pert nose.

"Hey." She rubbed the tip with her hand.

"Leigh?"

"No, thanks. I don't need the extra fat."

Uh-oh, he wasn't touching that comment with a ten foot barge pole. "Right. One bowl of chocolate *and* vanilla ice cream coming up."

Dan quickly made up a bowl for Amy and took it back to the games room. Certain they were both occupied for the moment, he went in search of Jody to confess he'd blundered into a parent-type conversation with her eldest daughter. He might not be a father, but he was pretty sure he'd handled the discussion correctly. Hopefully, Jody thought the same.

He found her on the floor in the laundry. She had three piles of folded clothes around her. Hunkering down beside her, he picked up a shirt from the basket and attempted to fold it. Jody laughed and took it out of his hands.

"Give me that. Watch." She grabbed the shirt under the armpits and shook it out. Then she folded the thing in half, bringing her hands together. After that, she tucked in the sleeves and folded it twice lengthways until it was a neat little square of fabric. "See. Easy."

"Yeah, right," he grumbled as he picked up another shirt to give it a try.

"How do you fold yours then?" she asked as she quickly made another neat square with a pair of shorts.

"I don't. I hang them all up." He dipped his chin close to his chest. "It's easier."

Smiling, she turned her head to look at him. "Why do men always take the easy way?"

"I can't speak for all men, but I'm all for cutting corners where I can."

"Yeah, cutting corners." She snatched up a pair of shorts and snapped them out, making them crack like a whip.

"Hey, just because I cut corners with my laundry doesn't mean I cut them everywhere."

She let out a burst of air. "Sorry. I shouldn't have implied you do."

"Speaking of the easy way, I, um, may have overstepped the lines of our friendship just now with Leigh."

Her gaze snapped up to his. "What?"

"Oh, wait, that didn't sound right. Let me explain."

She glared at him with narrowed eyes. "Go on."

"Amy let it slip why Leigh has been sulking all night and we got into a conversation about some guy she thinks is going to ask her out."

"Oh, that." Jody's shoulders drooped. "I'm not sure what to think about that."

"Well, anyway, I asked what the problem was and then offered some advice."

"What did you say?"

Dan wasn't sure what was going through Jody's head. For all he knew, she was about to thump him for interfering. "I told her that if this guy couldn't get her tonight, if he was really interested he'd talk to her tomorrow at school or try ringing her again tomorrow night. I also tried to tell her that if he didn't try again after missing her tonight then he wasn't worth her time."

She remained quiet and Dan couldn't take the suspense for longer than a few seconds.

"Well? Did I fuck up?"

A smile tilted the corner of her mouth. "No. In fact, what you told her was good advice and probably more acceptable coming from you than me."

"Really?"

"Yeah, ever since the weekend we've been butting heads. I'm not sure she'd have listened to me if I'd said the same thing word for word. I seem to have been relegated to the enemy camp."

"I'm sure it won't last long. I remember my teenage years being like a pendulum swinging between love and hate when it came to my mum and dad." He picked up another shirt and this time managed to fold it in a semi-neat square.

Jody took the top off him and put it on one of the piles. "You're right. I know that. It's just frustrating not knowing what tips the scale in either direction."

The drier beeped and he leaned over and popped the door open. Together, they pulled the second load of clothes out and dumped them in the basket. "Oh, I forgot, I gave Amy some ice cream. I didn't even think to ask if she could have it." Damn, he was an idiot. The kid could be allergic or something.

"That's fine. She's the ice-cream ho in our house."

"Yeah, Leigh said she didn't need the extra fat." He still couldn't believe a fifteen-year-old was worried about fat intake.

"Jesus. Another confusing, worrying aspect of raising a teenager in this era of thin is beautiful." Jody shook her head. "Lucky for me, she's fairly sensible and loves food." She laughed. "She'd never starve herself."

"I think West's sister had an eating disorder. She does a whole heap of seminars at high schools about food and nutrition. West helps put her menus together. You could ask him for some advice if you're really concerned."

"That's not a bad idea. I know their school has sent home a few notes about healthier options in lunch boxes. Maybe they've seen or heard something to be alarmed about."

"Maybe." Dan continued to help her fold. Unfortunately, he wasn't getting any better at it and Jody had to refold half of what he did. "Sorry. I should stop trying to help. I think I'm making more work."

"I'll have to remember to ask West in the morning." She grabbed the last piece of clothing before he could.

"I can remind you. I think he's in to make a cake for that kid's party Cassie is doing in the afternoon." Dan got to his feet and offered Jody his hand.

"Thanks." She got to her feet and they stood there just staring at each other for long moments. "I should get going. It's late and the girls have school."

"Yeah, you probably should." But neither of them moved.

Jody licked her lips and Dan couldn't resist leaning in for a taste. He pressed his mouth to hers and nibbled the sweet curves before sweeping over them with his tongue. She trembled against him before parting her lips and inviting him inside with the hesitant touch of her tongue. That was all it took for him to lose it and go deep. Thrusting his tongue between her teeth, he stroked and teased until they were caught up in a frenzied give and take.

Dan skimmed his hands over her hips and up her ribcage to her breasts. He cupped them, squeezed with his fingers and flicked her hard nipples with his thumbs. It wasn't enough—he wanted to feel her skin on skin, so he slid his hands back down until he could tuck them up under her T-shirt. Her flesh was warm and rippled beneath his fingers as he trailed them up her bare torso. She moaned into his mouth when he pushed her bra aside and palmed her bare breasts.

He wanted more. Pulling his lips from hers, he breathed her in as he nipped his way along her jaw to her ear. Scraping his teeth over the delicate flap of her lobe, he toyed with it until she whimpered. Then he sucked the whole thing into his mouth and tongued it with rapid flicks. She gasped and shuddered against him.

"I want you," he growled in her ear.

"Yes." The word left her lips in a rush of air.

"Mum?"

And just like that Dan's body went stone cold.

Chapter Twelve

Jody still hadn't gotten over almost being caught making out with Dan by Leigh. The thought still made her shiver with fear. He'd been so accepting and even a little relieved when she'd hustled the girls out of there. And the text he'd sent her late last night had only made her soften towards him more. He was so understanding of her lightning-quick changes of mind. She really didn't deserve his patience or persistence, but she was more than willing to take it.

"Hey, wanna get some lunch?" Cassie strode into Jody's office.

"Sure. What did you have in mind?" Jody glanced at Dan who was busy on the phone with a client.

"I thought we could go to the sushi place again."

"Sounds good." Jody shuffled some papers back into their folder. "Give me five minutes?"

"I'll meet you downstairs." Cassie left with a small wave in Dan's direction.

Jody busied herself with putting the few files on her desk away while she waited for Dan to get off the phone. She wasn't sure why she was waiting to talk to him, but she couldn't leave before she did. When he finally said goodbye and put the phone back on its cradle, she took a deep breath. But he spoke before she could get a word out.

"Can you bring me back something?"

"Ah, sure. What do you want?"

"Just get me an assortment. There isn't anything I don't eat, so whatever looks good." He stood up and pulled his wallet out of his pocket.

She waved him off. "No, I've got it. It's the least I can do after you let me use your washer."

"I thought dinner was payment for that?" He smiled.

"Well, yeah, but then the girls did the whole war of the teenagers thing, so I figure I owe you for that too." She'd tried to apologise this morning when she'd first arrived at work, but he wouldn't let her. At least now she could assuage some of her guilt over subjecting him to her warring teens.

"I told you that wasn't a problem." He came around his desk. "They were perfectly well-behaved, and I'd be more than happy to spend time with them again."

"You would?" She couldn't imagine why. He was single and none of his siblings had children, so it wasn't as though he was used to being around kids.

"Yep. In fact, what about doing something together this weekend? You can come over early Saturday and use the washer again. Then we can head out for lunch somewhere. What do the girls like to eat?" He held up a hand. "Wait, let me guess. MacDonald's."

"I don't think that's a good idea…"

Dan frowned. The corners of his mouth creased and his brows scrunched together above his nose. "Why?"

"Look I know we've kind of moved beyond workmates but—"

"Don't say it." He leaned in close. "Can you for one second forget about everything except whether or not you want to hang out with me? Don't think about work. Don't think about anything but spending the day doing something fun with me. And the girls."

Jody opened her mouth, except Dan put two fingers over her lips before she could say a word.

"Think about it over lunch. Give me your answer when you deliver my food." He bent forward and planted a quick, hard kiss on her mouth.

Shocked by his bold action, she stood frozen in place until the sound of Cassie yelling her name up the stairwell registered. Shaking herself, she glanced around to see Dan had left the room and she hadn't even realised he'd gone. He really did short-circuit her brain. She grabbed her bag and hightailed it downstairs to a waiting Cassie.

"About time. I was thinking of sending out a search party. What kept you so long?" Cassie asked as they headed across the warehouse.

Jody's cheeks heated and she knew they'd be flaming red. She wasn't about to tell Cassie Dan had kissed in the office. "Sorry, filing took longer than I thought it would."

"You could have left it until we got back."

"I know, but I sort of lost track of time." Boy had she ever. Only it wasn't the filing that had kept her spellbound.

"Never mind. It's still early so we shouldn't have trouble getting a seat next to the train."

Jody laughed when she remembered her boss's fascination with the sushi train. Cassie seemed more excited about the moving plates than what was on them. "You just want to watch the food go round."

"Oh, c'mon. It is kinda cool." Cassie bumped her shoulder into Jody's. "So wanna talk about Dan?"

"What?" Jody choked.

Cassie wrapped her arm around Jody's waist and gave her a quick squeeze. "You don't have to, but I thought you might want to. I'm not listening as your boss, so chuck that notion right out. I'm your friend. The woman dating your brother. Hell, I'm all but living with him now days."

"I'm not sure what you expect me to say."

"Look, let's lay the cards on the table. From the minute you started working for me, I've seen the sparks between you two. You were both so intent on disliking each other to begin with that neither of you worked out those sparks weren't hatred." Cassie glanced at her as they walked down the sidewalk. "Am I right?"

Jody sighed. "Yeah."

"So something happen last weekend?"

She laughed. "You could say that."

"Good or bad?"

"Oh, good. Very, very good." Jody's body flushed hot with the memory of just how *good* Dan was.

"Judging by your flushed face and breathless voice, I'm going to assume you got laid but good." Cassie grinned. "And can I just say about damn time. High five for you, honey."

Cassie held up her hand and Jody slapped her palm with hers. She couldn't stop the giggle that bubbled up her throat. "Jesus. I feel like a sixteen-year-old talking boys and high fiving."

"Hey, guys regress all the time, I figure we should too." They reached the end of the street and stopped to wait for the light to change. "So, are you seeing Dan now or are you going to do the whole I'm-a-single mum, he's-a-younger-man thing?"

"What makes you think I'd use that argument not to see him?"

"I noticed you didn't deny the not-seeing-him part."

Jody grimaced. "I don't know what to do."

"Why not?"

"I don't need any more complications. The girls and I are doing great. I love my new job and don't want to jeopardise it by having an affair with a workmate—"

"Too late for that." Cassie turned to face her. "Look, I can't say what will happen, but I can say that you would not lose your job if things between you and Dan didn't work out. There are plenty of options to keep the two of you from working together. The only reason you're sharing the office and quite a few of your early jobs was so you could learn the ropes. I can easily move either of you out into another space and make sure you're rostered on different events."

"I'm scared to get involved." There. She'd said it. She was scared. Colin had been her one true relationship and look how she'd fucked that up.

"Not scared to get involved with Dan but involved in general?" Cassie asked as the walk light turned green and they stepped off the curb. "Because I can tell you now, I don't think he'd ever do anything to hurt you or the girls. If he's pursuing you, he's serious. I've never known him to go after any woman. They all usually fall at his feet."

"So I'm a challenge then?" That idea didn't make Jody feel any better. In fact, it made the whole situation worse.

"No. No, I don't think it's that. He's not the type to go after something just because it's a challenge. More the type to only work for those things he really wants. What he's serious about."

Jody mulled that over for a minute. They entered the sushi restaurant and were directed to two seats in the back near where the chefs loaded the fresh food on the train.

"Yes. First pick." Cassie slipped onto her stool and nabbed a plate straight away.

"Good Lord, woman, at least put your arse on the seat before you start eating."

Cassie grinned at her around a mouthful of prawn and rice. "I'm starving. I skipped breakfast. Actually, Luc made me skip breakfast."

Jody put up a hand. "Do not start talking about you and my brother and before breakfast. I don't need to know what you two get up to in the hours between sunset and sunrise."

"Oh, we don't restrict our activities to the cover of darkness."

"Shit." She stuck her fingers in her ears and hummed.

Cassie laughed hysterically, drawing the gazes of a number

of surrounding customers and penetrating Jody's makeshift earplugs.

Jody pulled her fingers free and searched her handbag for the little bottle of sanitiser she kept in there. It was a shame she couldn't use it to clean her mind of the thought of her brother and Cassie doing something that made them so late they had to skip breakfast.

The last thing Dan wanted to be doing on a Friday night was stocktake. But he'd drawn the short straw this month, so here he was, going from one tub to the next, counting every damn thing in the place. Thank God, he didn't have to count all those beads, just the little boxes of them, although that was bad enough. And if anyone else interrupted him while he was counting, he was throwing the clipboard at their head. He was on the final row. Luckily, West was taking care of the kitchen supplies. He'd definitely go insane if he had to do those as well.

One thing about this job was he had plenty of time to think. Something he'd been doing a lot of since Jody had agreed to see him again. He wasn't sure what had changed her mind, but he knew she wouldn't back out because the girls knew they were going ice skating. He'd tried to come up with something different and fun to do. When he'd asked Jody if they skated and she'd told him none of them had ever been, he knew he had to take them the first time.

He better get a move on with the rest of the count or he'd still be here when they arrived on his doorstep to do their washing in the morning. Glancing at his watch, he saw it was ten minutes until midnight. He'd hoped to be home by now. The house could do with a bit of a tidy up before the girls arrived. Especially the one who'd cleaned his kitchen so well on Monday night that he'd discovered the section of counter behind the cook top wasn't black. It was silver.

His mother would have his head if she knew he'd let a

woman deal with his neglect. Then again, if she knew about Jody and the girls she'd be in his ear about bringing them round. That was something he wasn't ready for. Yet.

"Hey, you're still here." Cassie walked towards him.

"Yep, almost done though. Party over already?"

"Just about. I let Kerry take over. I wanted to get home before midnight because I've got the Winter's birthday tomorrow morning." She indicated the clipboard in his hand. "How much left?"

He nodded to the rack beside her. "Last few boxes."

"Good. Want me to help out so you get out of here faster?" she asked.

"No. You go on. I'm sure Luc is waiting up for you."

"Actually, he's at Jody's."

Dan's head snapped around. "What? Why?"

Cassie chewed her lip and diverted her gaze. "I'm not sure I should say anything."

"Cassie. Tell me."

"Fine. But if Jody wanted you to know, I'm pretty sure she would have told you herself."

"Just spill it." If she didn't tell him in the next few seconds he was out the door.

"Colin turned up at her house earlier tonight drunk. Apparently, he took a bat to Jody's car after she wouldn't let him in the house."

He'd dropped the clipboard and was at the end of the row before Cassie had finished speaking. He pulled his phone out of his pocket and checked for missed calls. Messages. Nothing. She hadn't rung him. Dan wasn't sure how he felt about that. He only knew he had to go to her now and make sure she was all right.

"I'll finish the stocktake," Cassie yelled behind him.

Dan didn't bother to acknowledge her. He sprinted across

the warehouse and slammed out the door. He'd ridden his bike this morning and was thankful because he could dodge through traffic a hell of a lot faster on the Ducati than in his Jeep. Throwing his leg over the seat, he snagged his helmet off the handlebar and strapped it on. In seconds, he had the motor thrumming between his legs as he sped out of the parking lot.

Traffic was light, and with him sitting ten or so kilometres above the speed limit, he was pulling into Jody's driveway in record time. Luc's car remained at the curb and Jody's SUV sat in the driveway next to where Dan had stopped, every window was smashed and most of the panels had taken a beating too. Dan switched off the bike and kicked the stand down. Jody's front door opened as he pulled his helmet off and Dan's heart stuttered until he realised it was Luc standing there and not Jody.

"Hey." Luc nodded at him. "Cassie rang."

"Is Jody okay? The girls?" Dan's long strides ate up the distance to Luc.

"They're all asleep. The girls are in with Jody. None of them would tell me what went on before I got here, but they all have to go to the police station in the morning to make statements. I was planning on going with them."

"I'll be there." Dan waited for Luc to step aside, but he didn't. "Are you going to make me sit out here all night?"

Luc sighed. "I guess not, but considering she asked me not to call you when Cassie suggested it, I'm not sure if it's good for my health. She's pissed, man. I've never seen her so angry before."

"Good. Maybe she'll finally give Colin what he deserves instead of treating him like a respected friend."

Luc arched an eyebrow. "She told you about him?"

"Enough for me to know he doesn't deserve her loyalty even if he is the girls' father."

"C'mon, let me get you a beer and we'll talk. There are a few things I'd like to do besides let the police take care of the situation."

Dan knew in Luc's line of business he could probably have a man disappear, and while he would love for Jody to be free of her ex-husband, he didn't think getting rid of the man completely was the right move. "As long as you're not going to ask me to help you hide the body, I'm in."

Luc laughed as he led Dan into the kitchen. "Nothing as dramatic. But we are going to make him wish we'd chosen that avenue."

The sinister grin that spread across Luc's face made Dan's blood run cold. If he wasn't serious about this man's sister, now would be the time to back out. Even with that threat hanging over his head, Dan didn't plan on going anywhere. He wasn't sure how this thing with Jody would play out, or whether they were meant to be together, but he was more than ready to find out. And definitely ready to put in the effort necessary to make a relationship between them work. He'd even grown fond of the girls, and they'd only spent one evening together so far.

"Dan?"

Jody's voice had both him and Luc spinning around. "Hey. You okay?" Dan asked.

She stood in the doorway, her hair all messed up, half in, half out of her ponytail. "What are you doing here?"

"Checking up on you and the girls." He walked towards her in slow, measured steps. She seemed fragile somehow. "Do you need something?"

"No. I heard voices."

"Sorry, we didn't mean to wake you." Dan got within touching distance and couldn't help but put his hands on her. He cupped her shoulders then ran his hands up and down her arms. "Are you cold?"

"Stop." She stepped away. "I don't need coddling."

"Okay." He moved back a step. "But maybe I do."

"What?" Her sleepy gaze met his.

"I need to know you're okay. I saw what he did outside..." Dan shuddered. "I need to know he didn't hurt you, Jody."

Jody's mouth kicked up on one end. "Physically? No, I'm fine and so are the girls. Emotionally, he may as well have taken that bat to my heart and soul because of what he said in front of the girls." She closed her eyes and a single tear slid down her cheek.

He couldn't do it. Couldn't stand back and watch her struggle to hold it together. Stepping close, he wrapped his arms around her and pulled her in. This time she came. It was like a dam bursting. Her whole body shook with the sobs racking her chest. Dan glanced over at Luc to see the other man clenching his fists, a jaw muscle ticking, and wondered if they were having the same murderous thoughts right now.

Dan indicated the living room with his head then scooped Jody into his arms and carried her into the darkness. He sat on the couch and held her in his lap. She cried and cried, her tears soaking the front of his shirt, but he didn't care. If he could, he'd take away every one of those drops, every bit of her pain. Except the only thing he could do was hold her tight and let her fall apart somewhere safe. Luc moved in front of him and placed a box of tissue on the coffee table. Nodding thanks, Dan went back to soothing Jody until her sobs turned to the occasional hiccup and she slipped off to sleep.

Sitting in the dark, Dan held her while she slept and came to a startling realisation. He'd fallen for this woman. Hook, line and sinker, he was done. She'd found her way under his skin and he'd never seen it coming. He wanted to laugh. To shout it from the rooftops, but he figured she'd think he was insane for admitting to such deep emotions when they'd barely moved into being friends. Sure, they'd had sex. But if anyone knew sex wasn't love it was him. He'd spent half his life having sex, and not once had he loved any of those women.

Instead, it had taken someone not looking for love, or a

relationship, to snag his heart. And didn't that just fuck with his head. He could have professed his love to any other woman and she'd have been glad to hear it. Except, like his mother always said, nothing worth having comes easy, and Jody would have to be the least easy woman he'd ever dealt with. Now he had to figure out how to convince her he was serious. And how to make her fall in love with him in return.

Chapter Thirteen

Jody wasn't sure why she was annoyed. She should be more than happy to have everyone's support. And she was. Kind of. Cassie had taken the girls to Luc's house a little while ago, but she was still stuck at the police station going over and over her statement. The officers had been wonderful with the girls. She'd been worried about letting them talk about what had happened with their father, but there had been a police psychologist waiting when they'd arrived and then Luc had pulled some strings somewhere and had a private counsellor come in to help them deal with the trauma.

The counsellor had gone with Cassie to spend the rest of the day with Leigh and Amy. Jody couldn't believe any of this was even necessary. Colin had really gone off the deep end this time. Mind you, in all the years she'd known him, last night was the most emotion she'd ever seen from him. Shame he'd chosen to put that level of intensity into a negative sentiment. She took a deep breath and tried to shake off the black cloud hanging over her. She'd be more than happy for this ordeal to be over. Now.

Unfortunately, she now had to file papers with the courts restricting Colin's access to the girls. The idea made her sick, but the two lawyers either side of her—and the police—had insisted it was the best option. Luc had pulled more strings to get her the best representation in Sydney. Mackenzie Harris wasn't even in family law, but here he was on her right, taking charge of all the legal proceedings. On her left was Mackenzie's family-law expert. Jody was pretty sure this guy was smart enough to convince the court Colin wasn't the girls' father even with DNA proof.

"Can we take a break?" Dan asked from his position leaning on the wall.

She'd almost forgotten he was here. Almost. The low hum vibrating over her nerves didn't allow her to eradicate him completely from her mind. Her eyes met his and the sudden sting of tears blinded her.

"Never mind. We're taking one." He strode over and pulled her from the chair. "We'll be back in five." Dan didn't wait for anyone to agree or disagree, he slipped his arm around her shoulders and ushered her from the room.

They walked a short way down the hall then entered the men's restroom where he locked the door after checking they were alone. He yanked a bunch of paper from one of the cubicles and handed it to her.

"Let it go." He pulled her back into his arms and held her. "I've got you."

She leaned on him. Let him take her weight—and not just the physical kind. Her tears were muffled against his chest, but the wretched sound of her sobs echoed off the walls. He held her close, ran his hands up and down her back and let her cry herself out. For the second time in twelve hours, she took advantage of Dan's generosity, of his compassion, and gave in to the need to be weak—to allow someone else to hold her up.

Jody knew she couldn't keep doing this. It wasn't his problem to deal with, and it was less than fair to expect him to put up with her messy life. God, she'd give anything to go back to being just a single mum dealing with a couple of emotional teenagers. Now she was the woman with the psycho ex as well. Not something she'd ever thought to be. Or something Dan had signed on for. With strength she didn't think she had, she pulled out of his arms and moved over to the sink.

She turned on the cold water and ran some clean paper towel under the flow then pressed it against her closed eyes. The cool pads brought a little relief to her stinging eyes, but nothing would help the red puffiness that greeted her when she looked in the cracked mirror. Even the chipped and peeling glass couldn't hide the ravages of hours of crying. She'd tried to conceal some of the damage this morning, except she'd washed that away with her latest jag. Her purse was back in the room so there'd be no emergency repairs.

"Better?"

She met Dan's gaze in their reflection. "I'm sorry."

"For what?" He stepped closer behind her. "You've got nothing to be sorry about."

He cupped his hands on her shoulders and she was so tempted to lean back into his solid strength, but she didn't. She couldn't afford to rely on him, not when it was her battle to fight. "I'm sorry you got dragged into this. I told Luc not to call you."

Dan spun her around to face him and brought his face down to within an inch of hers. "I didn't get dragged into this, and we'll talk about why you think I didn't deserve to know about this later. For now, let's get you ready to finish what you have to do to make sure you ex-arsehole doesn't do this again."

"But—"

His hand covered her mouth. "Nope. Not listening to anything except 'thanks, Dan, I really needed a few minutes out of the room to regroup'."

God, he was so right. That nagging sense of annoyance had gone, and she felt ready to face the last of the necessary actions to deal with the fallout of Colin's behaviour. "Thank you," she mumbled against his palm.

He smiled. "Much better." Dan removed his hand and replaced it with his lips. But just when she thought he might really kiss her, he pulled away and reached for the wet towel. With gentle pats, he wiped her face.

Her bottom lip trembled and Jody knew she was on the verge of crying again. Only this time it wasn't sad tears that clogged her throat. Instead, it was his simple act of caring that

143

had her on the brink of another meltdown. This man who'd been in her life less than a year had given her more of himself than her husband had in over a decade. How did she keep her heart from getting involved when Dan was doing everything her heart wanted?

He'd not once pushed her for more than she was willing to give. Sure, he'd made it perfectly clear what his intentions were, but he'd not forced her to become involved with him at any stage. Not really. He may have ambushed her with the occasional kiss, but she'd willingly surrendered when he had. And she wouldn't have done that if her heart wasn't already involved on some level.

"Ready?"

Was she? Jody wasn't sure she was ready for anything right now. Not when she'd just come to a shocking conclusion. She was falling for Dan. She might not be completely in love with the man, but it wasn't far away, probably as close as one kind gesture or simple acceptance of her suddenly crazy life. He studied her with a probing gaze and she had to turn away to gather some composure—to bolster her walls.

"Jody?"

She turned back to him and nodded. "I'm ready."

"Are you sure? 'Cause we can take as long as you need. They aren't going anywhere."

"No, they're not, but they're busy men who need to get back to their lives, and I really need to move on with mine. Can't do that until I've sorted out this mess, and I need Luc's friends to do that."

"I know you'd do it without them if you could or had to. Don't for one minute think it says you're weak for accepting their help." Dan rubbed his hands up and down her arms.

One more thing in the Dan-is-a-great-guy column. He got her. Totally understood that she needed to prove she was capable of taking care of herself and her girls. But he was right.

Accepting help didn't make her helpless, it made her smart.

Nodding, she said, "I know. I'm just not used to anyone except Lucas and my parents helping out or needing help with something this big. Colin has never gone off the rails like this before. Not even when I filed the divorce papers."

"So what set him off now?"

Jody sighed. She knew. Colin had made sure it was perfectly clear what had pissed him off enough to come after her and the girls this late in the game. As usual though, it was too little too late. "He was served the divorce papers yesterday. We've been officially divorced in the eyes of the law for a few months, but he's been MIA so he hadn't gotten the final paperwork before now. And for some reason that is beyond my comprehension, he didn't take it too well."

Dan's eyebrows shot up his forehead. "But he knew the papers were filed and would be processed in due course."

"Again, beyond my comprehension." Jody took a deep breath and let it go slowly. "Okay, let's get this over with. I want to get home to Leigh and Amy."

"After you." He swept his hand out to indicate she lead the way.

She smiled but didn't quite feel it. The sadness that settled over her wouldn't shift. It was extremely depressing to think her marriage had come to this. She'd had such high hopes and dreams for so many years. And for a while, she thought she'd found them only to have the rug pulled out from underneath her when she'd discovered Colin's cheating. Even then she'd stuck it out, listened to his apologies and promises. Until she'd been confronted by the blonde. There was no way to ignore the fiasco that was her marriage then.

Of course, she hadn't walked or even insisted Colin leave even after that confrontation. No. He'd walked. And for that she would always hate a part of herself. But that was in the past and she wasn't going to let him ruin any more of her self-esteem or her life—or the girls'. With that in mind, Jody made her way back to the interview room and the papers that would sever all ties she had with her ex and keep him away from Leigh and Amy until they reached the age of eighteen.

Dan stood behind Jody as she signed her name to legal papers that would remove her arsehole of an ex from her life. He should be thrilled with this development, and part of him was, but there was also the complete sadness radiating off her that ate at his gut. She'd been forced into this by her ex's actions, and no matter how right it was, she didn't like doing it.

He'd understood the basics of what Mackenzie was advising even with all the legal jargon the man had used. And Luc trusted the guy, so Dan was inclined to do whatever he suggested. Except it wasn't up to him to make the decision. Jody hadn't agreed immediately. She'd been full of questions, and only after thirty minutes of asking did she agree to lodge the documents to prevent her ex from seeing her or the girls. She made sure there was a provision for the girls to change their mind before they were adults but their father had no say in it and couldn't contact them until they reached eighteen.

Dan thought it was a good compromise considering both lawyers wanted her to block all contact between now and when Leigh and Amy were older. She signed the last paper and the officer who'd been in charge of the domestic-violence case added his reports and the two suited lawyers left them to file the paperwork with the court.

"Please, take my card, and if you need anything further from me, don't hesitate to get in contact." The officer handed over a business card before he left the room.

"I guess that's it then." Jody glanced around. "I thought I'd feel more relieved than I do."

"Give yourself some time. It's been a crazy twenty-four

hours." Dan helped her from her seat. "Let's get you home to the girls."

"Thanks." She grabbed her purse from the table. "Where did Luc go?"

Dan didn't want to lie to her, but he also didn't want to reveal where her brother had gone. "He said he had something to do."

She eyed him wearily. "He better not be doing anything that will jeopardise the papers I just signed."

He smiled. She knew her brother well. "Haven't a clue." With a hand to her lower back, he ushered her out of the police station and down the street to where they'd parked hours ago.

Luc was there, leaning against the hood of his black Explorer, arms crossed, dark shades covering his eyes, in a tough-guy stance that had people veering right to the edge of the sidewalk near the building to avoid him. As they got closer, Jody tensed until she all by vibrated beside Dan.

"Do not tell me you did something I'm not going to like," she said when they were a few feet away.

Luc straightened to his full height. "Okay, I won't tell you."

"Lucas!"

"Relax. All I did was make sure he saw me when that weasel of a lawyer got him released on bail." Luc walked to the passenger side and opened the door. "Hop in, the girls have decided we're having barbeque for dinner at my house. Cassie has taken them to the shops to pick up some food, so you have time to go home for a change of clothes."

"Why do I need a change of clothes?" Jody asked as Dan helped her up into Luc's SUV.

"Oh, did I not mention they want to have a sleepover at Uncle Luc's house?" Luc grinned, but Dan didn't miss the worry lines creasing his forehead.

"I don't think that's a good idea. I'd rather just pick up the girls and go home." Dan could hear the strain—the exhaustion—in Jody's voice.

"At least have dinner at Luc's. Besides, you won't have to worry about cooking and Leigh and Amy will be occupied by the three of us and not constantly thinking back to last night." Dan wasn't sure his arguments were enough to sway her. "It'll be good for all of you to have a number of distractions."

Dan saw the moment she gave in. And while he was happy she agreed to Luc's suggestion, he didn't like watching the fight drain out of her. He hoped it was just the results of the long stressful day. He'd never seen her look so vulnerable before. She buckled up and he closed the door and turned to Luc.

"I'm worried," Dan murmured.

"You and me both, which is why I'm not letting her stay at the house alone tonight," Luc said.

"They can stay at my place." The offer was out before Dan thought better of it.

"Yeah, well, I don't like that idea any more than I like the one of her going home." Luc seemed to grow two inches as he leaned over Dan.

Stifling a smile, Dan stood his ground. "Look, I get the whole big-brother-protection thing. I'm guilty of the actions myself, but I can guarantee you I'm not going to hurt Jody or the girls."

"Big talk for a guy she didn't want me to call last night."

"Did she call you?" Dan already knew the answer to his question but felt the need to point it out.

"Shit. No." Luc rubbed his jaw. "How'd you know that?"

"I overheard a couple of the officers talking earlier. Do you think she would have called you?"

Luc looked away for a few seconds before meeting Dan's gaze again. "No. Leigh freaked out when her father started yelling and rang me. I was on the phone when he started killing her car. The hardest thing I've ever done was tell that kid to hang up and call the police. For those few minutes, I was scared out of my mind I'd get there and find them all dead."

Fuck. Dan hadn't known the details, and hearing it from Luc sent a chill down his spine. "We need to thank Leigh for keeping it together enough to ring you and then do what you told her to."

"Agreed." Luc took a step away and stopped. "Oh, and for the record, I don't ever want to feel that way again."

Dan nodded. He didn't want Luc to feel that way again either. "Do you think he'll leave them alone when the court order is granted?"

Luc shrugged. "Hard to say. Before last night I'd have said he was a harmless loser. Now he's a dangerous loser."

Tapping on glass grabbed their attention. Jody sat in the car scowling at them. "We better get going," Dan said.

"Are you ready for the third degree when we get in?" Luc asked.

Dan laughed. "Yeah."

Luc grinned. "She's going to be relentless."

"I hope so. I'm a little worried this whole thing has taken the wind out of her sails."

"Nah, it'll take more than this to keep Jody down." Luc clapped Dan on the back as he walked past and headed for the driver's side. Taking a deep breath, Dan steeled himself for the coming questions and opened the rear passenger door.

"What were you two plotting?" Jody twisted around to peer between her seat and the door.

"Nothing. We were just talking about today." He didn't meet her gaze, which he knew would have given the half-lie away.

"Ha. Bullshit."

"Oh, she's swearing. Always a good sign," Luc said as he climbed in behind the wheel.

"You." Jody spun around and levelled a finger at her brother. "Don't you do your zipped-lip security-man impersonation on me."

Luc laughed. "Jody, Jody, Jody. Would I do that to you?"

"*Argh.* Yes, you would. Now I want to know what is going on. Don't feed me a line, Lucas Wilhelm. I might not be able to stop you from going all macho-protective big brother on me, but you can at least do me the courtesy of treating me like the adult I am and tell me what the hell you're doing."

Luc sighed as he started the car and then moved them out into the flow of traffic. "I'm not planning anything other than making sure he sticks by the court order when the judge puts his stamp on it."

"How?"

"I'll have someone keep an eye on him for a while."

"You're not going to have me or the girls followed are you? I won't stand for that, Luc."

Dan sat quietly listening to the two of them interact. They were close, and he wondered if they'd always been that way or just since Jody had separated from her ex.

"I promise not to have either you or the girls under watch. Just the loser ex who suddenly went from harmless to dangerous with the swing of a bat. What the fuck set him off anyway?" Luc asked.

"He was raving about getting the divorce papers before he started remodelling my car."

"But that's been in the works for well over a year and final for months."

"I know." Jody sighed and slumped down in her seat. "I don't get why he had a sudden objection to it."

"Did you see him before he showed up with the bat?" Dan asked. He wasn't convinced the guy had gone off the deep end over the finalisation of their divorce.

"No." She bolted upright. "Wait. Leigh said he'd come around before I got home but she hadn't answered the door."

Dan caught Luc's eye in the rear view mirror. "Do you think she said something to set him off?"

"What could she possibly say? And why would she even talk to him? Leigh said she didn't answer the door and I believe her. She has no reason to lie about it."

"Maybe not, then again, maybe she doesn't want to tell you what happened," Luc offered.

"I still don't see why she wouldn't, but I'll ask her when we get to your place." Jody settled back in her seat and Dan put his hands over the top of her seat and gave her neck and shoulders a rub.

"Don't worry about it. I'm sure you're right and Leigh didn't answer the door."

Chapter Fourteen

"You told him what?" Jody couldn't catch her breath. "Why would you do that, Leigh?"

"Well." Leigh's gaze dart over to Dan before coming back to her. "I thought—"

"You thought wrong, young lady, and that may have been the trigger that set your father off." Jody paced between the couch and the television.

"Jody—"

She quieted her brother with a look and continued to pace. Leigh's confession explained a lot. Colin's behaviour had been so out of character. Even when they were together he'd never gotten violent when drunk. Then again, his daughter hadn't told him he was being replaced in their lives by another man before. Dan stepped in front of her and grabbed her arms.

"Stop." He gave her a slight shake. "Leigh didn't do it out of spite."

Jody was appalled that he would even suggest that. "Of course not."

"Then take a breath and calm down before you scare Leigh to death," Dan whispered as he turned her around to face her daughter.

Oh God. Jody rushed over to where Leigh sat curled up on the couch beside Luc. The poor thing was crying her eyes out and all because Jody hadn't thought Leigh might misinterpret her reaction to Leigh's admission.

Jody pulled Leigh into her arms and rocked her like she had when she was a baby. "Oh, sweetie, I'm not mad at you. I'm mad at your father for even thinking he has the right to care about who's in our lives."

"I hate him!" Leigh sobbed against Jody's shoulder.

"Leigh, don't say that. Hate is such a strong word. Things are okay to hate, but not people."

"But he's horrible. And he said he didn't want us to be happy."

Jody's gaze darted up to meet Luc's as she ran a hand over her daughter's head. "Baby, what he wants doesn't matter."

"But, but, he trashed our car so we couldn't spend the day with Dan. Because I told him that's what we were supposed to do today." Leigh sobbed so hard she choked and all Jody could do was hold her and let her cry. She wasn't sure what else to do or say to soothe her daughter's fears.

Cassie came over and held out a box of tissues. Jody tugged a couple from the box and waited for Leigh to calm down a little. Luc indicated he was getting up and she glanced over to see Amy standing in the doorway, thumbnail caught between her front teeth. She hadn't chewed her nails in years, and Jody prayed this incident hadn't set her back on that bad habit.

She was grateful when Luc and Cassie ushered Amy out with the incentive of helping make the hamburger patties for dinner. Jody smiled. Amy loved to get her hands into food. And unlike Jody, her youngest daughter showed a real aptitude for cooking. Dan slid into the space vacated by Luc but remained quiet. She'd love to know what was going on inside his head right now. The poor man had been thrown into the middle of her family's drama without consent, and she was surprised he wasn't running for the hills by now.

When Leigh quieted and her sobs had turned to sniffles, Jody eased her away and handed her some tissues. "Feel better?"

Leigh shook her head. "Why does he hate us?"

The million-dollar question. No mother wants to have to

answer that. Not when the *he* in question is the child's father. "I don't think he hates you, Leigh."

"But he doesn't love us either."

Jody closed her eyes and prayed for strength. She wouldn't lie, but at fifteen Jody didn't think Leigh was old enough to process the truth either. "He loves you the best he can." Jody wasn't about to include herself in that notion.

"Well, it's a seriously shitty way." Leigh pouted and Jody breathed a little easier. If she was resorting to childish pouting then she wasn't as upset by the lack of fatherly love Colin possessed as Jody feared.

"Life is shitty sometimes. But we can't let those bad things destroy the good," Jody said.

"I know." Leigh sniffed into her handful of tissues. "But it still fucking sucks."

"Leigh, language." It didn't matter how crappy the situation, Jody wouldn't let her rule about swearing slide.

"Aw, Mum, c'mon. It's not like Amy's in the room," she whined.

Dan chuckled and Jody gave him the evil eye, prompting him to cover up with a fake cough.

Leigh's head swivelled back and forth, her gaze bouncing between the adults like spectators at a tennis match. Before her daughter could say anything, Jody said, "Why don't you go wash your face and I'll see if Uncle Luc has any of that ice cream you love."

"Ice cream before dinner?" Leigh's voice rose with hope.

"Yep. I think today calls for dessert first, don't you?"

"Yes." Leigh bounded off the couch and ran from the room.

"So is that a treat, a reward, bribery or distraction?" Dan asked.

"I have no idea, but I figure we could all do with something frivolous and pleasurable right now." Her gaze caught his just as she said the word pleasurable and all sorts of adult pleasures flitted through her mind. She'd love to lose herself in his arms right now. Sink into the oblivion of pure ecstasy Dan delivered. Except that wasn't happening any time soon. After last night and today, Jody wasn't ready to add another complication to her life.

And Dan O'Conner was one huge complication.

Dan had no idea what was going on. Jody had gone completely cold on him. It was like a switch had been flicked. Dinner had been interesting. She'd avoided looking at him, and if she'd said more than two words directly to him he'd hand over his beloved Ducati. Luc had given him a questioning look across the table that Dan couldn't even begin to answer. Luckily, the girls and Cassie had carried the conversation enough to cover up any lag in talk.

Jody was currently in Luc's living room with the girls. They were watching a movie from Luc's collection. A chick flick. Which meant he and Luc were more than happy to be stuck in the kitchen cleaning up after dinner.

"Wanna tell me what happened?" Luc asked as he took a stack of dirty dishes from Dan.

He shrugged. "If I had a clue I would."

Luc straightened. "You two didn't have a fight or something?"

"Hell, no. I can't even pin-point when exactly she started giving me the cold shoulder."

"What happened with Leigh after we took Amy out of there?"

"Nothing. There were no more big revelations. Although it does appear as though Leigh mentioning me set off the ex."

"I wouldn't have thought he'd care. There has to be something else driving the sudden shift in behaviour." Luc began loading the dishwasher. "I've got someone looking into his recent activity."

"Does Jody know?" Dan could only imagine her reaction if she didn't.

"Not specifics, but she knows I'm not staying out of it this time. I did that when she caught him cheating on her and look where that got her, years of crappy treatment."

"He cheated on her? Is he an idiot?" Dan didn't expect an answer really. As far as he was concerned, the guy had to be stupid to let Jody go.

Luc chuckled. "Among other things."

"Look." Dan tried to collect his thoughts. "I'm not sure where this thing between me and Jody is going, but I can tell you where I want it to end up. I like her. A lot. I like spending time with the girls already, and we've barely managed a few hours. She intrigues me, not to mention gets my engine revved with just a look."

"Whoa." Luc put up a hand. "I don't need to know any of that. And I'm not just talking about you two getting it on. All I need to know is that you're serious, and I think you've proven that in the last twenty-four hours."

Dan nodded.

"But you've just been given a front row seat to her less-than-pleasant past, and I'm not all that sure that all the emotions and drama associated with it aren't still weighing on her mind. She swore she'd never get involved with a guy again when Colin walked, and I believe she meant it, which is why you and her raises more than my eyebrows."

Dan pretty much figured the spectre of her past stood between them. He just had to work out how big of an obstacle it was. "Neither of us expected to connect the way we do."

"Maybe that's a good thing, because if she's got time to think about something she'll worry it to death before she ever gets started."

"So what are you saying?" Dan asked. If anyone could give him some insight it would be Jody's brother.

"It'll be an uphill battle."

"But it's winnable, right? You're not suggesting I give up?"

"What? No. I'm making sure you understand how difficult and stubborn she can be. Shit, she stayed married to that idiot out of stubbornness. She'd probably still be married to him if he hadn't been the one to walk."

"He walked? She didn't tell him to go?"

"Put it this way, I think he got to the punch line first. She was ready to leave, had made the decision, but the girls made it harder to just up and go." Luc ran his hand over his head. "Look. I shouldn't be telling you any of this. It should come from her. I just think you need to really be sure you want to continue seeing her. Those girls, all of them, have been through enough, and if you're not in it for the long haul then back out now."

"I'm in it as deep as a man can get." It wasn't a confession of love. He'd save that for Jody, but he figured Luc would understand what he was saying.

"Good. Good then."

Neither of them had a chance to say anything further because the bundle of energy that was Amy came barrelling into the kitchen. "Uncle Luc, Uncle Luc. Cassie said you can make us popcorn. Can you?"

At thirteen she hadn't quite given up some of her childishness, but Dan could see the woman starting to unfold inside her. "Aren't you still full from those two hamburgers you ate at dinner?" he asked.

"No. In fact my tummy is so empty it's aching."

Luc laughed. "Yeah, right, your eyes have always been bigger than your belly. Give me five minutes and I'll bring a bowl of salt and vinegar popcorn in."

"Yes!" She fist-pumped the air and disappeared back the way she'd come.

Luc shook his head. "Her energy levels always amaze me. I wish I could bottle it. I'd make a fortune."

"She'll lose some of that when she gets older. My sister was the same. Then she hit puberty and turned into a slug that we had to drag out of bed every morning." Dan leaned against the kitchen counter. "Do you have a popcorn machine or do you use the trusty old saucepan?"

Rubbing his hands together, Luc opened the pantry. "Neither. I'm a microwave man all the way." He pulled out a box of microwave popcorn and tossed it at Dan. "You pop, I'll get the toping ready."

Jody could not believe she'd agreed to this. After she'd made the decision—again—to distance herself from Dan, she'd done the complete opposite. Again. Okay, so the girls—or more pointedly, Amy—were the reason she'd said yes, but she still had to take responsibility for her own actions. If it were anyone but her, she'd conclude the woman chopping and changing her mind was bipolar. Instead, she had to admit she was totally smitten and not willing to do what her brain kept telling her she should.

"C'mon, Mum." Amy grabbed her hand and tugged her towards the ice. "Quick."

"What's the rush?" Jody stumbled as she tried to walk on the thin blade of metal on the bottom of the very uncomfortable boots she'd spent the last ten minutes lacing up.

"I want to beat Leigh." Amy let go and raced for the opening in the barrier that surrounded the ice rink.

"Be careful," Jody called out. She shouldn't have wasted her breath. Amy was off and running. Literally. Her long, colt-like legs took her across the icy surface so fast Jody's head spun. "Jesus."

Dan chuckled behind her. "I doubt *he* can even help you

with that one."

She sighed and glanced over her shoulder at him. "You're right. Nothing short of Valium can help with that one once she gets going."

"I don't think you need to worry." He indicated the ice rink with his chin. "She's already got the hang of it."

Jody turned back to see Amy skating past as though she'd been doing it all her life. "Oh my God, look at her."

"She's a natural." Dan moved beside her and took her elbow. "C'mon, your turn."

She allowed him to guide her onto the ice. Her knees shook, which didn't help, but she did manage to stay upright. At least she did the first time around. The second saw her getting a little too confident and paying the price. One slightly bruised backside. And while the fall had hurt, it wasn't enough to have her leaving the ice. Both the girls were whizzing past with the speed and skill only the young possessed.

And Dan. Well, he'd obviously done this more than once. He spun circles around her, tugged her along when she was steady and picked her up off the ground when she wasn't. In spite of all her doubts and fears where this man was concerned, she couldn't deny she always had a good time with him. The girls did too. They laughed and joked and played like they'd been doing it together forever, and Jody couldn't remember the last truly carefree day they'd had.

She made her way off the ice and sat on a bench to watch the three of them play tag around the rink. She was pretty sure Dan could catch either of the girls without any trouble, but he made it a game by stumbling and slipping whenever he got close to one of them. After Friday night and Saturday, she was eternally grateful for the happy smiles on the girls' faces—the rippling joy of their laughter as they chased each other around. Tears stung the backs of her eyes and throat. They owed Dan for today.

Jody quickly wiped at her eyes as the three of them headed her way. The girls giggled as they both tried to barge through the exit together. Dan scooped his arm around Amy's waist and pulled her off her feet to break the standoff. He swung her around and plonked her back on her blades as Leigh bounced in front of her.

"Dan said we can get an ice cream. I want a strawberry one."

"I want chocolate and vanilla," Amy yelled.

"Okay, keep it down. I'm right here, Amy." Jody laughed as both of them shouted yes and raced off in the direction of the kiosk.

"You want one?" Dan asked.

She turned back to face him. "Are you kidding? It's freezing in here already. I'm not making it worse by eating ice cream."

"Yeah, I'm not sure I'm up for a cone, but what about a hot chocolate? We can sit over by the kiosk where it's a little warmer."

Jody glanced over to where Leigh and Amy waited impatiently for someone to come and order their ice creams. "Okay. A hot chocolate sounds good."

"If you're not up for more skating we can take your boots back now. I'm happy to supervise the girls for the rest of our allotted time." He offered her his hand.

She slipped her cold fingers inside his warmer ones and let him pull her to her feet. "I think I'll take you up on that. These things are killing me. I think I've got blisters on my heels."

"I'll get the first aid kit from the counter. They should have some cream and Band-Aids."

They made their way over to the girls and it wasn't until they reached the counter that Jody realised they still held hands. Dan didn't make a big deal out of it, he just casually slipped his hand from hers to retrieve his wallet out of his pocket.

"Why don't you go grab that table?" He pointed to the table farthest from the rink. "The girls and I will carry everything over."

"Okay." She limped away, her feet suddenly hurting beyond a mild ache.

"And get those boots off so I can take a look at your feet," Dan called out behind her.

Jody waved her hand and kept going. She was afraid she'd never make it if she stopped to answer. Sliding into a cushioned seat, she immediately began unlacing the hundreds of hooks. Hundreds was an exaggeration, but it certainly felt that many by the time she had both boots unhooked and her wet-socked feet out.

"Mum, you're bleeding!" Leigh cried as she rushed over.

"What?" Looking down, Jody saw a patch of blood on the back of one heel. Okay, blisters were a tame definition. Gingerly, she peeled her sock down and off. Sure enough, she'd rubbed her heel raw.

"Damn, Jody, you should have said the boots were too small." Dan put two steaming mugs on the table and dropped to his knees in front of her. "Amy, hand me that kit you've got."

Amy handed over the small plastic container she carried while licking the side of her ice cream cone. "Does it hurt?" she asked.

"Just a little," Jody said.

"It looks like it hurts a lot. Do we have to go home now?" Amy asked.

"No, sweetie, you can finish your ice cream and skate some more. I'll just put some cream and a Band-Aid on and it'll be fine." Trying to reassure both her daughters, she smiled. "Who's going to give me a taste of their ice cream?"

As distractions went, it worked. While Dan doctored both her feet, she shared Leigh and Amy's cones. She ended up eating most of Amy's as she'd ordered a double scoop and couldn't finish. Sitting back, she sipped at her no-longer-hot hot chocolate. It managed to remove some of the chill a belly full of ice cream delivered.

"Will you be all right while we go skate some more?" Dan asked.

"Yes. Please. Go have fun." She shooed them off with her hand. "I'll stay right here where it's warmer."

"You want another drink?"

"Actually, yes, a refill would be good."

"Coming right up. Girls, why don't you go ahead and I'll be there as soon as I've gotten your mother another hot chocolate."

Without a word, Leigh and Amy raced back towards the rink. Concern for their mother's bleeding foot was forgotten in the face of more fun on the ice. Jody waited for Dan to order another drink before saying what needed to be said.

"Thank you."

"You're welcome. Just wave if you want another one, but I'll come check on you in a few minutes anyway."

"That's not what I'm thanking you for."

"It's not?"

"Well, yes, thank you for the drink, but I want to thank you for today. You've given us all something we desperately needed, and I was a little ungrateful when you used the girls to convince me to accept your invitation. I'm sorry."

"Jody, never be sorry for a genuine feeling no matter how misplaced it is. And I'll accept your thank you if you agree to have dinner with me."

Chapter Fifteen

Dinner hadn't been in the plan, but he couldn't resist taking any opportunity to spend more time with Jody. She'd wanted the girls home at a reasonable hour as they had school tomorrow, so they'd picked up Chinese on the way to her place after their ice skating adventure. Things were a little tense between them again and Dan wasn't sure how to get around this latest setback. Hell, he didn't even know what had made her pull back this time.

"Sorry, the girls won't be a minute. We can start dishing up the food if you like." Jody entered her kitchen. She'd changed into a pair of comfy looking sweat pants and a hoodie. Both looked a size too big but neither did anything to curb his libido. She looked hot.

"I'm happy to wait."

"Oh, but you must want to get home soon." She started opening containers and adding serving spoons. "Dish up what you want."

Dan wanted something other than food. He wanted an explanation, but as he went to open his mouth the girls came rushing in.

"I'm starving," Amy said as she sank into a chair.

"Me too. Did you get that spicy chicken that I like, Mum?"

Jody pushed the container of Szechuan chicken across the table. "Yes. And there's salt 'n' pepper calamari if you want some."

"Oh, yes, please." Leigh was already dishing up a mound of the chicken.

Dan passed the container of calamari over and picked up the fried rice. He dished up a couple of spoonfuls and waited until everyone else had taken what they wanted before filling his plate. Conversation was non-existent for a few minutes while they ate, but then Dan decided the quiet should end.

"When does the repairman come to look at your washer?" he asked.

"Oh, I forgot all about that. Tomorrow afternoon. Why?"

"I just wondered if you needed me to take any dirty clothes home with me to wash and dry. I can bring them to work in the morning."

"No, no, I can't ask you to do that. We've got enough to get us through until the machine is fixed."

"There's no point piling it all up until then. And what if it's not a simple fix? Give me a small-essentials load and I'll get them back to you first thing." Her objections to his help were really starting to grate on his nerves, and Dan was determined to get her to agree. "It's no trouble. I have to do laundry when I get home anyway."

She chewed her lip and he knew she was trying to come up with another protest.

"Honestly, it's just a few clothes, Jody, one load. It's not like I'm asking to do it for the rest of your life." Although he would. In a heartbeat.

"Fine. I'll get a basket together after dinner."

Leigh kept her gaze glued to her mother as though she were waiting for the other shoe to drop. She might only be fifteen, but she was extremely aware of her mother's moods and Dan had to agree with the wary look. He was waiting too.

They finished dinner in silence, a squirm-in-your-seat quiet that left the hairs on Dan's neck standing on end and his teeth on edge. The girls got up and cleared the table, which left him and Jody alone again. She fiddled with the cord on her jacket and looked everywhere except at him. Something snapped inside him. He'd had enough of this back and forth between them, and he planned to have it out with her before he left tonight.

"Well, I better get the girls organised for school tomorrow." She pushed back her chair. "I'll get a basket of stuff together for you too."

Before Dan could say or do anything, Jody bolted from the room like her pants were on fire. With a sigh, he leaned back in his chair and pulled out his phone. He shot a quick text to Cassie to let her and Luc know Jody and the girls were home and that he'd be leaving soon. Jody might not be happy about it, but Luc had arranged for someone to watch the house last night and tonight. It was the only reason Dan hadn't slept in his car outside overnight and why he was okay with her shoving him out the door in the next few minutes.

Which was exactly what she did about five minutes later. He found himself on her doorstep with a basket of clothes in his arms and not so much as a goodnight peck on the cheek. It was not the way he wanted to end their fun day together but he didn't seem to have a choice. Once again, she was in the driver's seat and was driving off without him. He was getting really tired of chasing after her. Except he didn't have any other option. If he wanted to get anywhere, he had to play the game her way.

Or at least he had to keep her within his sights, and to do that he had to follow where she lead even if that was round and round the mulberry bush. Carrying his load, he headed for the Jeep. Stashing the basket on the backseat, he took one last look at Jody's house before climbing in the driver's seat. He thought he saw movement in one of the windows but dismissed it when he didn't see anything else. Dan cranked the engine with a rev before shifting into reverse and backing out of the driveway.

His hands were tied for now. He'd give her some space and then he'd be sure she knew he wasn't going anywhere. Unlike her ex, Dan had no intention of letting the best woman he'd ever met get away. Come tomorrow morning, he'd have his next step ready to go. And as much as he hated using the girls, he figured they were the way to get to her. Luckily for him, he thought they were great fun and wanted to hang out with them as much as he did their mother.

As he made the ten-minute journey to his house, he tried to come up with another outing that would grab their interest. Jody had mentioned they went bowling, so perhaps he should suggest disco bowling next weekend. He'd have to check the roster, but he was pretty sure both he and Jody had Saturday night off.

He pulled into his driveway with a smile on his face. Cassie had already volunteered to pick Jody up for work and drop her off until her car was repaired, but it made more sense for Dan to do it seeing how they lived so close. He'd work it out with Cassie tomorrow. One way or another, he was going to get more time with Jody.

Jody couldn't get away from him. And other than her irrational need to run, she really had no reason to avoid him. He was everywhere she went, and if he wasn't then her stupid traitorous mind conjured him up in technicolour splendour to remind her of what she was trying to walk away from. She tossed her handbag on her bed on the way to her wardrobe. He'd used the girls to get her to agree to go out again, and while she was glad Leigh and Amy were being kept busy and therefore distracted from the mess that was last weekend, she didn't like Dan's manipulative ways.

She'd heard from Mackenzie Harris that Colin was fighting the restraining order and the no-contact request. She should have known he wouldn't go for it. Not because he wanted to have contact with his own children, but because she didn't want him to have it. Colin's lawyer was arguing that the girls were old enough to have their say and wanted them in court to do so when the paperwork went before the judge next week. Jody felt sick to the stomach just thinking about it. Then again, she'd been queasy the last two days, so it might just be a bug she'd picked up and not the anxiety of the coming court visit.

She glanced at her bedside clock. Dan would be here in an hour and her mum had said she'd drop the girls off in about fifteen minutes, so if she was going to shower she needed to do it now. Today's party had been an easy one, but an excited father-to-be had spilt champagne all down Jody's back and she really did need to shower off the smell of alcohol as well as the stickiness. Pulling jeans and a sweater out of the cupboard, she then grabbed undies and a bra from her top drawer and headed for the bathroom.

A wave of dizziness struck her as she bent over to turn on the shower. Jody grabbed the edge of the bath and held on until the flashes of light before her eyes cleared and she didn't feel like she was going to fall over anymore. Her breathing was a little shallow and her pulse raced, so she sat on the closed toilet seat to give herself a minute. She needed to eat something, her sugar levels were obviously down seeing how she hadn't consumed any food since the toast she'd rushed down before heading out to work.

The front door slammed a second before Amy yelled at the top of her lungs. "We're home!"

Pushing up, Jody stuck her head out the bathroom door. "I'm just about to jump in the shower."

"Hey, honey, I'll hang around until you're done if you like," her mother said.

"Hi, Mum, were they good?"

"Always." Her mother waved her arm. "Now go shower and I'll get these two sorted."

Jody did as her mother suggested but she made it quick. She didn't want Dan to arrive before her mother had gone home. That would just invite questions she wasn't ready to answer. Dressed and feeling a lot better, she headed to the kitchen where her mum had a cup of tea and a slice of chocolate cake waiting for her.

"Oh my God, I love you." Jody lunged for the cake. Her mother made the best chocolate cake in the world. "Mmm..." she moaned around her first mouthful.

"Did I not teach you manners, Jody Maree?" Her mother clucked her tongue.

Jody smiled and swallowed. "Sorry. But you have no idea how much I needed that."

"Good thing I brought the whole cake over then." Frances Wilhelm smiled as she brought her mug to her lips. "So I hear you girls are all going on a date with some man named Dan."

Jody sprayed tea across the counter as she choked. She coughed a couple of times before catching her breath. "What?" she asked from behind her hand.

"Leigh and Amy have been telling me all about him. He sounds lovely."

"Lovely?" Dan? Lovely wasn't the word that came to mind when Jody thought of him. More like yummy. "He's a guy I work with."

"And you're seeing him?"

The mother inquisition had begun. "No, not really. We've just hung out a few times." She shrugged. No point giving her mother the wrong idea. It was bad enough that her brother knew about her see-sawing relationship with Dan, the last thing she needed was for her mother to get involved.

"Dan's here!" Amy screamed from the direction of the front door.

Too late.

Jody dropped her head and prayed for strength.

"Do you want some chocolate cake? My gran makes the

best cake." Amy chatted behind her and Jody knew she had to do the introductions before her mother slapped her upside the head.

She turned on her stool. "Hey, Dan, this is my mum, Fran. Mum, this is Dan."

A genuine smile covered Dan's mouth and Jody wondered why he was so happy to meet her mother. "Hello, Fran. It's nice to meet you. I hear you make the best chocolate cake." He held out his hand.

Her mother sat taller and smiled while taking his hand in hers. "I do. And it's lovely to meet you. The girls talked about you non-stop today. Sit down and I'll cut you a slice of cake. Do you want coffee with that?"

One thing that could be said for Jody's mother was that she was the ultimate hostess. Even when not in her own home. Jody popped up off her stool. "I can get it."

Fran waved her away. "Nonsense. You've been working all day. Let me get it."

Jody sank back onto her seat and let her mother go. She knew from experience she'd not be swayed, and really, she was too tired to bother.

"You all right, Jody? You look a little pale." Dan ran the back of his fingers down her cheek.

She jerked away, frightened her mother would see the gesture for more than it was. "I'm fine. A little tired, that's all."

"We don't have to take the girls bowling if you're not feeling up to it," he said.

"What? No! Can't we go without Mum?" Amy wailed.

"Stop that right now Amy Catherine. If your mother isn't up to going out then you won't be going." Jody's mother rushed around the counter and put her hand to Jody's forehead. "Dan's right, you do look at bit pale. Are you sure you're okay?"

Jody pushed her mother's hand away. "Yes, I'm fine. It's been a long week, and to be honest, I'd rather be out than at home where I'll just brood over what's going to happen in court next week."

"Ah, yes, that's probably it. I dare say you aren't sleeping properly, are you?"

"No, Mum, not really." She shrugged and quickly changed the subject to get everyone focused on something else. "Amy, are you and Leigh ready to go?"

"Yes. Leigh's in the other room talking to that boy on the phone again." Amy's dramatic rolling of her eyes made everyone laugh.

"Well, go tell her to get off because as soon as we finish our cake we're out of here." Jody took a sip of her tea and hoped the conversation about her health was over. "If you don't mind, Dan, can we cut the evening short and perhaps get a pizza to bring back here instead of eating out?"

"Sure. But we don't have to go at all if you're not up to it." He took a big bite of her mother's cake. "Oh my God, this is amazing." He covered his mouth with his hand so he could speak with his mouthful.

Jody's mum frowned at him. "I see you have as little manners as Jody does."

Dan turned to her with one eyebrow raised.

"She scolded me earlier for talking with my mouth full too."

He grinned while he chewed, but he wisely waited until he'd swallowed before speaking again. "Ah, yes, well, it's a good thing my mother isn't here or she'd be giving me a slap on the head and taking away my cake." As if it just occurred to him Jody's mother could do the same, he picked up his plate and held it close to his chest.

Jody laughed and her mother frowned so heavily her eyebrows joined above her nose, making Jody laugh harder. In the meantime Dan scoffed down the last of his cake.

Dan didn't like the look of Jody. She was pale and the dark

circles under her eyes worried him. He knew she had a lot going on. It was hard to miss her conversations with her lawyer when they shared an office. With a restraint he had no idea he possessed, he'd refrained from asking what was going on, but tonight, while he had her complete attention and the girls were busy bowling, he wanted answers to some questions.

"Are you allowing the girls to appear in front of the judge?"

She sighed. "I don't have a choice."

"Really? But they're just kids."

"According to the law, they're old enough to have a say, and Colin is within his rights to insist that they do." Jody watched Leigh as she took her turn.

"Have you told them?"

"No. I don't want to colour their opinion or coach them at all." She turned to face him. "Mackenzie assures me that they'll be asked questions by the judge in the privacy of his chambers. There will also be a court-appointed counsellor and of course Mackenzie and his partner. I'm trying not to worry, but I can't help thinking it might be best to just drop the whole thing."

Dan straightened. "Don't you dare. Don't let him force you into something you know isn't the right thing. Leigh and Amy are strong. Neither of them wants anything to do with their father, and after the other weekend he doesn't deserve to have any contact with them. It's for their safety. You know that."

"I know." She buried her head in her hands. "It's just so hard to let them do this without being with them."

"You trust Mackenzie, right?"

She glanced up at him through her fingers. "Yes."

"Then you know he's going to do his best to protect them and make sure they're heard." Dan turned to be sure both girls were still occupied. "Do you think maybe you should talk to them about it before it happens?"

"I've gone back and forth on that so many times I'm sick to my stomach, but I think I'm just avoiding the inevitable. Do you mind if we head home early? Tonight is probably a good night to talk to them about it."

"No worries. I'll go order us a couple of pizzas to take away while the girls finish their game. One supreme and a pepperoni, right?"

"Yeah. Thanks."

Dan went to order. He could only imagine what Jody was going through, and he wanted to do anything he could to support her during this ordeal. If she'd let him. So far she had to a point, but he knew if he suggested going to court with her—like he wanted to—she'd shoot him down. Meeting her mother this evening had been a pleasant surprise that he had the feeling Jody would have loved to avoid. And the fact the girls had been talking about him to their grandmother could only be good.

He grabbed a couple of cans of soft drink and made his way back to the lanes where Leigh was bowling the final ball in their game. She was pretty good and knocked down the two remaining pins to get a spare, which of course meant she got another bowl. Amy sat pouting next to her mother, and when he glanced at the scoreboard he saw why. Amy hadn't managed to get the extra shot at the pins in her last frame. A distraction might help brighten that gloomy face.

"Hey, Amy, wanna come pick out some dessert for after pizza?"

"Yes." Her face lit up and he wondered how many more years before the simple things like dessert couldn't cheer her up. Leigh wasn't as easy to impress, and Dan figured Amy was headed that way with the teenage years spread out in front of her.

"C'mon then." He held out his hand and she didn't hesitate to put hers in it. Dan smiled at Jody and led her daughter over to the shop where a selection of take-home ice-cream tubs awaited.

As they made their selections, Dan kept thinking about what lay ahead for all of them. He hoped Jody would let him stay while she talked to the girls, but he'd respect her wishes if she asked him to leave. As hard as it was to accept, he knew he wasn't a part of this small family unit, and what they were going through really wasn't his concern. Except he felt part of it, and he was concerned so much that he hadn't slept more than a few hours at a stretch.

No matter what happened this coming week, he was not walking away from this woman and her two daughters. He'd had lots of time to think, to ponder, to contemplate life with and without these three females, and he'd come to the conclusion that it wasn't acceptable to live out his days without them. No matter what it took he had to convince Jody they had a future. But first they had to deal with her past.

Chapter Sixteen

On Monday, Jody woke to a rolling stomach and the urge to vomit. Bounding out of bed, she made it to the bathroom just in time to empty everything in her belly. Hot from head to toe, she broke out in sweat as she continued to dry heave. She leaned her forehead against the cool toilet seat and waited out the spasms. When she was convinced it was safe to leave the bathroom, she washed her face then wobbled on shaky legs to the kitchen where she braved a glass of water.

When that stayed down, Jody breathed a sigh of relief. She had too much to do today to be sick. Tomorrow was the big court appearance so she had to do two days' worth of work in one to have the time off. Of course, Cassie insisted she not worry, but the last thing Jody wanted was to feel guilty about not pulling her weight, especially when it would fall to Dan to pick up the slack.

He'd been more than generous to her over the last few weeks. Since the weekend they'd gone away, he'd found a way to help her out at every turn and while she more than appreciated it, she didn't want to get used to it. At some point he'd no longer be interested in her and find something else to do with his time. If she let herself—or the girls—become dependent on him, they'd be in all sorts of strife when he finally walked away.

The sound of shuffling feet had her turning to see Amy, hair sticking up every which way, dragging herself into the kitchen. "Morning, sweetie. You're up early."

"Bad dream," she murmured as she came over and wrapped her arms around Jody.

"Want to talk about it?" They hadn't had to discuss nightmares for years, and she hoped this wasn't due to their conversation on Saturday night. That hope was soon squashed.

"The court man said we had to go live with Daddy," she sobbed into Jody's side.

She wrapped her arms around Amy tightly and rubbed her back. "Sweetheart, the judge isn't going to do that. He can't make that decision. All he's going to do is say whether or not your father can contact you. It has nothing to do with who you live with."

How did she explain that their father had already given her full custody in the divorce without making him sound unloving? As much as Jody wanted to tell both her daughters what an arse their father was, she wouldn't. Easing onto one of the breakfast stools, she pulled Amy between her legs and cuddled her close.

Leigh came wandering in and stopped short when she saw the two of them. "What's wrong?"

"Amy had a nightmare." Jody held out her hand to Leigh, who walked over and took it. "You know this court thing tomorrow is just for you to talk to the judge about your dad, right? It has nothing to do with who you're going to live with. That decision was made already. The court awarded me full custody and your dad visitation. Tomorrow is not about that."

"Yeah, I know. The judge is going to ask questions about us and Dad," Leigh said. "Why does Amy think it's about going to live with Dad?"

"No, she knows it's not, but she had a bad dream about it anyway. I just wanted to make it perfectly clear that where you live isn't in question."

Leigh wrapped her arms around both of them and Jody enjoyed the quiet moments with both her babies close. Now that the girls were older, cuddles were few and far between. Regardless of the circumstances, she'd take these minutes and soak them up.

She thought Amy might have fallen back to sleep, but when she angled her head for a look, Jody discovered her staring off into space and chewing on her thumbnail. "Hey, none of that." She pulled Amy's thumb away.

"Sorry. I forget I don't do that anymore." She pulled out of Jody's arms. "Can we have pancakes for breakfast?"

Jody glanced at the time and calculated they could manage pancakes. "Yeah, why not. Grab the packet out of the pantry while I get the frypan ready."

They worked together and soon had the first one cooking. Of course, it was easy when you had a jug of pancake mix on hand. Amy poured, Jody flipped and Leigh ferried them to the table when they were done. A stack of twelve pancakes later, they were sitting down to breakfast. Unfortunately Jody's stomach rebelled at the idea of food and she just picked at hers until the girls were finished and heading to their rooms to get ready for school. She packed up the leftovers and cleared away the dirty dishes before making her way to her room to get ready for work.

Dan jumped when Jody doubled over and threw up into her waste bin. There was no warning. Only a little stifled, "Oh God," and then she was head down, stomach contents up. He rushed over and held her ponytail out of the way. After a few more heaves, she was done and Dan helped her sit back in her chair.

"Wait right there. I'll go get a damp cloth and some water."

Jody laughed, well, as much as she could manage under the circumstances. "Yeah, like I'm going anywhere right now."

He raced to the bathroom and grabbed a wad of paper towel. He turned on the tap and held the bundle under the water until it was wet through. Next, he detoured past the small staffroom and the water cooler Cassie kept there. With cup in one hand and wet towel in the other, he headed back to Jody. She hadn't moved and his step stuttered until he saw her chest rising with a shallow breath.

"Here. Try a sip of this." Dan handed her the cup of cold water.

"Thanks." She sipped cautiously, and while she did he had a good long look at her.

She was paler than Saturday, and those circles were so deep her eyes looked like they were going to pop out. "I think you need to see a doctor."

Her gaze snapped to his. "Why?"

"You're paler than you were the other day and you don't look like you've slept a wink in months. Your cheeks are sunken too. Are you eating properly? I know you're worried about tomorrow, but making yourself sick over it isn't going to help."

"I think it's a little worry and something I ate yesterday. I'll be fine." She pushed him away and stood on shaky legs. Picking up the waste basket, she said, "I'm going to the bathroom to wash my face and get rid of this."

Dan watched her go. Her explanation sounded plausible, but something nagged at him and yet he couldn't put his finger on what. He'd give her ten minutes and then he was following to make sure she was okay.

He didn't even make it to five. She was back, and if he hadn't seen it with his own eyes he would not believe she'd just been sick. The dark smudges under her eyes were still there but her colour had returned and her eyes no longer had that spaced-out, glassy look to them.

"Better?"

"Yes, much, thanks." She sat behind her desk and began to work.

"Aren't you going to head home?"

"No." Jody looked up with one eyebrow raised. "Why would

I?"

"Because you're not well and tomorrow is a big day. Go home and get some rest." He checked his watch. "If you leave now you can be home before the girls and spend some time with them before you all have to deal with tomorrow."

"Thanks for the suggestion, but I still have things to sort out before I take the day off." She returned her gaze to the file in front of her.

He could not believe she thought work was more important than time with the girls, especially with everything that was going on. Snatching the file out from under her, he leaned in until their noses almost touched. "Go home."

"Dan—"

"No. I don't want to hear it. Go home. Everything is under control. There's absolutely nothing that can't wait until you get back if I can't sort it out." Dan grabbed her arm and helped her out of the chair. "Please, for me, go home and spend time relaxing with the girls. Rent a movie or take them to a movie, whatever, just go be with them."

"Okay, fine. But don't get shitty when something comes up that I should have dealt with." She bent over and grabbed her purse from the bottom drawer of her desk. "If things go quickly in the morning, I'll come in afterwards. Mum and Dad are going to be there so they can take the girls out or something so I can come in."

"Don't even think it. If you're out of there early you can all go spend time with your parents."

"But—"

"No buts. Take the time, Jody." Dan was on the verge of begging her to take it when he felt her soften next to him. It was like every muscle she had took a breath and relaxed.

"Okay, but I owe you for this."

"Sure. Dinner."

"What?" She went a little pale.

"Have dinner with me."

The colour drained right out of her face and she slammed a hand over her mouth before dashing to the bathroom. Dan didn't care what she said, it was more than worrying about tomorrow, and if something she ate yesterday messed her up this bad then it was food poisoning and that could be deadly.

He walked down the corridor and knocked on Cassie's door.

"Come in," she called out.

"Hey, mind if I shoot through for a few hours?"

"Everything okay?"

"Yeah, Jody's sick and I want to be sure she gets home all right."

"Sure. No worries, but isn't tomorrow the court thing?"

"Yeah, which is why I want to be sure she's okay." He paused to check no one was in the hallway. "I think I'll take tomorrow too. There's nothing that either of us needs to do, and this week is a quiet one, thank God. So if you're cool with it I think I'll take the day and help Jody out."

"Definitely. You've got Luc's number, right? He'll be there tomorrow anyway, but if you need him at all today, ring him."

"Thanks, Cassie, but I'm pretty sure having me hovering around is going to piss her off, we don't need to aggravate the situation by adding Luc." He grinned.

Cassie laughed. "You're right. He can be a little over the top when he worries."

"I'll text you later." Dan heard the bathroom door open. "Gotta go. See you on Wednesday."

"Catch you then."

Dan quickly caught up to Jody. "Here give me that."

"What the hell are you doing?" She pulled away from him.

"Trying to carry your bag for you." He was worried she might still be a little shaky, and the last thing he wanted was for her to topple down the stairs.

"I can carry my handbag. I'm not an invalid."

Whoa. He hadn't heard that tone from her in weeks. "Sorry. Didn't mean to offend."

"No. I'm sorry. I was snapping at you for no reason."

"You've got a lot going on. Add in feeling sick and I imagine just breathing is making you snappy." He grinned to soften his words. Heaven forbid she take offense and snap at him again.

"Probably." They were almost to the bottom of the stairs when it twigged he was walking out with her. "What are you doing?"

"Going out with you."

"What?"

"Coming with you." Dan cupped her elbow and kept her moving when she stopped. "I'm going to make sure you take it easy. I'll organise dinner and occupy the girls if you want to rest or think of something we can all do to pass the time."

"You can't do that."

"Why not?"

"Because...well...because...argh! I have no idea why not exactly, but you can't."

Dan laughed. As arguments went it was a complete wash, but he'd give her credit for trying. He ushered her through the door and out into the sunlight before he turned her to face him. "Here's the thing. I either follow you home and come in and do all I just suggested. Or I follow you home and sit outside your house in my car. Your choice."

"That's not a choice." She was right. There was no way she'd let him sit outside and he was counting on it. "Fine. But when the girls get home you can explain why we're not at work. Oh, and you get to help with homework."

Homework was the least he'd do to spend the afternoon with Jody and the girls. He smiled. "Deal. Unless it's English. I suck at English."

Jody laughed. "Too bad. You already made the deal. No changing the rules now."

Dan followed her over to her car and made sure she was okay to drive before racing over to his Jeep and starting the engine. He knew where she lived so didn't need to tail her, but he was worried she'd have another bout of vomiting, and if she did he wanted to be there to take care of her.

Jody was stretched out on the couch wondering when it was that Dan had taken over her life. He was currently at the dining table with the girls doing their homework. She could hear them giggling and generally having fun, which she couldn't remember them doing whenever she helped them. He'd ordered dinner, which would be delivered around seven. And he ordered her to take a nap. Ha. Fat chance that would happen when all she could hear was her girls and how happy they sounded.

She hadn't been sick again but the nausea was still hanging around. The thought of food made it worse, so she tried to not think about it. But she was thinking about something that made her feel even sicker. It had been a while, a good long while, but she had a sinking feeling she knew exactly what was wrong with her. If she was right, her world—and Dan's—was about to be turned on its head.

She'd put it off long enough. Forcing herself to move, she got to her feet and headed to her bathroom. She found the packet of pills she was looking for and studied it carefully. The sugar pills had kicked in five days ago and she still hadn't got her period. This wasn't good. She checked to see she'd taken all the other pills before she suddenly remembered something that not only confirmed her suspicions but dropped the bomb on her world.

During the first week of this packet of contraceptives, she'd had a throat infection and had to take antibiotics for fourteen days. How could she have been so stupid? She knew the drill.

Knew the meds would affect the pill and put her at risk, but she hadn't thought about that when she'd assured Dan that she was safe. Sinking to the edge of the bath, she stared at the empty pouches and wondered what to do. Telling him was out of the question. Not until she knew for sure. There was no point stressing out both of them until she'd either peed on a stick or in a jar.

"Hey, you all right?" Dan asked from the doorway. He noticed the packet in her hand and came into the room, closing the door behind him. "What's wrong?"

"I, um, I'm not sure…" Did she just blurt it out? Oh God. She'd been here before. Pregnant, unmarried and facing an uncertain future. Except this time she was older—wiser—and she had no intention of being forced into something she didn't want. "I was just taking some medicine."

"Do you have a headache, fever?" he asked as he placed the back of his hand on her forehead.

"A slight one," Jody lied.

"Why don't you have a shower and get in your pyjamas. If you want to skip dinner and go straight to bed, I'll take care of the girls."

Tears stung her eyes. He was being so nice and she was keeping a huge secret from him. But until she knew for sure, she wasn't about to reveal what she'd discovered. Instead, she'd play the sick card and keep out of his way as much as possible. "If you don't mind, I'd really like that. I can always ring Mum though."

"Nonsense. I'm already here and dinner is taken care of, so there isn't any point dragging her out when I'm more than capable." He grinned at her, which made her want to cry more. Why did he have to be so nice when she was feeling so crappy?

"Thanks."

He backed away. "Yell if you need anything."

"Okay."

"I mean it. Anything."

"I will."

"Good. I'll get you a glass of water for beside your bed. Do you want anything else, food?"

"No. I don't think I could stomach anything right now."

"All right. I'll check on you in a bit."

He was out the door and gone before Jody breathed easy. She had some major decisions to make. Having a baby was not in her plans. She'd been there and done that. The idea of more children had never entered her head after she'd had Amy. Her hand slid over her belly. If she was pregnant, did she want to keep it? Could she even get rid of it? No. There was no way she could abort a child. It just wasn't in her to take that step.

Pushing to her feet, she turned and twisted the hot-water tap in the shower. Steam rose almost instantly, and she adjusted the cold until the water was the right temperature. She stripped out of her clothes and stepped under the warm spray. The heat and massage showerhead did wonders for her tight muscles and she stayed under longer than she should have.

When her fingers began to wrinkle, she decided it was time to get out. The end of her ponytail had gotten wet so she grabbed a handtowel to squeeze the water out before picking up her large bath towel and rubbing the soft cotton over her skin. With the towel wrapped around her, Jody made her way out into the bedroom to find Dan had done exactly what he said he would. On her bedside drawers sat a glass of water.

She fought off the onslaught of tears that suddenly pressed against her eyes and quickly got into some pyjamas. Turning back the covers, she climbed beneath and snuggled into the thick quilt. First thing tomorrow, she'd sneak off and buy a home-pregnancy kit. The sooner she knew for sure, the sooner she could make some decisions and plans.

Chapter Seventeen

Jody stared at the stick in her hand and couldn't believe it when a tiny pink plus sign appeared in the clear window. That couldn't be right. She shook the damn thing in case it was stuck. No change. She grabbed the box and re-read the instructions. Had she peed on the stupid thing right? Maybe she was supposed to pee in a cup and soak the end for a minute or something. She scanned the words as they blurred before her eyes. *Oh God!* She'd done everything exactly as instructed.

Full-blown panic took over. She trembled from head to toe and sweat broke out, slicking her palms so much that the reason for her sudden terror slipped from her grip. It dropped to the bathroom floor and she scrambled to pick it up before someone in another cubical saw.

"Oh God." *This can't be happening again.* "Oh God, oh God, oh God."

She couldn't breathe. Couldn't think. Couldn't get past the terrifying reality that at thirty-four she was a divorced mother of two teenagers and pregnant from what had essentially been a one-night stand.

"Oh God."

It had to be wrong. She couldn't be pregnant. Did these things have used-by dates? Surely it was broken or something—anything other than finding herself in the same position as sixteen years ago. A wave of nausea swamped her and she spun around, flipping up the toilet seat before emptying her stomach into the bowl. Again. She'd never been this sick with either of the girls. That had to be a sign the stick lied. Didn't it? When the last of the spasms passed, Jody got to her feet and almost toppled headfirst into the toilet when someone knocked on the door.

"Are you all right in there, love?" The voice was shaky with age and Jody thanked God it wasn't the smartly dressed twenty-something who'd been her constant shadow since arriving at the courthouse.

"Y-yes." Jody licked her dry lips and bile rose in her throat at the foul taste. "I'm fine. Thank you." Her own voice shook, but it had nothing to do with age.

She needed to pull it together. Revealing her secret here was not an option, and if she didn't get control of her emotions the first person to look at her funny would send her into a meltdown. Water ran in one of the sinks and Jody hoped the elderly woman was about to leave. Drawing in a deep breath, she turned the lock on the door and stepped out of the cubicle.

"Here you go, dear." The smallest woman Jody had ever seen held out a handful of wet paper towel. "Put that against your neck. I always found that helpful when I was suffering morning sickness."

Jody's hand froze in mid-air as she reached for the wadded up towel. "How—"

The gray-haired woman chuckled. "My dear, nothing other than a coming baby can empty a woman's stomach quite like that." She patted Jody's arm. "Now take these and a deep breath. I'm sure it'll pass in a few moments."

Jody took the bundle of wet paper and pressed it against her neck. Dumbfounded, she stood there as the kind old woman turned to leave. At the last second, she remembered her manners and muttered, "Thank you."

"You're welcome, dear. And congratulations. It's an exciting time when you're expecting." With a wave, she disappeared through the outer door, leaving Jody alone in the cold marble room with her decidedly unexcited emotions.

She still held the stick in her hand and she brought it up to look at it one more time before tossing it in the bin when she discovered the plus sign hadn't changed. Remembering her bag, Jody turned around and retrieved it from the hook on the back of the toilet door. The test kit sat on the floor where she'd dropped it when she'd thrown up and she picked it up and shoved it back in the brown paper bag in her purse. There were another two test sticks in the box. She'd wait until later, at home, to do the test a second time. Possibly a third. If the results were the same, she'd make an appointment with her doctor as soon as she could get in.

"Ms. Walsh?" Blonde twenty-something stuck her head in the bathroom door. "The girls are finished and the judge is going to make his decision in the next few minutes."

Jody breathed a sigh of relief. Finally, Leigh and Amy were out. They'd been in with the judge for over an hour, and the longer it went on the more she'd worried. Not about what either of them might say, but about how they'd cope being peppered with questions about a man they barely knew.

"I'll be right there." She dumped the wad of towel in the bin and checked her appearance before deciding she was none the worse for wear after her latest vomiting episode. She'd been doing it so regularly this morning that haggard was her permanent look, and she figured she'd get away with it because of the nature of today's proceedings.

Exiting the bathroom, she found both her lawyers, her parents, her brother and the girls waiting for her. It was the person between the girls that surprised her. Dan smiled, and even with the emotions currently swirling around inside, she smiled back and felt a heavy weight lift off her, like he'd taken heavy grocery bags from her hands. She took her time, nerves about the decision, about how the girls went and about the man who'd turned her life on its head, collided together to make her cautious even when it was just approaching those who were here to support her and the girls.

Mackenzie stepped forward. "Leigh and Amy did brilliantly. You should be very proud of both of them."

"Thank you. But I don't need them to answer questions in front of a judge to make me proud." Jody held out her arms and both girls rushed into them. She buried her nose in Amy's hair and breathed in the scent of her familiar shampoo. The three of them held on for longer than normal, but today was anything but normal.

"We'll know for sure in the next few minutes, but I'm confident the judge is going to grant the order," Mackenzie added.

Jody looked up and met Mackenzie's gaze. "Thank you. For everything."

"You're welcome."

The girls started talking at once as they pulled away and Jody had to hold up her hand to stop the excited flow. "One at a time, please."

"Gran and Gramps want to take us to the movies. Can we go?" Leigh asked.

Jody glanced at her mother and father. "Are you sure?"

"Of course. We'll bring them home after dinner." He father pulled her into a big hug and she leaned into him, soaking up his warmth and comfort.

"Thanks, Dad."

"You hang in there, kiddo. Everything is going to be fine." He gave her a final squeeze before letting go. "We'll see you later. Me and my favourite girls have a date."

"Hey, I thought I was your favourite girl."

Her dad tweaked her nose. "Always. But if I don't share it around the others will get upset." He winked, making her laugh.

Her mother gave her a quick hug before grabbing the girls' hands and leading them away.

"Bye. Behave, girls," she called out. They were already

halfway down the corridor, their mother and this morning's ordeal completely forgotten. Which delivered equal pangs of relief and sadness.

"You okay?" Dan's warm hand spread across her spine. "Still feeling a little queasy?"

"Yes, how can you tell?" She turned to look at him. He couldn't tell anything else could he?

"You're still a little pale and your eyes have that glazed look you get when you've been tossing your cookies." He rubbed his hand in circles and Jody couldn't help but lean into the support he offered.

"You can stop worrying now. In a few minutes, the judge will hand down his decision and everything will go back to normal," Dan said.

Jody covered a snort of laughter with her hand and a fake cough. If only he knew. Nothing was ever going to be normal again.

Dan hadn't meant to snoop. But when he'd dropped Jody's handbag on the counter and everything had tumbled out...the brown paper bag had snagged his attention first. Then the box with words *Early Test Kit* half hanging out had grabbed him by the gut. He wasn't proud of himself for pulling it out the rest of the way, but nothing could compete with the roller coaster of emotions that followed.

He wasn't sure what to think. Okay, he knew exactly what he was thinking, but what to do about it was the question. Jody hadn't said a word, and he couldn't decide if he should wait to see if she did, or bring up the topic himself. She'd obviously taken the test. The box was open and one of the three test sticks was missing. A burst of excitement exploded inside him quickly followed by anger.

Had she lied to him about being on the pill? Reason quickly

asserted itself. Why would she? It didn't make sense or fit with the woman Dan had come to know. He shoved everything back in her bag and put it down on the breakfast counter. She'd raced off to the bathroom the minute she'd opened her front door and he had a pretty good idea why. So far he'd counted four dashes to the toilet today, and he'd only been with her for as many hours. He'd honestly thought she was sick due to the stress of going to court, but if he was reading the signs right—and a box of home pregnancy test kits was a pretty big sign—it wasn't the threat her ex represented that had her throwing up her lunch.

"Sorry. Can I get you a coffee?"

She breezed into the room, her face flushed, her eyes glassy, and he couldn't think of a thing to say that didn't start and end with, "Are you pregnant?" He figured blurting it out was the wrong way to deal with it, so he held his tongue and nodded.

He slid onto a barstool and watched her move around. She wasn't as animated as usual, but after the last few weeks and today that was to be expected. And if she was pregnant—his gaze dropped to her belly, but he couldn't see any evidence of a baby bump—then he was surprised she was functioning at all. Other than the dark circles beneath her eyes and the tired, pale look, Dan couldn't see any physical difference. He'd heard the female body went through numerous changes before it became obvious there was a baby on the way, but other than the obvious swollen belly he didn't know what they were.

A thought occurred to him and he pulled his phone from his pocket and opened his calendar app. He counted back to their weekend job. Seventeen days. She wasn't even three weeks. Things were barely getting started inside her.

"Dan!"

He jerked his gaze up to meet Jody's. "Huh?"

"Do you have milk?"

Oh, his coffee. "Yes, please."

"Where were you? You spaced out on me. I don't think you heard anything I said in the last five minutes." She filled two mugs with boiling water and the aroma of coffee filled the air.

He waved his phone. "Just checking email."

"Oh." She leaned across the counter and put his coffee in front of him.

Dan had to admit he could get used to watching her make him coffee every day. And if she was pregnant, he'd get to do exactly that. He wondered if she'd want a big wedding or if they'd have something small and intimate. He'd never thought about how he'd get married or even if he would. But now that he was thinking about it, Dan had to acknowledge a small wedding would be more his style. Of course, he was putting the cart before the horse. She hadn't even mentioned the possibility of a pregnancy.

He decided to lead her in the direction of a confession. "How are you feeling?"

"Better. I'm sure it'll pass now that the drama is over."

"Are you happy the judge granted your order?" Dan had to wonder how much she cared for her ex when she very rarely badmouthed him. Although he was more inclined to think she pitied the man she was once married to.

"Yes. There won't be any real difference day to day, except the girls and I are protected from another incident like the other night." Jody took a sip of her drink before continuing. "Colin's not in the girls lives anyway. Since he moved out five years ago, he's seen them a total of twelve times. He does the obligatory Christmas and birthday visits and that's it—although he's missed both of their last birthdays and Christmas. Other than the child-support money that drops into my account once a month, I don't even think about him most of the time."

"I don't understand how anyone can walk away from their children like that." He wanted his position on any children he might father clear before Jody brought up her possible pregnancy. "I'd never abandon a child of mine even if I was no longer involved with their mother."

He thought she stiffened for a second, but then she turned around and, opening the dishwasher, began emptying it. "Not all fathers feel the same way obviously."

Dan bit his tongue. He wanted to confront her. Wanted to know for sure so they could make plans, except something told him she wasn't ready to face this yet. He'd been chasing after her from the start, and he suddenly had the sinking feeling that he'd always be trying to catch her. In this, he had to let her come to him. And if she didn't by the end of the week, he'd say something.

He got up and walked around the breakfast bar and helped her put away the clean dishes. He was beginning to know where most things were in her kitchen. And while he liked that they'd become close in that way, he wanted to get closer. What he'd really like was for her to move in with him. His place was bigger and the girls could still attend the same school, keep in touch with their existing friends and not disrupt their lives at all.

When she told him about the baby, he'd suggest they combine their households before the wedding, although he wanted a ring on her finger—and his—as soon as possible, he understood she might want to wait. Either way, in the next few months they'd build the foundations of their future together.

Jody woke with a start. Her nose was pressed into the hard wall of Dan's chest while one of his arms was wrapped around her back holding her close. They were on the sofa in her living room, the television turned down low and the darkness of dusk shrouding the room in shadows.

"What time is it?" She stretched her arms over her head as she sat up.

"Not quite six. You slept for about two hours."

"Oh God. Why didn't you wake me?" She went to stand up but Dan stopped her with a hand on her arm.

"Because you needed it and there was nothing urgent that you had to do. The girls are with your parents and won't be home for a while yet. For once, just sit and relax, Jody."

He pulled her back against him and she gave in. The warmth of his body, the scent of his skin, the sound of him breathing, it all calmed her in a way she'd never experienced before. It was as though just having him close would make all her problems go away—or at least make them easier to deal with—and Jody couldn't decide if she liked the sensation or not. For now, she'd let him hold her while it was just the two of them. The outside world would intrude soon enough.

She watched the sitcom Dan had on. She wasn't a fan of much on TV, but she had to admit this particular show always made her laugh and tonight was no different. She'd seen the episode before and even that didn't dull the impact of the humour. He'd wrapped his arm back around her and Jody soon found herself dozing off again. When she did it for the third time, she decided she'd better get up or getting to sleep tonight would be impossible.

"I think I need to get up and do something."

"Why?"

"Because I keep nodding off."

"And?" He pulled her up and over his legs until she was draped across his lap. "You've had a big few days. Take the time and rest while you can."

She knew he was right. It was beyond rare for her to have a few moments to herself, never mind hours. Usually when the girls were with her parents it was because she had to work. Settling into Dan's arms, Jody allowed herself this indulgence while she could. Things would be different once he knew about the possible baby. Her decision to keep it from him until she'd had it confirmed by her doctor weighed on her mind.

He deserved to know. And if she were honest, she'd concede the need to have his support. She had no doubt he'd stand up and take responsibility once he knew, and the longer she mulled over it the more she realised waiting until she saw her doctor was her way of putting the inevitable off. And that wasn't fair to either of them.

"Dan."

"Mmm."

Jody couldn't work out how to tell him in a way that wouldn't blindside him. Then again, she doubted that was even possible. "Um, remember the other weekend?"

He turned his gaze her way and muted the television. "Which weekend? We've spent the last few together."

"The one in the Hunter." Her mouth went dry and her tongue stuck to her teeth as she spoke. "When we...you know."

"Had sex?" He waggled his eyebrows.

She smiled. "Yeah, well, I was sick a couple of weeks before that, remember?"

"Didn't you and the girls all have tonsillitis or something?" Dan skimmed his fingers over her waist, sending tingles through her, and she struggled to stay focused.

"Yes. We were on antibiotics."

"Okay. Any reason we're taking this medical history trip?"

"Medicine can make contraceptive pills ineffective." There. She'd said it.

"Meaning?"

Oh God. She was going to have to spell it out—say the words out loud. She'd avoided it until now. The words might have sounded in her head, but they hadn't once passed her lips. Scrunching her eyes closed, she buried her face against his chest and let the words out. "I think I'm pregnant."

"Okay."

Her eyes popped open as she jerked her head backwards. "What? Okay? That's all you have to say?" She tried to get off his lap, but he held her down by wrapping both arms around her waist.

"I have to confess I saw the kit in your handbag earlier."

"You looked in my bag?"

"I didn't mean to snoop, but it fell out when I dropped your bag on the counter and well, I added that to the frequent trips to toss your cookies and figured you had something to tell me."

Jody stumbled over what to say next. Until Dan opened his mouth again.

"As soon as we're sure, we'll get married, but we can move you and the girls into my place this weekend."

"Wow. Wait a second." This time she did scramble off his lap. She got to her feet and stood, legs apart, hands on hips. "Who said anything about getting married or moving in together? I'm not uprooting the girls again. They've had enough uncertainty in their short lives."

"Then I'll move in here, but I thought it made sense to move into my place because it's bigger. And the girls will still be in the same area so they won't have to change schools or lose friends."

"No."

"Jody, be reasonable. If we're having a baby we need to combine our lives to give our child the security and stability of a family."

"I did that already and look where it got me. I'm not getting married or moving in with you just because we made a baby together. Jesus, we haven't even slept together since it happened." Couldn't Dan see how stupid it was to get married or move in together at this point?

"Is that what happened? You got pregnant with Leigh and married the guy? And now you're comparing me with him? I'm going to pretend I didn't hear you say that."

Jody opened her mouth to speak when the front door flew open and Amy came rushing in talking a mile a minute. Their conversation was officially over and it hadn't gone anything like she'd expected.

Chapter Eighteen

Two and a half days. Dan hadn't spoken to Jody in over forty-eight hours, and he was starting to go stir crazy. He'd left her house not long after the girls had arrived home on Tuesday night thinking he'd see her Wednesday, only she hadn't come into work. Cassie had come into his office to tell him Jody had called to say one of the girls was sick, except he was pretty sure it was Jody who was sick. He hoped she'd used the day to visit the doctor and confirm her pregnancy. The sooner she did that the sooner they could move forward.

And then she hadn't shown up on Thursday or today. He'd dialled her number numerous times but only allowed the call to go through a few of them. He didn't want to pester her if she was resting, except now that she hadn't returned any of the five messages he had left in the last three days, he was beginning to worry. Tonight he was turning up on her doorstep whether she wanted him there or not and he'd see for himself she was okay even if he had to peer in through the damn window.

"Hey."

Dan looked up to see Cassie leaning on the doorjamb. "What's up?"

She came into the room and closed the door. "Mind if I sit down?"

"Um, no." He arched one eyebrow. "Is there a problem?"

"No." She chewed her lip as she slid into the seat across from him. "More that I just want to have a chat. Friend to friend."

"Jody. Luc asked you to talk to me about Jody didn't he?"

Cassie laughed. "Actually, no. He told me to stay out of it."

She grinned. "As you can see, I'm taking his advice."

"Oh?"

"Look, I don't know what's going on and I don't want details, but I think you need some advice from a woman who might understand the working mind of another woman better than you."

Dan wasn't sure if he followed that correctly or not, but at this point he'd take any and all advice under consideration. "Go on."

"Jody is ready to move on from her disastrous marriage, so don't think she doesn't have feelings for you. Quite the opposite. If she didn't she wouldn't have let you close. Her problem is she's been hurt by someone she trusted before. Badly. You know that, so I don't need to go into details. Unfortunately for you, she's going to tar you with the same brush."

She already had. When she'd insinuated marrying him or moving in with him for the baby's sake would end up the same way her relationship with her ex had, Dan was pretty sure he'd been tarred by that arsehole's brush. He nodded for Cassie to continue.

"Straight out, no lies, Dan. Are you serious about Jody?"

"Yes."

"Okay." She stood. "That's good then."

Dan watched puzzled as Cassie got up to leave. Where was the advice in any of what she'd just said? "Is that it?"

She glanced over her shoulder. "Oh, no. See you Monday."

"What? I didn't think you had a job off site today."

"I don't. But you're heading home early. Oh, and I gave your Saturday party to Kerry."

"What?" He pushed his chair back and got to his feet.

"I'm giving you the rest of the day and the weekend off. Go fix whatever the hell needs fixing with Jody."

With that, Cassie disappeared into the hallway, leaving Dan

wondering if he'd been dropped into the twilight zone. Cassie's head popped around the door. "The girls are at school and Jody's home resting, but you didn't hear that from me."

He stared at the space his boss's head had just occupied for ages before he shook himself out of his daze and glanced at his watch. It wasn't even eleven o'clock. If he headed to Jody's now, they'd have a few hours of alone time to get things sorted out. With a plan in place, he scooped his keys off the edge of his desk and headed out.

Perhaps he should pick up some lunch? Although he wasn't sure what she'd be able to eat with her tummy upset the way it had been the last time he'd seen her. He'd done some research and he knew morning sickness often lasted months. He hoped she didn't suffer that long or get it as severe as some of the information suggested was possible. Dan hit the outer warehouse door just as West was coming in.

"Hey, man, leaving early? I didn't forget a job, did I?" West asked.

"What? No. I've got some personal stuff to deal with so I'm cutting out early."

"Lucky you. I've got at least another twelve hours before I can call it a day." West held the door for Dan to pass through.

"But busy means you're making money, right?"

"According to my accountant, I'm making too much money and should hire a manager. Hey, you're not looking for a job are you?" West asked.

"You trying to poach me from Cassie?" Dan arched one eyebrow. "Brave. If I take you up on the offer she'll be serving testicles at the next function."

West laughed as he covered his groin and glanced around. "It'll be our secret. But I'm serious. If you ever want out of Are You Game? come knock on my door. Whether I'm looking or not I'd hire you on the spot."

"I'll take that as a compliment."

"Hell no. I'm complimenting Cassie. She's got your arse so shipshape you'd be a fantastic addition to my team." West slapped him on the back. "Anyway, you go enjoy your time off while I go slave over a hot stove."

"Yeah, right, you love your job. Meanwhile, there's not much enjoyment in what I have to do." Dan hoped there would be, but he had to be realistic. Jody was avoiding him and their last words had been spoken in mild anger.

"Ah, woman troubles." West nodded.

"That obvious?" Dan asked.

"Only because I've seen that look in the mirror a time or two lately."

"Oh? Anyone I know?"

West mimed zipping his lips and throwing away the key.

"So that means I do know her." Dan grinned. "Which means it has to be someone who works for you…"

"You want me to start speculating on what you did to fuck things up with Jody?" West asked.

"Who said anything about Jody?"

"C'mon, you'd have to be deaf, blind and stupid to miss the fireworks shooting between you two."

Dan frowned. He hadn't realised they'd been obvious in their attraction.

"Relax. Nobody's talking if that's what you're worried about."

He wasn't, but Dan was relieved to know it anyway. Except the lack of workplace talk would change once Jody's pregnancy became public knowledge. Everyone would be talking then. "Look, I gotta go."

"Sure thing. Catch you later. Oh, and that job offer stands." West grinned as he ducked inside, the door closing behind him.

Dan wondered what was going on with his friend. He'd been so wrapped up in his own life that he hadn't spent much time with West in recent months. Not that he should be worrying about someone else's problems when he had his own to sort out. Shaking his head, he opened the door on his Jeep and climbed in. In the next hour he'd know if he had any hope of fixing the situation between him and Jody.

Jody dragged herself off the couch and crawled towards the door. She hadn't kept any food down since Monday and her muscles just weren't up to walking. Holding onto the wall, she barely made it into the hallway when the banging started. God, it sounded like someone had snuck into her skull and was hammering away at her brain with an axe.

"I'm coming." Her voice was hoarse and scarcely more than a whisper. Her throat and mouth were so dry her tongue stuck to her teeth, and her lips stung in places where she knew they had to be cracked.

The thumping on the door continued and Jody grabbed her head, cupping her ears to try and lessen the noise. She collapsed against the wall and slid the rest of the way to the floor. Her arms and legs were like lead weights that an Olympic lifter would struggle to get off the ground. Curling in a ball, Jody cried, except she was so dehydrated that no tears formed and her eyelids grated against her eyes as she lowered them and prayed whoever was at the door would stop bashing on it soon.

"Jody?" She had no idea how much time had passed before Dan kneeled on the floor beside her. He shook her shoulder and she moaned.

"Jody? Can you hear me?"

"Yes," she whispered over dry lips.

"C'mon, baby, let's get you off the floor." He scooped her up and stood, sending her head spinning and her stomach flipping.

"Oh God, gonna be sick." She slammed a hand over her

mouth as he dashed her towards the bathroom where she dry heaved for what felt like an eternity.

He pressed a damp cloth to her forehead when the wave of nausea had gone. "Can you hold that there?"

Jody couldn't manage a shake of her head never mind move her arm. The only thing she could do was groan as Dan picked her up once more. She closed her eyes and fought against the bile rising in her throat as he moved out of the bathroom and into her bedroom. He laid her on the bed and she could hear him moving around but she had no strength to even open her eyes.

The bed dipped and Dan's warmth brushed her side. "C'mon, try a sip of this." He held her head up and pressed a cool glass against her mouth.

She parted her lips on a breath and let him tip a little water inside. He waited for her to swallow before repeating the process.

"How long since you ate anything? Drank anything?"

Jody's head swam, her mind spinning as she tried to remember what day it was. "No."

"No, you don't want to tell me or you don't know? C'mon, Jody, help me out here. Have you kept anything down since Tuesday?"

She knew that answer. "No."

"Damn, Jody, have you been to the doctor?" He wiped the cloth over her face and her eyes fluttered open.

When her eyes focused, she saw his face twisted in deep concern. Tears stung, and her throat constricted, making it difficult to swallow even with the water he'd recently fed her. "Couldn't." She licked her lips. "Get in."

"Where's the number? If they won't see you now I'm taking you to emergency."

"Phone." Her eyes closed as fatigue threatened to take her under again. She seemed to spend all her time sleeping. "In. My bag."

The bed rose as Dan left her to go in search of her bag. She couldn't tell him where it was because she couldn't remember what she'd done with it. Turning on her side, she curled into herself and hoped her stomach didn't repel the fluid churning in her belly.

"Jody?" Dan's hand smoothed over her cheek. "Jody, you have to wake up, baby. I spoke to your doctor. She said to take you straight to casualty. She's ringing ahead so they'll take you right in."

"Girls?"

"I'll take care of them, but let's get you sorted first." He wrapped the quilt around her and picked her up once more. She snuggled close and let his warmth and comfort surround her.

Dan was going out of his mind. He'd lied to the nurse so they'd let him behind the security doors, but that hadn't done him any good because they'd whisked Jody away on a bed and hadn't brought her back yet. It had been an hour. He ran his fingers through his hair again. At this rate he'd be bald by the end of the day. Glancing at his watch, he noticed the time and pulled out his phone to call Luc. Someone had to be there for the girls and he didn't want to leave Jody yet. Not until he knew how she was.

He thumbed through his phonebook until he came to Luc's number and hit call. It rang twice when Jody's brother answered.

"Dan? What's up?"

"Someone needs to go to Jody's and get the girls. I'd go but I don't want to leave Jody."

"What do you mean leave her? Where the fuck are you?"

"We're at the hospital." Dan sighed. He'd have to talk fast

or Luc would put him six feet under before his next heartbeat. "She's sick. I think it's the baby but the doctor hasn't come back yet and they're still running tests."

"Baby! What baby?" Dan pulled the phone away from his ear but didn't have any trouble hearing Luc yelling at him. "Did you get my sister pregnant? Jesus H. Christ, O'Conner, what the hell were you thinking?"

"Let's not do this now. Can you get the girls or not?"

"Yes. Shit, of course I can. Which hospital are you at?"

"North Shore." Dan turned at the clatter of metal behind him to see two nurses pushing Jody back into the room. "Gotta go, I'll call you back."

Dan hung up to Luc screaming at him not to. He stepped out of the way so they could wheel the bed into the correct position. "Is she okay?"

The nurse who'd greeted him at reception smiled. "She will be. We've started an IV and the doctor is going over her results now. He should be in with you shortly."

He wanted to ask more—know more—but the nurses left before he could get another word out. Dan looked at Jody. She looked so small curled on her side, the IV tube running into the back of one hand. Her hair was matted and the black circles beneath her eyes were so dark—so deep—he wondered how her eyes remained in her head. Gently, he ran his fingertips down her cheek, along her jaw. His phone rang and he quickly hit reject and turned it to silent so it wouldn't disturb her.

She stirred, her eyes fluttering open and the ghost of a smile tipped the corner of her mouth. "Dan."

"Hey, baby." He leaned down and dropped a kiss on her forehead. "You'll feel better soon."

"Girls?"

"Luc is going to pick them up. Do you want them to come here?"

She licked her lips and he looked around for some water.

"No. Scare them."

"All right, I'll ring Luc back and tell him to take them home with him or to your mum and dad's."

"Please." Her eyelids lowered and he wanted to let her rest but he wanted answers too.

"Why didn't you ring me, Jody? You're far too sick for this to be normal."

"Too tired." Her mouth went lax as exhaustion took her under again.

A throat cleared behind him and he turned to find an older stout man in a white coat in the doorway. "Daniel O'Conner?"

"Yes?"

The man held out his hand as he came into the room. "Doctor Moore, I'm in charge of Jody's care. I've spoken with her GP, Doctor Simmons, and we believe the best thing is to admit her. She's suffering from hyperemesis gravidarum, or in layman's terms, severe morning sickness. She is very dehydrated so I'd like to administer fluids intravenously for at least twenty-four hours. I've also started her on some medication to counteract the nausea, though it won't stop it altogether. But she should at least begin to eat and drink normally before we send her home tomorrow if she responds to the treatment well."

"Will that affect the baby?"

"No, no, it's fine, and she's not the first woman to experience such extreme morning sickness. Doctor Simmons did mention that she wasn't this ill with either of her other two pregnancies though, and as she's a good deal older now I'd like to run some other tests. I'll get a nurse to bring in some pamphlets about Jody's condition and also some information on the tests I'd like her to have in the next few weeks."

"Okay."

"We'll get her up and going again before we do anything more though. I can tell you the ultrasound showed everything is otherwise progressing normally for a three week foetus."

"Thank God," Dan breathed the words out in a rush of air.

"This extreme form of morning sickness can be very frightening, but I assure you she and the baby will be fine as long as we control the nausea and make sure she keeps up her fluids and nourishment."

Dan held out his hand. "Thank you."

Doctor Moore shook Dan's hand. "I take it this is your first?"

"Yes." Dan smiled. "Does it show?"

"A little." The doctor smiled and stepped around Dan to check Jody's IV. "All looks good. I'll come by once they move her up to her room to make sure she's settled in."

"Do I need to fill in any paperwork?"

"Not now. I'll get the nurse to bring it to her room later."

"Thanks." Dan turned back to Jody. She'd slept through the whole exchange, and even though they hadn't been here long, he swore some colour was returning to her face. It was the most welcome thing he'd ever seen.

Chapter Nineteen

Something tugged at the back of Jody's hand when she tried to roll over.

"Hey, hey, careful now."

Dan's soothing voice filled her ears and she turned her head in his direction. Her eyelids felt heavy but she forced them open to see him standing beside her. "Where...?" She scanned the room around her.

"The hospital. You don't remember?"

"No." She licked her lips. "How did I get here?"

"You don't recall me finding you on the floor at your house?"

Jody shook her head, but the action brought on a wave of dizziness that made her moan and her stomach roll. "N-no."

"Well, that might be for the best. What's the last thing you do remember?"

She thought about it for a moment. "Sending the girls to school?" Was that this morning? What day was it? Jody could see through the window that it was dark outside.

"Today, yesterday or Wednesday?"

"It's Friday?" Jody tried to sit up only to be forced back by her spinning head and her pitching stomach.

"Take it easy." Dan stroked her hair back from her face with the fingertips of one hand while he held her hand—the one with the tube snaking out from under a bandage—with the other. "Yes, it's Friday, and from what I can gather you've been sick since I left Tuesday night."

A horrible thought occurred. "The baby?"

"Is fine. You have hyper-something or other. Severe morning sickness. It has a fancy name but I don't remember it, and even if I did I probably couldn't pronounce it correctly. The doctor said he was going to give us some leaflets that explain what's going on and how to help make it more bearable."

"So I am pregnant?"

"Yep. Three weeks according to the ultrasound they did when I brought you in earlier."

"I guess there's no denying it now."

"Nope. We're going to have a baby."

Dan grinned at her like it was the best thing in the world, and she supposed for some it would seem that way. But right now all she could think was she hadn't planned for this—hadn't wanted to find herself in the same situation a second time in her life. But she'd learned a valuable lesson the first time. Forcing two people together for the sake of a baby was the worst possible way to begin a relationship of any sort, especially marriage, and Dan had been adamant that they get married if she was pregnant.

"I won't marry you," Jody blurted out.

He jerked back, his eyes widening, his eyebrows shooting up into his hairline. "Wow. Okay. How about we leave that discussion for later, when you're better and home."

Why was he being so accommodating? What happened to giving their child security and family? "I won't change my mind. I'm not going through that again."

"Jody." Dan sighed. "I understand you're frightened by what's happening, but I swear I'm not going to treat you the way your ex has."

"He was fine in the beginning too. Then when reality set in it all changed." She folded her arms around her waist, hugging herself tightly. "I can't do it again. I *won't* go through that again."

"Stop." He stepped closer and leaned over the bed until

their faces were inches apart. "I don't want you to work yourself up. It's not good for you or the baby. We'll talk about this more later, when you're back on your feet and not lying in that bed looking like you're at death's door, because I have to tell you I feel partly responsible for that look and it's killing me to know that carrying my baby—our baby—has put you through this."

"But—"

"No buts. Just rest. Get better so we can argue later when it won't feel like I'm kicking a sick puppy." He stroked her face with a fingertip, back and forth across her cheek. "I don't like this Jody. I like the one who fights with me. The Jody who doesn't look like she'll fall over if I breathe on her."

Jody didn't want to talk about the baby or the future or them any more than he did, so she changed the subject and felt a slam of guilt for not thinking to ask before now. "Where are Leigh and Amy?"

"Luc has them with him. He and Cassie will keep them overnight, and if they let you go home tomorrow then you can all stay with me or I'll stay with you." He held up a hand. "And don't even think about arguing with me on that one. It's not negotiable. You're going to need someone to take care of you until you get better."

She wasn't stupid enough to open her mouth this time. She'd wait until he went then she'd ring her brother and organise for their mum and dad to have her and the girls at their place until she got her strength back. They'd happily taken them in when she'd separated from Colin and they'd been sad to see them move out into their own place, so Jody was sure her parents would be more than pleased for the three of them to move back in indefinitely.

"What are you smiling about?" Dan asked.

"Was I smiling?"

"Yes. And I know that smile. It's the one you get when you're planning something."

"I have no idea what you mean."

"And why do I not believe that?"

Jody really did smile then. "You've got a suspicious mind?"

"Me? *Ha.* I'm not the one thinking the worst of the other every step of the way." He stood back and crossed his arms over his chest.

Her smile faded. He was right. She thought the worst of him a lot. And if they were having a baby together that had to change. It wasn't fair to him or their baby if she continued to expect him to let her down or turn away. But the lessons of a lifetime were hard to unlearn, and Jody knew there was no way she'd be able to open herself to him. She'd locked a part of her heart away when Colin had sliced into it with his indifference, and she wasn't about to let any other man have the same opportunity to hurt her.

Dan met Luc on the street in front of the hospital. He'd asked him to bring some of Jody's clothes over so she'd have something clean to change into after her shower. They'd seen the doctor this morning and he'd told them Jody could go home this afternoon as long as she kept her breakfast and lunch down. Doctor Moore was more than happy with her progress, which pleased Dan because even though he could see a marked physical difference, having the doctor's reassurance made him breathe easier.

"How is she?" Luc asked as he handed over a backpack.

"Tired still. Grumpy about being here even if it is for just a few more hours and pissed at me for not fighting with her when she's clearly spoiling for one." Dan ran his fingers though his hair.

"And what does she want to fight about other than the fact you got her pregnant?" Luc asked.

"First, *we* got her pregnant. It takes two. And second, she's feeling trapped." Dan shrugged. "Nothing I can do about that. I want to get married, she doesn't. We're at a stalemate."

"You asked her to marry you?"

"Ah, not in so many words..."

"Oh my God. You didn't?" Luc laughed. "You did." His laughter got louder.

Dan crossed his arms and waited him out.

"Sorry." Luc sucked in a breath. "Man, you really fucked that up, didn't you?"

Dan sighed. There was no avoiding it. "Yeah. I might have fudged the delivery of my proposal but my intentions are serious. She thinks it's because of the baby, and she's partially right, but the baby isn't the only reason I want to marry your sister."

"Does she know the other reason?" Luc asked. "Do you?"

"You know I do." He wasn't about to declare his love for Jody to her brother. No. The first person to hear those words from him would be the woman he'd fallen in love with. Only she wasn't ready to hear them. "Look, I know I've got some ground work to do and not all of it is to repair the damage I've done. In fact, most of it is because some arsehole took her love and her trust and crushed them under his feet as he was walking out the door.

"Is that fair? Fuck no. But it's the way it is and it's my reality and hers. Now I have to work out how to show her I'm serious and ready to stand beside her every step of the way, so what I need from you is support. As a friend and her brother. Can you do that?" Dan asked.

"All I want is for Jody to be happy. If that's being with you then I'm all for it, but I don't see how I can help you prove you're serious about her. I couldn't convince her not to marry Colin all those years ago, so even if I want her to marry you—which I will admit I'm leaning towards—she isn't going to listen to me sprouting off your virtues."

"Okay, maybe support is the wrong word." Dan scratched his chin. What was he asking Luc for?

"How about I agree to stay out of it?" Luc asked. "I won't offer advice to either of you or interfere."

"Thanks." Dan held out his hand. "I appreciate your understanding. We need to work this out between the two of us."

Luc shook his hand. "I'll be honest and tell you I think you're good for both her and the girls. And you're a thousand times a better man than Colin is or was. As stubborn as my sister is, my money's on you."

Dan smiled. "Let's see if you still think that way in a few weeks." He turned to go but then remembered something he wanted to ask. "Hey, you didn't tell the girls about the baby did you?"

"And risk my sister removing any future chance of me having babies of my own? Not on your life." Luc shuddered.

Dan had to laugh. The idea of this six-foot-five-inch solid wall of muscle being frightened of his much smaller sister was ludicrous. "Good. Although I'm not happy with her decision to keep quiet about the baby, I see her point in not telling anyone until she's further along."

"Me too. But they're asking questions—lots of them—so expect to be subjected to their brand of the Spanish Inquisition the second I bring them home."

"We'll let Jody handle it. I'll let you know when we're back at her place. I'm expecting around five, so if you guys want to stick around we can order pizza for dinner."

"Sounds like a plan. I'll see you then." Luc waved before he headed across the street to where he'd parked.

Dan waited until Luc was out of sight before heading back inside. He'd left Jody's room about thirty minutes ago. She'd been napping on and off all morning, and he wasn't sure how she thought she was going back to work on Monday, but he'd let her think whatever made her happy for now. Cassie had already decided she wasn't going in. Of course, Dan had to be the bearer of that news flash. He figured he'd wait until Sunday night to let that piece of info out.

When he made it back to the room, Jody was out of bed, the IV had been removed and a nurse was helping her get ready to shower.

"Looks like I made it back just in time," he said as he walked over with the bag of clothes. "Here, I got Luc to bring you some clean clothes."

"Really?" Jody's face lit up and the smile that stretched her lips made him smile in return.

"Yep. I didn't check what he brought, but anything would be better than what you came in here wearing yesterday."

"Oh my God, yes. I was contemplating going home in a hospital gown. The idea of re-wearing the clothes I'm sure I wore for three days straight is too repulsive to think about, never mind do."

He leaned over and planted a kiss on her forehead. "Good thing you've got me around to think of these things then, isn't it?"

"I wish my man was so thoughtful," the nurse said. "Come on. Let's get you in the shower so you can go home with that gorgeous man of yours."

Jody frowned but Dan smiled. He couldn't have paid the woman to sing his praises better. Now all he needed was for Jody to see those good points and realise they weren't booby trapped.

Jody wasn't ready to go home with that gorgeous man of hers. For a start, he wasn't hers. And *he* was the reason she'd ended up in here. Okay, that wasn't fair. If anyone was to blame for this accidental pregnancy, it was her. He'd accepted in good faith that she was safe and look where that had gotten him. A father-to-be. She was the one who'd proven untrustworthy, and yet not once had he uttered a word of blame in her direction.

The nurse made sure she was all right before leaving her in the bathroom to shower. It felt good washing away four days of sweat and sickness. She remembered showering Tuesday night after Dan left, but everything else was a blur except sending the girls off to school on Wednesday morning. Lord knows what they'd been doing while she'd been so sick. Or what they'd been eating. Another wave of guilt swamped her. She'd left the girls to fend for themselves. Anything could have happened to them while she'd been out of it.

She ducked her head under the water to wet her hair then grabbed the little bottle of shampoo the nurse had left her. It didn't smell the best, but anything would be better than the foul odour emanating from her hair right now. Lathering up, she scrubbed at her scalp with her nails before rinsing and repeating. A palm-full of conditioner left her hair silky smooth and she made quick work of washing the rest of her body. She'd been in here a while and the last thing she wanted was for Dan to come in to check on her.

Jody stepped out and used the scratchy hospital towel to dry off then pulled out the clothes Luc had brought over. She was surprised her brother hadn't come in to see her. Then again, he probably didn't want to for fear they'd end up in an argument about being stupid and getting pregnant again. When she'd conceived Leigh he'd been so angry, but that had been nothing compared to when she'd told him she was marrying Colin for the sake of their baby. He'd exploded. They'd had a huge argument and the result had been months of not speaking to each other. Jody could only imagine how pissed off he was that she'd managed to do it again.

Shaking off the memories, she got dressed, gathered her things and left the bathroom. Dan waited in the chair next to the bed. He was flicking through a magazine he'd picked up for her last night. Jody didn't think there was anything appealing in the gossip mag for him to read, but there wasn't anything else for him to do while he waited for her.

He glanced up. "Ready? The nurse dropped off your paperwork." He pointed at the bed.

She picked up the bundle of papers and tucked them into the backpack. "So I'm clear to go then?"

"Yep. We just have to buzz the nurse and she'll bring a wheelchair in."

"A wheelchair? I can walk." The idea of being pushed out of here grated. She wanted to walk out. Probably a trivial thing, but she needed to be in control of something right now.

"You can argue with the nurse over it." Dan leaned over and pressed the call button.

A nurse arrived within a minute, a wheelchair leading the way.

"I'm not getting in that thing." Jody didn't wait for the woman to get all the way in the room before voicing her protest.

"You think you're up to walking out?" the nurse asked.

"Yes."

"Okay, but I'll still have to come down to street level with you. Hospital policy." She pushed the wheelchair off to the corner.

"Let's go then," Jody said.

"In a hurry?" Dan asked.

"Aren't you ready to get out of here? And you didn't even have to stay. You chose to be here overnight." Jody shook her head. She still couldn't believe he'd spent the night in the recliner in her room. And now that she looked at him, she realised he looked a little worse for wear. "You need a shower."

Dan laughed. "Thanks. I'll grab one when we get home."

Her heart skipped a beat. Going home with Dan was the last thing she wanted. She wasn't ready to face the future. The stay in hospital might have been uncomfortable—and annoying—but at least she'd been able to avoid the whole Dan and baby situation to a certain degree.

"C'mon, I thought you wanted out of here?" Dan stood in the doorway, the nurse already out in the hall.

Jody had been too busy thinking about something she had no power of stopping instead of paying attention to what was going on around her. "Sorry. I was just wondering what to cook the girls for dinner," she lied.

"Already sorted. We're ordering pizza when Luc and Cassie drop them off."

He held out his hand, and without thought she closed the distance between them and slid her hand into his, weaving their fingers together instantly. And didn't that say it all about their relationship. When she didn't think, when she went on gut instinct, she walked straight towards him. It was only when her brain—her wounded heart—got involved that she ran in the opposite direction out of fear.

Chapter Twenty

"Dan!" West clicked his fingers in front of Dan's face.

"Shit. Sorry. What?" He'd been doing that a lot in the last few weeks. Ever since he'd taken Jody to the hospital, he'd pretty much spent twenty-four hours a day awake.

"You look like crap man. Are you sleeping at all?" West's face creased in concern.

"Yeah, a few hours a night."

"You can't keep this up. Something's got to give."

Dan agreed. "I know, but Jody's barely tolerating me as it is. The only way to get more sleep is to leave her to take care of herself and the girls every night after she's been at work all day. And there's no way I'm doing that."

"Running yourself into the ground won't help anyone either," West protested.

"I know, and I'm working on solving the problem." And he was. It was just taking a lot longer than he thought it would to win Jody over.

"Jody seems to have taken Cassie's change to her hours okay."

Dan laughed. If only. "Ah, yeah, no. I thought Jody was going to pop a blood vessel when Cassie said she was changing her to nine to five, Monday to Friday. Of course, Jody blamed me for that and let me know it."

"Surely she's happier not working weekends. She gets to be at home with her girls. Which reminds me, does anyone know she's pregnant yet?"

Dan had confided in West weeks ago, but other than Cassie

and Luc, Jody's pregnancy was still a state secret. He shook his head. "No. She wants to wait until the twelve-week mark to tell Leigh, Amy and her parents. Of course, that means I haven't been able to tell my family either. I'm not looking forward to the earbashing I'm going to get over that."

"They'll get over it. C'mon, let's get this food loaded so you can get on your way."

Glancing at his watch, Dan saw he'd be late if he didn't get a move on. "Shit. I seem to be constantly running five minutes behind."

West smiled and handed him a cooler box of food. "Better late than never."

"Can't be late. This stuff has to be there by eleven-thirty ready for lunch."

"You've got plenty of time. Traffic isn't bad this time of day. You'll be across town and back again before one." West picked up a crate of drinks.

"I know, but I was hoping to have enough time to duck home to Jody's and check on her before I came back to the warehouse."

"Everything okay? She's not sick again is she?"

"No. She's doing really well actually, but that's what worries me. Yesterday I found her up a ladder dusting the ceiling fans." Dan shook his head. "A picture of her sprawled on the floor flashed in my mind and I yelled at her, which of course made her start and the ladder wobbled…took ten years off my life."

West frowned. "She's pregnant, not a cripple. Surely she's capable of climbing a ladder and cleaning the fans."

Dan slid the cooler into the back of the van with a sigh. "Yeah. She is. It's me that isn't capable of seeing her do it."

"Ah, I see. You need to go home because you're in the dog house again."

"I'm always in the dog house." Dan laughed as he headed

back to the kitchen for the second cooler of food. "But I figure if she's seeing me she can't forget about me."

West chuckled. "I doubt that's possible, mate. She's carrying your kid. Kind of hard to forget you when she's feeling sick every day."

One more strike against him as far as Dan was concerned. Jody had told him she'd breezed through her other pregnancies without so much as an up-chuck. His baby, however, was determined to make his mother throw up every damn day. At least she was only sick first thing in the morning now. And once that initial wave of nausea passed, it was smooth sailing for the rest of the day.

"Not exactly an endearing effect though," Dan said.

"No. I guess not." West grabbed the second crate of drinks while Dan picked up the cooler. "But look on the bright side."

"There's a bright side?" Dan arched an eyebrow.

"Hell yes. You're gonna be a dad."

Dan grinned. "Yeah, that is definitely one of the highlights of this whole thing."

"One of?"

"Being connected to Jody for the rest of my life is another. And Leigh and Amy. They're a bright spot in all this."

"I can't believe they haven't worked out their mother is having a baby."

Dan frowned when he remembered the conversation he'd had with Leigh yesterday. "I think Leigh is suspicious, but she hasn't outright asked me or her mother yet. She's a smart kid. I think she's biding her time. I just hope Jody's the one she asks and not me. I won't lie to her if she asks me directly if her mother is pregnant."

"I'll cross my fingers for you."

They loaded the rest of the food and beverages without further conversation, and Dan was soon moving through the congested streets of Sydney's CBD. He parked in the loading zone outside the office building where Maggie was running today's corporate event. She met him in the lobby with a couple of guys she'd roped into helping and Dan didn't even have to leave street level to deliver lunch, which meant he was back on the road and heading for Jody's with plenty of time to spare before his job this afternoon.

He glanced at the dashboard clock and figured they wouldn't have had lunch yet. Dan pulled over and reached for his phone. He'd give Jody a call and see if she was okay with him picking up something. Leigh answered on the fifth ring. "Hey, Leigh, where's your mum?"

"Outside in the garden with Amy. They're trying to grow herbs or something." Dan could image her rolling her eyes.

Dan smiled. They'd picked up the seeds and pots for Amy's herb garden last weekend and he was happy to know Jody was up to helping her daughter plant the seeds. "Okay, tell her I'm on my way through from one job to another and I'll drop off some chicken and salads for lunch. Sound good?"

"Yes. I was just looking at the fridge thinking we need to go shopping again."

"We can do that tomorrow. Do me a favour and write a list for me."

"Sure. See you soon."

Dan hung up then pulled back into traffic. He'd stop at the little shopping centre near his place for the charcoal chicken. The place near Jody's wasn't nearly as nice and often didn't have a good selection of salads on hand. Distracted by his thoughts, Dan didn't see the truck speed through the red light until it was too late. Squealing tires and shattering glass filled the air just before the airbag exploded in his face and everything went black.

Jody fumed as she paced the kitchen. She should have

known she couldn't trust him. Except he'd been so attentive in the two months since she'd been admitted to hospital that she'd softened. He'd been so good with her and the girls that she'd looked forward to his visits—to his care. Still, she should have known better than to get sucked in by his kindness. Dan couldn't be trusted any more than Colin could.

It had been three hours since he'd called Leigh and told her he was bringing lunch, and he wasn't answering his phone so Jody couldn't even give him a piece of her mind. The doorbell rang and she hoped it was him with some flimsy excuse so she could slam the door in his face without a word. She stormed down the hallway and flung the door open to find Luc and Cassie on her doorstep.

"Oh, hey, I wasn't expecting you guys." Jody moved out of the way to let them in. "Come in."

"Thanks, but I can't stay, I'm just dropping Luc off," Cassie said.

"Huh?" Confused, Jody studied them more closely and the look on Luc's face registered. Narrowing her eyes as she moved in front of her brother she said, "What's going on?"

"Let's go sit down."

"No." Jody knew this wasn't going to be good. "Whatever it is, just tell me."

"Jody."

"Don't you Jody me. Tell me, Lucas. Now." She crossed her arms and barred the entry. Not that she'd be a barrier to him if he really wanted to get in.

"It's about Dan."

Jody held up her hand. "I don't want to even hear his name. He's proven I was right and shouldn't have trusted him."

"What the hell are you talking about?" Luc asked as he pushed his way into the house, Cassie following behind.

"I thought you were just dropping him off?" Jody looked at Cassie.

"I was, but I don't think I want to miss this. Why are you mad with Dan now?"

"Mad? I'm not mad, I'm furious. He comes here and takes over, does things, looks after us and makes it easy for us to rely on him—to care about him. Then he just doesn't show up. Says he will but doesn't. And he's not answering his damn phone or I'd tell him to never step foot in my house again." Jody couldn't believe how angry she was. She'd never gotten this upset when Colin let her down. Never felt this gut-deep burn of rage.

"Jody." Luc grabbed her shoulders and held her still. "Dan's been in an accident."

Cold settled over her. It started at her head and sank lower as though she was diving into a pool of liquid nitrogen headfirst in slow motion until every inch of her between scalp and toenails was frozen solid. "Accident?"

Luc nodded. "He was hit by a truck."

Bile rose in her throat. "Oh God." Jody slapped a hand over her mouth and ran for the bathroom.

The cheese toast she'd eaten not thirty minutes ago hit the toilet bowl as Cassie slipped into the bathroom behind her.

"Go away."

"Not on your life, Jody."

Water ran then Cassie was pressing a wet towel to Jody's forehead and pushing her hair off her face. She wanted to push Cassie away but the cool cloth felt wonderful against her hot, sweaty face. "How bad?" Jody got the question out around another wave of heaving.

"He's okay. Wait until your stomach settles and then we'll talk."

Jody cried then. Big fat horrible body-jerking sobs. Cassie waited through a few before wrapping an arm around her waist. "C'mon, I think you've finished being sick. Luc!"

"No." Too late. Jody found herself being lifted against her brother's chest.

He carried her out to the lounge room where the girls were waiting, huddled together on the couch. "Leigh, can you go grab your mum a glass of water, please?" Luc asked as he sat down with Jody in his lap.

"Is Dan going to be okay?" Amy asked.

"Yes, sweetie. He's got a concussion, a couple of bruised ribs and some minor cuts, but other than that he's fine," Cassie explained.

"Fine? That doesn't sound fine." Jody pushed out of Luc's arms. "Let me go. I have to go see him."

"Hang on." Luc held her tight. "I'll drive you to him in a minute, but first calm down."

"I don't want to calm down until I see for myself that he's okay." She yanked out of her brother's hold and headed for the kitchen and her car keys.

"Jody." Cassie stepped in her way. "Wait."

"Why?"

"Because you need to think about this."

"Think about what? Dan's hurt and I need to go to him."

"Why?"

Why? "Because he's hurt, that's why."

"And?"

"And? And? And I have to see he's okay." Why was Cassie trying to stop her? Jody had no clue what her boss was getting at and really didn't care. She brushed past her and ran to the kitchen.

"Stop!" When Jody turned around Luc stood in the doorway. "Why are you racing off to a man you were angry at only minutes ago?"

"Angry?" Why was she mad at Dan? "I don't know what…" But she did know what Luc was talking about. Dan hadn't shown up with lunch and she'd put him right in the untrustworthy box beside Colin. Jody hung her head forward on a groan.

Luc's shoes came into view just as he tipped her chin up with his hand. "Why are you racing off to check on Dan?"

Jody met his gaze and her eyes blurred. She'd been an emotional wreck the last few weeks because of the pregnancy hormones, so the urge to cry didn't surprise her, it was the reason she wanted to cry that did. Oh God. She was in love with Dan. Even with all the barriers she'd thrown up, with all the lectures and reminders of what had happened last time she'd agreed to be with the father of her unplanned baby, she'd still opened herself up in a way that could tear her apart if it went wrong. It would destroy her if Dan walked away.

Luc pulled her into his arms and held her against his chest. "Let it out, Budgie."

The childhood nickname worked like a switch. She cried into Luc's shirt until her eyes were dry and her throat sore. And still she stayed in the safety of his arms for a few more minutes. Pulling away, she snagged a handful of tissues from the box on the kitchen counter and dried her face. "What am I going to do now?"

"I'm thinking that was meant as a rhetorical question, but I'm going to answer it anyway." Luc turned her around to face him. "Marry him."

"What?" Jody's mouth dropped open.

"He's the best damn thing to happen to you in forever, Jody. Even mad at him and fighting, you're the happiest I've seen you in years. And the girls are thriving. If you're not ready for marriage then at least let the guy in here." Luc tapped her chest. "Try to make it work because it's obvious to everyone but you that you're in love with each other."

"What?" Jody couldn't get over the fact her brother was telling her to get married this time. "But last time this happened you tried to talk me out of getting married."

"Because Colin was and is a loser who never deserved you."

"Oh."

"I know you're still carrying the scars from your first marriage. And I know the idea of going through that again terrifies you. But, Jody, this is Dan. You said it yourself earlier. He's been here every day. He's taken care of you and the girls, and if you're honest you'll admit he was doing it before you found out you were pregnant."

Jody nodded. Luc was right. Dan had been there for her when Colin had shown up all enraged about her and the girls moving on with their lives. She closed her eyes and sighed. She'd been so wrong to expect Dan to behave the same as Colin. To watch for every little sign that he would treat her badly. Her fear of being hurt again had blinded her to the good man Dan was, and she'd be lucky if he forgave her for the slight she'd shown him.

She opened her eyes and stared at her brother. "Take me to see him."

Luc smiled. "That's my girl."

"Is he really okay?"

"Yes. The airbag knocked him out for a few seconds and he's got bruises from the seatbelt and steering wheel, a couple of minor scratches from flying glass. Nothing major at all," Luc reassured her.

"Why didn't he ring me?" Did Dan think she wouldn't want to know he was hurt?

"His phone is trashed. A bystander called Are You Game? to let them know the van had been in an accident, which is how Cassie found out. She rang me because she thought you'd want to hear it from me in person instead of over the phone."

Jody smiled. "Thank you, for that and putting up with the crazy pregnant woman."

"Hey, it's easy when you're crazy all the time." Luc grinned and ducked out of the way of Jody's fist.

"Smartarse." She poked her tongue out. Turning around,

she located her handbag on the counter and grabbed the handles. "Can we go now?"

"Sure. But you might want to put some clothes on."

Jody glanced down at her pyjamas and groaned. Not only had she not dressed this morning, but her top and pants were smeared with dirt from when she'd helped Amy pot her herb seeds earlier. "Give me five minutes to change."

"Don't rush. I'll get the girls ready to go while you change." Luc called after her as she made a dash for her bedroom.

Jody made it back to the living room in three and a half minutes to find Luc waiting for her. "Where's Cassie and the girls?" she asked as she slipped her feet into her sneakers.

"Cassie took them to work with her. She said she's giving them a crash course in event management."

Jody's gaze darted up to meet Luc's. "What?"

"I'm kidding. I think she's making a cake or something for tomorrow's baby shower. She said the girls can hang with her until you find out if Dan has to stay in overnight or not."

She sucked in a breath. "You said he was okay."

"Relax." Luc placed his hand on her back and steered her towards the front door. "It's just a concussion. You know how careful they like to be with head injuries no matter how minor."

As far as Jody was concerned, no head injury was minor. A ball of lead sat on her chest and her tummy started churning. God, she hoped she didn't throw up again. She was getting tired of living in the bathroom with her head in the toilet. Mind you, she'd rather be making a dash to the loo instead of one to the hospital.

Chapter Twenty-One

Dan sat up in bed and cursed the idiot who'd phoned his mother. "I'm fine, Ma." Then he cursed himself for still having her listed as his emergency contact.

"You don't look fine." She leaned over and poked at the bandage near his temple.

"Shit! Keep doing that and I won't be fine." He batted her hand away.

"Daniel O'Conner. Language."

He rolled his eyes. "Why don't you get Reagan to take you home now? You don't need to be here and you've seen that I'm okay." Dan turned his gaze to his sister, pleading with his eyes to get her to take their mother out of here before Jody showed up.

"C'mon, Mum. We can't do anything for him and you've already spoken to the doctor and know his injuries aren't life threatening." Reagan placed her hand on their mother's arm. "Besides, you know as well as I do that Dan has the hardest head in the world."

"Who's going to watch him for complications? He lives alone. He could die in his sleep," Ma argued.

The gasp from the doorway had all three of them turning in that direction.

"D-die? But they said..."

Shit. Jody and Luc stood just inside the room. "Jody." Dan held out his hand. "My mother is exaggerating as usual. I'm not going to die."

To his surprise, she came forward and took his hand. He'd

expected to have to coax her into the room.

"You're really okay?" she asked as she wove their fingers together and squeezed them in a death grip.

Dan gave her hand a gentle squeeze in return and tugged her closer. "I'm fine. One more set of observations and they're letting me out of here."

"Really?" she murmured, her voice shaky with uncertainty.

He smiled at her. "Honest. I tried to ring you, but my phone got broken in the crash and I couldn't remember your number."

She brushed his hair away from his bandaged head. "Does it hurt?"

"No. The headache is gone and the pain in my ribs is bearable."

"Ahem."

Dan's gaze darted to his mother. Shit. "Um, Jody, this is my mother and sister, Susan and Reagan O'Conner."

Jody turned with a smile. "Hello. I wish we were meeting under better circumstances." She let go of his hand to offer it first to his mother and then his sister.

Dan avoided his mother's questioning look. A complete change of subject was in order. "Hey, Luc, how's the van?"

"Totalled according to the tow-truck driver, but Cassie said she'll wait until the insurance assessor takes a look. She's organised a rental for Monday."

"You wrecked the van?" Jody asked turning back and taking his hand again.

"No. The idiot who ran a red light wrecked the van."

"You're lucky a few bruises and a concussion is all you got." She stroked her fingers through his hair and he closed his eyes.

"That's what the policemen, the paramedics, the nurses *and* the doctor said."

"Are you supposed to go to sleep with a concussion?"

Reagan asked.

Dan opened his eyes. "I'm not sleeping, I'm resting. Doctor's orders. So you can all leave now." He pointed at Jody as he pulled her right up to the side of his bed. "You stay."

"Dan," Jody gasped.

"What? I'm grumpy and all I could think about was not being able to tell you I was going to be late and knowing you were going to get angry with me when I didn't show up with lunch." He used the hand he held to pull her closer until her face was near his. "Kiss me so I know I'm not having a drugged-up dream. Remind me I'm the luckiest man alive to walk away from that crash with nothing but bruises."

Her eyes darted to the side and he realised no one had left. But Dan didn't care who saw. He was done pretending he didn't love her. Wrapping a hand around her neck, he tugged her down the last few inches and pressed his mouth to hers.

He forgot about everyone else. Nothing matter except Jody and the way she surrendered to his kiss. Her lips were soft and warm and such a welcome touch. Their tongues tangled and their breath mingled and a part of Dan that had been wound tight since the accident unfurled. He'd thought of nothing but her since he'd regained consciousness sitting in the mangled wreck, the airbag deflating around him.

Dan pulled back, separated their mouths and leaned his forehead against hers. "No more. I can't fight this anymore, Jody. I want to marry you, and not because of the baby. I want to spend my life with you because you're the light in my days and the dark in my nights. You're everything I never dreamed I wanted and I can't take another day—another minute—without knowing you're mine."

"Dan." She breathed his name against his lips and the tightness in his chest eased.

"You. The girls. The baby. Are my life. My future. And I want it to start now." He locked his gaze to hers. "I love you,

Jody Walsh. Marry me."

Jody couldn't believe he'd blurted all that out in front of everyone. But she couldn't worry about it now. Not when he was kissing her again. Kissing her like she was the breath that would save his life. She lost herself then. Lost herself in him. Lost every last shred of wall between her and this man. He'd said he loved her. She'd thought—hoped—his feelings ran deep, knew hers did, but she'd never once believed it was possible to love this completely.

A clearing throat pulled them apart, but Dan didn't let her go far. He tugged until she sat on the edge of his bed. Jody turned to find a very familiar man in a white coat standing before them.

"Hi, Doctor Moore." Jody smiled at the man who'd treated her weeks ago.

"Well, I must say it's a pleasure to see you up and about. Can't say the same for your young man though." The doctor tipped his chin in Dan's direction. "I could have done without seeing him come in on a stretcher."

She shuddered. "I'm glad I didn't see that."

"So how are you feeling now? Keeping things down?" he asked as he picked up the chart from the end of Dan's bed.

"Yes. Things are going well and my doctor has scheduled those tests you requested."

"Good. Well, let's get to today's patient shall we?" Doctor Moore walked around the other side of the bed and checked Dan's pulse. One by one, he made his way through blood pressure, temperature and a quick listen to Dan's chest. "Well, young man, you're free to go home as long as you have someone who can be with you for the next twenty-four hours."

"I do."

"He does."

Dan and Jody spoke at once, drawing a chuckle for the older man.

"All right then, you can leave whenever you're ready, no paperwork as you weren't admitted." Doctor Moore pulled a card from his pocket and handed it to Jody. "Ring me if you're worried, but I doubt there'll be any problems. And I don't want to see either of you again until it's time to deliver that baby."

There was a split second of stunned silence before Dan's mother exploded with the kind of lecture only a mother can give. Jody tried to interrupt but the woman was a force she had no hope of stopping. In the end, Dan had to lean over and cover her mouth with his hand.

"Be quiet and listen for a minute." Dan indicated Jody should say what she had to.

"Please don't blame Dan for not telling you. I asked that he keep things between us until the twelve-week mark. I have two other children and I wanted to be sure everything was okay before I upset their world by telling them about the baby." It wasn't a complete lie, but Jody didn't think telling the truth would make a good first impression.

"You have other children?" Susan asked.

"Yes, two girls, they're thirteen and fifteen."

"And you are going to marry my Daniel, yes?"

It suddenly dawned on her that she'd never answered him. Spinning around she met his gaze. "Yes. Yes, I'll marry you."

He grinned then pulled her in for a kiss.

"Right, where are these granddaughters of mine?" Dan's mother brought them back to the here and now.

"They're with my brother's girlfriend, Cassie," Jody said a little breathlessly.

"You work with Dan?"

"Yes. And Cassie is dating my brother, Luc." Jody pointed to Luc leaning against the wall in the corner of the room.

"When can I meet them?"

"Ma, c'mon, give us a minute, would you?"

Jody watched mother and son stare each other down until Dan's sister stepped in and ushered their mother from the room with a promised return in five minutes. Luc pushed off the wall and walked to the door where he kicked the doorstop out of the way.

"I'll wait out here and hold her off as long as I can." He waved his phone. "I've got pictures of Leigh and Amy I can bribe her with."

The door whooshed close and Jody breathed out with a rush. "Oh my God. Did I really just meet your mother?"

"Yep. Now come here and kiss me again. Actually, better yet, use those lips for something else. Say it." Dan held her face in his hands. "I need to hear you say it."

She knew what he wanted. He'd told her, but she hadn't said the words yet, not to anyone but herself. She wasn't sure if she could, but for him—for them—she'd force aside the fear that was still an automatic reaction. "First, I need to say I'm sorry. For everything I've put us through but mostly to you for what I've made you put up with."

"Hey, Ma always says nothing worth having is easy. And you—" he tapped her nose with his thumb "—are the least easy person I know. And you're worth every painful second of it." His smile softened the blow of his words.

Jody smiled in return. "I love you," she whispered before pressing her lips to his.

Dan leaned back. "Again."

"I love you."

"Good, because I plan to love you for the rest of my life." He kissed her this time. Only he didn't keep it light. He took them deep. Fast. And it wasn't until his mother cleared her throat from the doorway that they came up for air with matching grins on their faces.

"Enough for now, I want to meet these granddaughters I plan to spoil." Suzan O'Conner spun around and disappeared out of sight.

Reagan stuck her head in the door. "I'll detour as much as I can, but you better give me an address of where she can meet those two beautiful girls we just saw on your brother's phone or Dan will need more than a few Band-Aids and rest to recover."

"What? Tonight?" Jody squeaked.

"Yeah, there's no stopping her when she's on a tear, and she's definitely on one," Reagan looked to the side. "Yes, I'm coming."

Dan laughed. "My place at six for dinner."

"See you then, big brother." Reagan disappeared.

"I think we better get going. We've got lots to do before my mother turns up and lets the cat out of the bag about the baby."

"Oh no. I didn't want to tell the girls yet."

"It'll be fine. Besides, you know you were keeping it a secret as much to keep me at a distance as to protect them."

Dan helped her off the bed and stood. Jody turned and was struck speechless by his state. "Oh my God. Look at you." His clothes were torn in several places and splattered with blood in others.

He shrugged. "Not much I can do about them until we get home."

Jody liked the way he put home and we together. It had been a long time since she'd thought in terms of home as anything except her, Leigh and Amy. Now, the thought of home brought images of Dan to mind.

She put her hand in his and pulled him towards the door. "C'mon, let's go home."

Epilogue

"Don't you dare lift that!" Dan yelled as he walked into the bedroom and saw Jody attempting to put her suitcase on the bed.

"It's not that heavy," she protested as she heaved it off the floor a couple of inches.

He raced over and replaced her hand with his and swung the bag up on the mattress. "There. Next time just ask."

She pouted. "But you were busy with the girls."

"I'm always busy with the girls. They find something they want me to do every other second." Not that he was upset by their constant need for his attention. In fact, he loved it.

"You shouldn't have told them they could do whatever they wanted in the house then," Jody said as she unzipped the bag and threw open the top.

"I want them to feel at home as soon as possible. I want you all to feel that way." He wrapped his arms around her thickened waist and splayed his hands over her protruding belly. "Is he moving?"

"*She* is asleep. For now." Dan could hear the smile in her voice.

They'd decided not to find out the sex of the baby, but each of them had their own thoughts on what was growing inside Jody's rounded stomach. "I love touching you like this."

"You just like touching me." She laughed.

"Well, yeah, I am a guy. But like this." He smoothed his hands over her curves. "It brings a lump to my throat and tears to my eyes. There's a part of you and me growing in here."

"Don't I know it." Jody cupped her hands over his and moved them lower. "She's kicking."

"I'll never get over how amazing that is."

He followed the movement with his fingertips. Their baby was so tiny. With less than three weeks to go, he worried their child wouldn't be big enough to survive. It didn't matter how many times the doctors told him everything was progressing normally, he wouldn't believe it until this little person was in his arms and breathing. Jody's stomach tensed beneath his hands.

"Whoa. What was that?" Dan's own stomach tightened.

"Mmm..." She leaned back against him and hummed out a breath.

"Jody?"

She dug her nails into his forearms as she hissed out a breath.

"Jody?" She had him worried now.

"Can you ring whoever drew the short straw for coming to sit with the girls while we're at the hospital?" She let go and stepped from his arms like she was doing nothing more than getting a drink of water.

"It's time?" Did his voice just go up two octaves? "It can't be time."

"Babies always have their own timetable. Ours has chosen today."

"But..." He watched as she pulled some things from her suitcase and piled them on the bed. Why was she unpacking now? "What are you doing? We have to go."

Dan wasn't proud to say he was beginning to panic. What if she had the baby before they made it to the hospital? He moved next to her and grabbed her hand.

"Jody. Talk to me. I'm freaking out here."

She patted his cheek. "Relax, these things take a whil—"

The word was cut off by a gasp and she doubled over just as water splashed over his bare feet.

"Fuck."

"Okay," she panted. "Maybe this won't take so long after all." She gripped his arm and dug her nails in so hard he had to clench his jaw to keep a cry of pain from escaping.

"Leigh! Amy!" he yelled.

Both girls came running and skidded to a stop in the doorway.

"Get the phone. Call 000," he ordered as another pain ripped through Jody.

"Is Mum having the baby now?" Leigh asked. "She can't have it now. It's not time."

"Try telling him that."

"Her," Jody got out through gritted teeth.

Dan eased her towards the bed.

"No. Not on the bed. I don't want to ruin the bedding or mattress."

"Screw that." Dan scooped her up into his arms and placed her on the bed. "We'll buy new ones if we have to."

"Dan." She grabbed his arm. "This is happening too fast. We aren't going to make it to the hospital."

"Clearly."

"Ring doctor—argh..." Jody gripped her stomach and groaned through the next contraction.

"How close are they? I haven't been keeping track." Dan glanced at the alarm clock, noting the time. "Where's the phone?"

"They're on the way," Leigh said.

Dan turned to see his step-daughter with the phone to her ear.

"The lady wants to know how close the contractions are."

Dan looked back at Jody just as another pain gripped her midsection. "Shit. Less than a minute."

Leigh relayed the information and then disappeared down the hall calling out, "I'll get Amy to direct them in."

The next few minutes were a blur of Jody's pain and Dan's panic. When the paramedics rushed into the room, Dan wasn't sure which one of them breathed the bigger sigh of relief. It didn't take them long to determine the baby wasn't waiting for a trip to the hospital to enter the world. He followed directions. Tried to remember the breathing from class but he couldn't, and when one of the paramedics said the baby was crowning, his whole existence boiled down to this monumental moment.

Leigh and Amy hovered near the door and he wondered if he should shoo them away or urge them closer. He sat on the bed behind Jody, propping her up so that she could concentrate on bringing their child into the world. And with the very next contraction, she did.

The hearty wail of a newborn filled the room and tears slid down Dan's face. It didn't matter what they had as long as the baby was healthy and his wife of three months didn't kill him for making her go through this. His world was complete.

"It's a boy. Here you go, Mum and Dad."

The paramedic passed the slippery bundle of squirming arms and legs. For a second, Dan's heart stopped. But he wasn't about to miss this catch. And with his son firmly in his grasp, he ended the game with a kiss on his wife's head.

About the Author

Years of slavery to four young aliens and their sire failed to squash the love of writing or reading hiding behind the facade of a boring stay-at-home mum. Escaping from the mother-ship with vivid imagination intact, Rhian uses her superpowers for good.

Okay, so that's not quite how it happened. A 20-year marriage to her very own hero and raising a family of four kept writing on the back burner, but with more time to spend on the things she loves most, Rhian and her accomplice, Mr. Muse, have taken over. Writing in a multiple of genres keeps life interesting and busy.

An Aussie who's spent years living overseas Rhian is now happily residing with her family back in their native land of down under. Rhian can be found in numerous places online where her love of talking is well satisfied.

To learn more about Rhian and her writing visit her website, www.rhiancahill.com. You can contact Rhian at rhian@rhiancahill.com.

It's all fun and games until their hearts are on the line.

7 Minutes in Heaven
© *2013 Rhian Cahill*
Are You Game?, Book 1

Cassandra Moreland's hard work to build her party-planning business is starting to pay off. There's only one thorn in her side—a six-foot-five wall of testosterone throwing his weight around while she supervises her friend Lil's first party. Butting heads doesn't work. Ignoring him *really* doesn't work. Not when he makes her pulse race and her palms sweat. But no way will she give in to his demand to shut the rowdy party down.

Lucas Wilhelm, head of McDermott Security, can't believe the pint-sized brunette has the balls to go toe-to-toe with him. Strangely enough, that sassy mouth of hers isn't ticking him off. It's tightening his groin and stirring something much hotter than anger.

A stolen moment in a pantry leads to a challenge that pushes each other's sexual boundaries to the limit. Except the rules go up in flames when they realize they're not just playing around. They're playing for keeps.

Warning: Contains an alpha male who's used to being in charge, and a tough-as-steel woman who isn't going down easy. Involves the use of beads, but not in the way you might think.

Available now in ebook and print from Samhain Publishing.

Romance

HORROR

www.samhainpublishing.com

Printed in Australia
AUOC02n1100130215
265838AU00002B/2/P